THE LIGHT THIEF

THE LIGHT THIEF

THE LIGHT THIEF

BOOK 1

DAVID WEBB

First paperback edition December 2019

ISBN 978-1-7343511-0-1 (paperback)
ISBN 978-1-7343511-1-8 (ebook)

www.jdavidwebb.com

This book is dedicated to Abby Simms.

This is the most I could show my appreciation for all your help and support without putting your name on the cover.

Thank you.

What is to give light must endure burning.

— Viktor E. Frankl

PART I

THE THIEF

1

A s seventeen-year-old Aniya Lyons sat across the table from her date, a forgotten man stumbled through the alleys of the Hole, slipping on blood that drained from his side.

As she avoided eye contact with her potential suitor, the man outside began to lose vision, forcing him to walk blindly through the already darkened town.

As she feigned interest in her admirer, the dying wanderer lost consciousness and fell in a pile of trash behind the very same tavern in which Aniya was currently trapped.

"Did you hear me?"

Aniya's eyes flickered upward. The warm roll she had stuffed inside her mouth had a wondrous taste, one that took her away from the dimly lit tavern, far from the underground city of Holendast, away from the Lightbringers, and somewhere into the free world far above, which would have been nice if it weren't for the blackened sun that hung in the air.

But her date's question had brought her crashing back down to her seat, across from her least-favorite Potential yet.

"Sorry, what?" Wet crumbs spat from her full mouth.

Noticing the grimace on his face, Aniya swallowed and wiped her chin. "I'm sorry, Everett. Have you tried these rolls?"

Everett's eyes narrowed. "I get the feeling you don't want to be here."

He was wrong about that. She could stare at the plates of food that drifted by her nose all night long. Rations were decent, but enough to always keep her wanting more. Seeing the hurt on his face, she softened.

It's not his fault.

"I'm sorry," she said again, this time putting effort into sounding sincere. She swept her black hair away from her face and let him look into her eyes. It wasn't that he was unattractive. In fact, his gaze was striking, his jaw chiseled, and his physique strong. But whether it was the way he introduced himself by his last name, the way his nails were immaculately trimmed, or the way he organized his food into neat piles on his plate, Aniya couldn't relate to the man at all.

Everett sighed. "Maybe we should have canceled after all."

"We could have tried, and they might have let us because of the blackout, but I'm running out of time to choose. I don't have the luxury of waiting for the power to come back on, so they would have made us do this whether it was a Black Day or not." She placed a hand on his, ignoring unpleasant chills as her skin touched his. "It's not you, I promise. It's just . . . do you really think you'll find love based on an algorithm?"

"They say it's pretty accurate."

She scoffed. "You trust your future to a bunch of whack-jobs with flashlights on their heads?"

At this, Everett's eyes widened, and he held a finger to his lips, but it was too late to stop her.

"You think the Lightbringers have your best interests in mind? You're okay signing away your love, your work, your family to—" Aniya couldn't go any further. She swallowed her words and hid behind her glass of water.

Everett glanced around the tavern and lowered his voice. "You're lucky none of them are close by."

She scoffed again. "In the middle of the Hole? We're not important enough for them. Just important enough to control us, herding us into the perfect lives they've laid out for us."

"Keep talking like that, and you'll probably lose whatever choices you have left. You'll wind up like your brother just like that." Everett snapped his fingers.

Aniya bristled. "Like you'd report me. This is the Hole. No one cares."

"I care. If anyone else finds out, I don't want to be associated with you, and I feel sorry for the poor soul you wind up with."

She let her fork fall to the table as she pushed her chair back. "Well, you won't have to worry about that." She walked away from the table, her anger winning out over her hurt.

Aniya crossed the tavern, sat on a stool, and slumped over the bar. "I need a drink, Gareth."

From the opposite end of the bar, a large man sauntered over, cleaning a glass with a wet rag. "Correct me if I'm wrong, Aniya, but you still have three months left before I can agree to that."

"Gareth, can't you pretend you haven't known me since I was born, just for tonight?" Aniya rolled her eyes. "I'm in the middle of one of my government-sponsored courting sessions."

Gareth nodded over her shoulder. "That him?"

Aniya turned to watch Everett staring at them, his sour mood hanging over him so richly that it should have spoiled his food. She turned back to Gareth. "Unfortunately, yes."

"For that, little one, I'd say tonight is an exception." Gareth laughed and poured her a drink from a large, brown jug.

Aniya took it, turned to the table by the wall, and raised

her glass toward her neglected date, who glared back at her. She smiled for the first time that night.

"You know, you'll have to choose eventually. You've been at this for nearly a year now. Most people choose within the first month."

"I think most people have a better pool of candidates," she said, downing half the glass in one swig. "Seriously, that's the best the Lightbringers can do?"

Gareth shrugged. "He's not your only option."

"No, but the other four jokers aren't much better." Another gulp, and the glass was empty. "Though I will say he is, without a doubt, the worst one yet."

"One of those jokers will be your husband, whether you like it or not," Gareth said grimly. "If you hadn't waited until now to decide, you could have gone through the six-month appeal process for a certain bricklayer."

"Nicholas?" Aniya laughed. "That would be the most awkward marriage imaginable. He's my best friend."

"Most people would count it a true treasure to marry their best friend. People like your parents."

"They got lucky, especially since they didn't get a choice." She furrowed her brow. "Why don't they understand that I don't need any of them? I can work just as hard as any of my suitors."

"No doubt," Gareth said. "But my heart would break if you had to take part in relocative servitude. It was hard enough to watch William go."

Aniya looked down, hiding a tear that inched down her face and dropped onto the bar, staining the surface with awful memories. The mental picture of her brother being taken away for good broke her heart all over again.

"You should count yourself lucky that girls are exempt from servitude. I wouldn't—"

"Doc!"

A young man came running from the back room. A quivering candle threatened to fall from his hand as he panted.

Gareth turned around with a stern rebuke. "Careful, boy. Unless you want to ferment the wine yourself, you'll not run inside and break half my inventory."

"Come quick!" The intruder turned to run again but was held back by Gareth's hand clutching his collar.

"What did I just say, Roland?"

Roland turned around, breaking free of Gareth's grasp. "There's a guy out back, Doc. He's bleeding out into the alley. It was the Silvers."

Gareth relaxed and shook his head. "You know I can't interfere in that business. I could lose my license."

"You don't understand. He's been shot!"

Gareth's eyes widened as his face turned to steel.

"Stay here."

"But Doc . . ."

"Stay here," Gareth repeated. With that, he disappeared into the back room.

Roland sighed and approached the counter. He snatched a cloth and began wiping down the bar, though his movements seemed aimless and distracted.

"Don't get many of those?"

"Huh?" Roland looked up.

Aniya gestured toward the back room. "Not many shootings?"

Roland shook his head. "The Silvers don't waste their bullets on just anyone. As much of an annoyance as they are, they don't often kill people."

"That's what my parents say. Not as many people to work for them if they do."

"And they don't need another revolt on their hands. I think the Chancellor learned his lesson after last time."

"Yeah, but we lost."

Roland shrugged and tossed the cloth backward toward

the sink. He missed, and it landed on the floor behind him, but he didn't seem to care. Instead, he turned his attention again to the bar, dipping his finger in a nearby puddle and moving it around into a shape.

"Why don't I ever see you in Assembly?" Aniya asked. "You're always here."

He smirked but didn't look up. "Why would I want to go somewhere I don't have to go?"

"Everyone has to go. Even I skip classes sometimes, but I'm always there for morning roll call. I missed it one time, and—" Aniya shuddered. "Let's just say I'm never doing that again."

Roland dipped his finger in the liquid again. Whether it was water or alcohol, Aniya couldn't tell. "They don't care about me."

"Of course they care. Well, not *care*, but you know what I mean."

He shrugged again. As he finished his tracing on the bar, Aniya studied the liquid drawing to try to figure out the pattern. It looked like a hand, but if it was, it was missing a finger.

Aniya regretted her disinterested behavior toward Everett as Roland gave her the same treatment. *I guess I deserve this.* "Do you know much about the Uprising?"

Roland looked up, and his eyes seemed to come alive. However, after a brief pause, he shook his head and looked back down.

"What's wrong with you?" Aniya rolled her eyes. "You used to talk to me all the time. You played with me and William when we were kids. But for the last year, I've only seen you here."

"Not my choice," Roland grumbled.

"What do you mean?"

Roland shook his head once again.

Before Aniya could grow any more frustrated, a young girl

approached the bar next to her and stood on her tiptoes to see over the edge.

The girl held up four fingers and asked in a timid voice, "Do you have any bread today?"

Roland pushed the girl's fingers down and looked around swiftly. "Careful, Milu. What did I say about coming around the side?"

The girl ran around Aniya to the side of the bar, away from the busy part of the tavern.

"It's too late, don't—" Roland rolled his eyes and walked over to the girl.

Aniya looked on, amused.

"Do you have any bread?" The girl gave a small, sweet smile, again holding up four fingers.

Roland looked at the floor. "I'm sorry, Milu. We were so busy today that we sold the last of our bread, and we can't bake any more right now because our oven has no power. I didn't even get a chance to save some for you like usual."

The girl's smile faded, and her eyes welled up with tears. "But Mama doesn't have enough for dinner. After the half-ration, we don't have anything left."

"I'm sorry," Roland said again. He stroked the top of her head and brushed a tear from her cheek, and it looked to Aniya like he was fighting back tears of his own.

Aniya stepped forward and knelt so that she was even with the girl's height. "I can get you some food. You just have to do one thing for me."

The girl nodded through her tears.

"Go to the door, open it wide, then shut it as hard as you can."

Milu looked up at Aniya quizzically.

"Go now."

The girl darted across the room, dodging much larger bodies.

Aniya stood and turned around to see Roland giving her a similar questioning glance. She flashed a smile and a wink.

Old hinges creaked loudly as the sheet metal door swung open.

Aniya took a deep breath and closed her eyes.

The door slammed shut, an impressive feat for the young girl.

Almost instantly, the torches that lined the walls were extinguished by a gust of air, and the tavern was plunged into darkness.

Aniya opened her eyes. Her vision had already adjusted to the dark, and she took advantage of the confusion to make her move, darting into the crowd and blending into the throng of people. Aided by her small frame, she bobbed and weaved between the raucous patrons, who grew louder now that they were subject to enjoy their food in complete darkness.

With a flourish of her fingers, a coin disappeared from one man's pocket and a meal voucher from the next. Almost as an afterthought, she slid past a table and snatched away two small dessert cakes, tossing one of them into her mouth as she moved.

Satisfied with her plunder, Aniya returned to the bar just as the first torch sparked back to life, and she reappeared before Roland and the girl, a smile gracing her face.

Roland stared at her with a look that seemed to be a mixture of confusion and wonder.

"Here you go, Milu." Aniya crouched down and gave her spoils to the girl, whose wide eyes darted between the prizes presented to her.

Rather than reaching for the food first, she leapt up and hugged Aniya's neck, then grabbed the food and disappeared into the crowd again.

"I think you've made a friend," Roland said. "Just be careful. You know the penalty for stealing, right?"

"Only for those who get caught," she said in a sing-song

voice as she poured herself another drink right in front of the young bartender.

"I wouldn't wish it on you, but you may be pushing your luck tonight. Someone seems very interested in you right now." Roland nodded toward the other side of the tavern, which was once again fully lit.

Aniya glanced back over to her forgotten date.

Everett's eyes, it seemed, had never left her. Now, he scowled, likely realizing that she didn't plan on coming back. Aniya grinned back in indifference, and that seemed to be the last straw. He shoved his plate of food away, knocked his chair over as he stood abruptly, and stormed out of the tavern.

"Don't worry about him," Aniya said, turning back to Roland. "He's nobody important."

Roland didn't seem convinced but remained silent.

At that moment, Gareth returned and pointed at the two of them. "Both of you, come."

"But who's going to tend the bar?" Roland asked.

"Now."

Gareth turned around and led them past the bar and into the back room, where an unconscious man lay in the middle of the floor. Without a word, Gareth closed the door behind them and sat down on the floor next to the injured man.

Aniya stared at the blood-soaked man lying before her. His body was decrepit, his rib cage showing through his unclothed chest. His face was saggy and worn, wrinkled and aged, accompanied by gray hair that grew in patches.

"Who is he?"

"I didn't recognize him at first either," Gareth said. "Take a closer look."

Aniya approached the man carefully, as if he could leap up and attack her at any moment.

"Given that those selected for relocative servitude spend the rest of their lives working for the Lightbringers in the Hub, I'm very curious to learn why he is here, about forty years older than he was when he left three years ago, and almost dead."

Even with Gareth's comment, it wasn't until she saw a familiar scar above the man's right eye that it all fell into place. She backed away, holding back tears as she held her hands to her mouth.

She turned to Roland. "It's William."

2

"We have ways of making you talk, Mr. Lyons."

This was true. One look at the small fire in the corner confirmed this. A poker could be heated and used to scorch human flesh. Or perhaps the knife sitting on the table a few feet away—it certainly looked sharp enough to slice off a finger or two.

But out of all the ways anyone could have extracted information from Theodore Lyons, his interrogator had chosen a much more effective approach.

He held back a smile from his wife, silently daring her to come closer as he gestured with his finger.

Catherine finally broke and flashed a wide grin as she jumped into bed with her husband, straddling his hips with her legs. She grabbed a candle from the nightstand and let hot wax drip onto Theodore's bare chest. "Torturous enough?"

"Wow, that's actually pretty warm." Theodore winced but chuckled. "Yes, I suppose that would work."

She set the candle back down and kissed him. "I'm glad we get to have this Black Day to ourselves for once, but I can't help but feel bad for Aniya right now."

Theodore nodded. "I know she wasn't exactly excited

about this, but at least she has a choice. You and I didn't have that luxury."

Catherine's grin turned to a pouting frown. "Are you saying you wish they chose someone else for you?"

"Very much so," Theodore said grimly before cracking a smile of his own, rolling his eyes. "You know I'm okay being stuck with you, darling. Especially considering how long I chased after you for. I may not have been your first choice, but we turned out okay after all. I guess the Lightbringers know how to play matchmaker." He picked up his wife off his body and threw her down next to him, wrapping his arms around her. "But do you really want to talk about the past or Aniya right now? We have *other* things to do."

"Good point." Catherine smiled again, and she leaned in to kiss her husband.

"Mom? Dad?"

The door shook, but the latch holding it shut held fast.

Catherine let out an audible sigh of exasperation.

"One night. Just one night." She got up from bed and put on a robe while Theodore picked his shirt up from the floor.

"Hello?" The door jiggled again, followed by multiple knocks.

"One moment, Aniya." Theodore got up from the bed and disengaged the latch, opening the door for his daughter. "What are you doing back so soon? I thought you were spending time with Everett tonight."

Aniya gave a nervous laugh. "Yeah, he's not going to make the cut. I assume you two are the only ones here?"

"Well, we were." Theodore chuckled sheepishly as he avoided his daughter's knowing glance.

Aniya's expression darkened. "Good." With that, she walked back out the door.

Theodore turned to his wife, who shrugged.

Within seconds, Aniya was back inside. She was followed by two men, one of them carrying a blanket-covered bundle.

"Roland? Gareth? What are you doing here?" Theodore frowned and stared at the strange sight. "What is that?"

The bartender ignored the question and placed his load on Theodore's bed. He stepped back to the door, replacing the latch and placing a chair underneath the handle.

Meanwhile, Catherine pulled the blanket off the mass on the bed, discovering the bleeding body that Gareth had brought. "Who is it? I haven't seen anything this bad since the last person who tried to dodge the Citizen Tax."

Roland nodded toward the bloody heap. "Keep looking."

Catherine turned back to the man on the bed and began pulling long strands of blood-soaked hair away from his face. After a moment, she shrieked and backed away from the bed, her trembling hands covering her mouth.

Theodore's eyes narrowed as he approached the bed to examine the man.

The victim was in terrible shape. His facial hair had grown to a point where his lips were invisible. His face was strained and worn. The man may as well have been fifty.

But despite the radical change in the man's appearance, Theodore still recognized his son.

"William," he whispered as he stepped back in disbelief.

Gareth pushed Theodore and Catherine aside. "Give me some room. This is going to take a miracle."

They stepped aside and let the bartender/doctor go to work. Theodore waited nervously, alternating between sitting on the second bed and standing over Gareth's shoulder. Catherine sat at the head of the bed, diligently wiping away the seemingly endless flow of blood that seeped from her son's wounds. Roland also pitched in, assisting Gareth in no small way. Apparently, Theodore surmised, Gareth had been teaching the boy more than just notions of rebellion. Aniya was the only one who did not move, and she sat in the corner, staring at the bed where her brother lay. It was the most still Theodore had ever seen his daughter.

As the hours stretched on, Theodore resorted to helplessly pacing back and forth in the small room that made up nearly the entirety of the Lyons' shack. "I don't understand," he muttered. "He was never supposed to come back. They said he was gone for good."

Gareth did not look up but replied, "I'm sure that was the idea. It looks like they tried pretty hard to keep him from leaving, and they almost succeeded. Good on him for getting past the Silvers, though. That's one trick he'll have to teach me before he passes."

Catherine visibly shuddered.

"Not here," Theodore said. He glanced at Aniya.

Gareth looked up at Theodore. "She'll find out soon enough. Change is coming, Theodore. If nothing else, this proves it," he said, motioning to William.

"If I have anything to say about it, she'll never be involved."

Aniya said nothing indicating her acknowledgment, and it was unclear whether she even heard. She simply stared at the bed. "No one's ever returned."

"Right you are, little one," Gareth said, turning back to William. "Though you won't be little for much longer now, will you? Your Day is coming before the month is out, isn't it?" Not waiting for an answer, he held his hand out to Roland. "Pincers."

Roland retrieved the requested tool from Gareth's large bag and handed them to the doctor without a word.

Aniya scoffed. "My Day? If I didn't want it before, I definitely don't want it now if I'm going to end up like William."

"You're a girl, Aniya. You know there's no risk of that," Catherine reassured her.

"Gareth, what happened to him?" Theodore asked. "How does he look so different? His eighteenth birthday was a mere three years ago, but he looks older than I do."

It was true. William's face was lined with wrinkles, his

body was emaciated, and his overgrown facial hair could have been the envy of every other young man his age.

"Clearly, your son was very poorly cared for in captivity." Gareth extracted the first bullet from William's back, dropping it in a bowl held by Catherine. "He must have been working at least twenty hours a day in the Hub. Not manual labor, or else his muscles would be more defined. Perhaps menial work that was just engaging enough to keep him from going mad. And to be honest, I can't even be sure of that. There's no telling what his mental state will be like when he wakes up." He paused and bowed his head. "If he wakes up."

Catherine held a hand to her mouth.

Theodore shook his head slowly and resumed pacing.

"You know what this means, don't you, Theodore?" After Theodore did not reply, Gareth continued. "They'll come looking for him. If they don't have a body, they won't make any assumptions. He has to be moved by the morning, whether he is awake, unconscious, or . . . otherwise."

"We have the basement," Catherine said.

"Basement?" Aniya looked up and rubbed her eyes, yawning. But Theodore knew his headstrong daughter well enough to recognize a veiled attempt to wipe her tears away. "We don't have a basement."

Theodore glanced at his wife.

She shrugged apologetically. "She'll find out anyway."

"I'm not sure the basement is sufficient," said Gareth. "It will do for tonight, but he will need to be moved as soon as he is stable."

"We'll have to be careful until then. Aniya, I'll make sure you are exempt from school tomorrow."

Gareth shook his head. "No, Theodore. You can't act like anything is wrong. If you hole yourself up here, it will only raise suspicions." He secured the last bandage on William's upper back and reached again for the pincers. "Go on with your business just as if this had never happened. The power will be back on tomorrow, so go to work, go to the tavern for a drink, and then come back here at your regular time. Catherine will keep him well cared for in your absence. In fact," he said, looking up at Aniya, "perhaps you should go to one of your Potentials' houses for the evening, just until we're done patching up your brother and he's hidden."

"It's a Black Day, Gareth," Theodore said, as if the doctor did not already know. "Curfew is in fifteen minutes."

"If she gets caught, she'll be in far less trouble than if she were to be found here with her brother on the bed. If the Silver Guard pay you a visit, they'll finish what they started and kill him. And if Aniya is still here and they think she helped shelter him, I truly have no idea what they'll do to her. The Chancellor might find it appropriate to lift the Female Restriction Act for a night just for her. I wouldn't put it past him."

At this, Catherine finally burst into tears. Her husband rushed to her side, taking her in his arms.

"Nothing is going to happen to Aniya, darling." But Theodore looked up at Gareth, and sighed in reluctant agreement. "I suppose it is wise that she leave, given the circumstances."

"Will you stop talking about me like I'm not here?" Aniya finally spoke and stood up, her clenched fists at her side. "I can take care of myself, and I'll die before I let them take me or William to the Hub."

"That's exactly what we're afraid of." Gareth frowned. "It's a dark world out there, and I'm not just talking about the blackouts. If you insist on relying on no one but yourself, you won't make it very far."

"I'm not leaving," she snapped at Gareth, folding her arms in defiance.

"Please, Aniya." Theodore released his wife and approached his daughter. "We'll keep him safe, but we want you to be safe too. Come back in an hour, and you can stay by his side in the basement as long as you want."

Gareth nodded in agreement.

After staring at the two of them for a moment, Aniya spun on her heels with a huff and exited the shack, leaving the door wide open.

"If I didn't know better, I would worry about her," Theodore said as he closed the door.

"She has a strong head on her shoulders, and a smart one at that. But I still worry for her, and you should too." Gareth dropped the final bullet into Catherine's bowl and reached for more bandages. "I've no doubt she's catching on to the roles we played in the war."

"You're nearly done, Gareth." Catherine took the bloody bowl to the counter and set it down gingerly. "Why did she need to leave for so long?"

Gareth sighed. "You're not going to like this." He turned again to Roland. "In my bag, there's a large syringe filled with green liquid. Give that to me, then go home. You've done enough, and it's not safe for you, either."

After a quick search in the bag, Roland handed the syringe to Gareth and offered a hug of consolation to Catherine. "I hope he wakes up soon."

Catherine hugged him tightly as a smile slipped through. "You're a sweet boy. Don't tell anyone you were here."

Roland left as quickly as Aniya had, gently closing the door behind him.

As she sniffed back a tear, Catherine kissed Gareth's cheek. "Thank you."

Theodore locked the door, then knelt next to his unconscious son as he squeezed Catherine's hand. "I second that. You've done well with him."

Gareth looked up with a sad smile, then returned to work, examining the green syringe.

"What is that?" Catherine asked.

"Roland hoped for William to wake up soon. Well, he's going to get his wish much sooner than he may expect. We have to talk to your son and find out what he knows before it's too late. Turn him over." Gareth squirted a small amount of the green liquid onto the floor as Theodore and Catherine carefully turned William's body over. "This is pure adrenaline."

Without another word, Gareth plunged the syringe deep into William's forearm and pressed the plunger down until it would go no further, shooting the green substance deep into William's body. He withdrew the syringe and massaged the injection point.

No one said a word as they stared at William's face, watching for any sign of life.

After a long moment, Gareth looked up and sighed. "I've done all I can. I'm sorry."

As Catherine threw herself over William's body, sobbing into her son's shoulder, Theodore backed away slowly, pressing his palms against his forehead. Was this how the Chancellor would make him pay for his crimes against the Lightbringers? Or was this Alpha's sick revenge?

With a shout, Theodore spun around and punched the wall.

3

Nicholas Kent stood up straight and looked in the mirror, examining himself by the light of the candle in his right hand. He took his other hand, licked it, and carefully put a stray hair back in its place. Taking a breath, he grabbed the piece of paper taped to the mirror and studied the words in the candlelight.

"This is why I think I should be reassigned to the programmers' division." He stopped, took his pencil and scratched out a couple words, and started over again. "This is why I should be reassigned to the programmers' division. I taught myself to code when I was eight years old, and it's been my passion ever since. I've been familiar with the govern-ment-issue UX-97 since it was first released because it was assigned to my father for his work in the Ambassadors' Program. I'm familiar with—" Another scratch of the pencil. "I am very familiar with—"

"Nicholas!"

The piece of paper fell to the floor as Nicholas jumped, his focus lost.

"What?" he shouted down the hole in the roof, annoyed that he had been caught off guard.

"It's time for bed!"

Nicholas sighed and muttered under his breath, "You'd think that would have stopped last month when I turned eighteen." He leaned down toward the trapdoor and called back, "Okay. I'm going to sleep up here tonight." Without waiting for a response, he closed the trapdoor and engaged the latch to ensure no more interruptions. Disregarding his cot in the corner, he went back to the mirror and cleared his throat. "This is why I should be reassigned to the programmers' division."

He was interrupted again, this time by a loud thump coming from behind him. He sighed and gritted his teeth. "I'm going to bed, ma!"

However, his annoyance faded as he discovered the source of the noise, evident by the rope near his feet stretching taut and grinding against the edge of the roof. Several more thumps later, a hand appeared in the darkness, accompanied by a feminine grunt.

Nicholas grinned and extended his hand past the ledge. As his best friend grabbed the hand and held on tight, he pulled her up and embraced her. "Aniya, what are you doing here? You haven't broken curfew in weeks." He let her go and pulled the rope onto the roof as Aniya fixed her hair from the strenuous climb.

"I thought it would be more fun to see you than dreary, old Axel again. Or worse, Everett. Besides, like you said, it's been weeks since I broke a rule. Life was getting pretty dull."

"You would say that," Nicholas said. He smiled at her, but she looked away. "Are you okay, Aniya?"

Her eyes flickered back to him. "What?"

"Are you okay?"

"Of course," she said, but her words trailed off into little more than a whisper.

Before Nicholas could speak, Aniya spotted the paper on the ground and snatched it up. Nicholas's eyes widened, and as he reached for it, she backed away with a smirk, keeping the paper away and bringing it closer to the candle to read. "This is why I should be reassigned to the programmers' division," she read out loud, exaggerating proper speech and deepening her voice as low as she could. She looked up and offered one word in mock derision before continuing: "Nerd."

Nicholas rolled his eyes.

Aniya looked back down at the paper but didn't keep reading out loud. She looked up again and frowned. "I didn't think we had a programmers' division in the Hole."

Avoiding her gaze, Nicholas turned and sat on a stool next to his cot. "Someone has to keep the sky ceiling turning."

Aniya smirked and looked up at the powerless, defunct dome far above their heads, a pure black surface that normally simulated an impressive starscape around this time of night. "Yeah, because that's going so well right now." She looked back down and cocked her head to the side, confused. "I thought they controlled that from the Hub."

He looked up and changed the subject. "How did your date with Everett go?"

Aniya grumbled, crumpling up the paper in her hand. "It wasn't a date, and you know it."

"Well, you're going to marry him. Sounds like a date to me."

"I'm not going to marry him!" She let herself fall on the cot and folded her arms.

"Let's review, shall we?" Nicholas counted off on his fingers. "Wesley is too snobbish, Sean's hair is too red, Calvin is too tall, and Axel is too lovey-dovey. What in the Web is wrong with Everett?"

"I'd rather not get into the specifics of tonight's so-called date." She let out a sigh and collapsed on the bed. "I thought the Lightbringers were supposed to be good at matching people up. Look at my parents. They seem happy enough.

But if this poor lot is the best they can do for me, I'm better off alone."

Nicholas laughed. "Have you ever considered that you, Aniya Lyons, are just unmarriable?"

Aniya grabbed the pillow from the cot and smacked him. "You're unmarriable."

"Nice comeback." He grabbed the pillow and tossed it back at his friend. "I'm sure one of the pretty ladies will choose me one day."

"I might have picked you if you were in my pool. At least then we could grow old together and be lonely together."

"You make it sound so awful," Nicholas said. "It wouldn't be the worst thing in the world."

Aniya covered her ears and grinned, "Now you're starting to sound like Axel."

"Hey, at least you get a choice. Not everyone got a happy ending like your parents did back when the Lightbringers chose for us." Nicholas grimaced and glanced toward the house below. "You know, I'm friends with a guy who actually has no family, but I honestly don't know which one of us has it worse."

Aniya's smile faded. "To have no parents or to have parents who don't care about each other or you? I vote you, but I can't imagine not having a family either way."

Nicholas shrugged. "You can't miss something you never had."

"The least they could have done was give you a brother or sister."

"I think it would have only made matters worse. Though I guess things are pretty bad when you file an appeal with the Lightbringers to have only one child just so you don't have to spend any more time with your family than necessary."

Aniya looked away. "I'm sorry."

"Don't be. I'm not." Nicholas sat down on the mattress next to her and gently placed a hand on her shoulder. "I do have a family, you know. And what family I have, I wouldn't trade for the world."

Aniya dropped her gaze as Nicholas's hand traveled down her arm.

"Why do you want to leave?" Aniya stood and cleared her throat. "And don't change the subject this time."

Nicholas looked up sharply. "Who said anything about leaving?"

"Come on, I'm not dumb." She looked away. "I know that Holendast is too far out from the Hub for any fancy programmers. Nobody cares enough to send anyone fancy our way. That's why it's the Hole. That's why we love it here. Why would you ever want to leave?"

"Because like you said, it's too far out for any fancy programmers," Nicholas said. "Programming is what I'm best at, and they're wasting my potential by putting a trowel in my hand and calling me a bricklayer. I had another brick fall on my shoulder today, and it's just a matter of time until one finds my head."

"You mean you don't like your random work assignment?" Aniya scoffed. "At least they didn't take you to the Hub against your will. Not like William, even though . . ." She trailed off and looked away.

"I know, Aniya. I'm grateful that I don't have to do that, and I don't wish it on anyone. I was almost as crushed as you when they took William."

Aniya fiddled with her fingernails, refusing to look up.

"Are you sure you're okay?"

Still no response.

Nicholas sighed. "Look, I can still visit occasionally. I wouldn't just leave and never see you again."

He reached for her hand, but she pulled it away.

"What do you want me to do, Aniya?" He finally gave up and stood, pacing away from her. "I can't just stay here for the rest of my life, stuck in this grueling job that will probably kill me. I know what I'm good at, and I need to go do it. I could actually make this messed-up world a better place. Who knows, I might even be able to help find an alternative to the energy problem so people like your brother don't have to go off to who knows where—"

"He's back," Aniya whispered.

"Who's back?" Nicholas grew more frustrated at her interruption, even though he had forgotten his point in the middle of his rant.

"William."

"William what?"

Aniya stood up and grabbed Nicholas's arms. "William is back, Nicholas. He's come back."

He stared at her. "That's impossible. They never would have let him go. That's the whole point of the Citizen Tax."

"They didn't." She blinked, her eyes growing moist. "He was shot."

Nicholas froze. "What did you say?"

"They shot him, Nicholas." Her tears now flowed freely. "It doesn't look good."

"How many times?"

Sniffling, she looked up. "What?"

"How many times did they shoot him?"

"Th-three times."

Nicholas didn't respond but stared at a point past Aniya's face as a wave of realization washed over him.

"Nicholas?"

He snapped out of it and grabbed Aniya's hand, pulling her to the other side of the roof. "You need to hear this." Nicholas sat down in front of a large radio wired to a small tablet. "The last time we lost power, I told you that I wanted to find out how it was happening. So, I set up a trigger on my equipment to detect voltage loss and retrospectively capture audio from the Hub's secure radio channels, which I've been able to gain access to thanks to brute-force reverse hashing."

Aniya groaned and wiped her tears from her eyes. "What did I tell you about English and Nerd being two different languages?"

"Sorry. Basically, I hacked into the Hub's secure communications and set it to record everything, automatically wiping all data every few days if I don't save it. When the power went out this time, I saved all audio recorded in the hour leading up to it."

"I'm confused," Aniya said. "How did you save it without power?"

"Don't make me explain batteries to you, you goof."

"Where did you get your hands on one? The Hole would be the last place I would expect to find one, and they're not exactly cheap."

"Perks of my dad's work. One of the few good things that man has given me. Anyway, this is the five minutes of the recording."

Nicholas pressed a button on his tablet, and a low voice spoke.

"This is Alpha, responding to the breach in the reactor chamber."

"Go ahead."

"The officers are gone. Perhaps dead. We have an empty pod over here. The chain is corrupted, and the pillar is down."

"Do you have eyes on the intruder?"

"Negative. They said there were two of them, but I don't see anyone else."

"Keep looking."

The transmission went quiet.

"No one else is down here. I can do a full sweep, but it would be faster to scan for biologics from the control room."

"Understood. Might as well get back here and run it. I don't have an authorization key for that."

It went quiet again for a few minutes. Aniya looked up at Nicholas, shrugging, but he held up a finger and shook his head.

The same low voice began speaking again, but it didn't seem to mean anything to Aniya. After a while, however, and another long pause, the man's voice took on a different tone.

"I see them, control."

"Good. Hold and wait for reinforcements."

"No need."

"Alpha, wait!"

BANG BANG.

BANG.

"Alpha, what is your status? We're reporting an energy surge. I think they overloaded the reactor."

BANG.

"Come in, Alpha. You need to get out of there before—"

A loud squeal of feedback buzzed from the radio, and Aniya covered her ears in pain.

"Sorry," Nicholas said as he turned down the volume of the recording.

"What was that?"

Nicholas took a deep breath. "Three gunshots the first time, Aniya. I think your brother is in more trouble than you realize. I think he took out the power."

4

William faded in and out of consciousness.

When he was awake, it was like he observed the world through a pane of glass. He could see everything but had no way of communicating, no way to warn his family of the imminent danger. And even if he could, there was nothing he could say that wouldn't put them at great risk.

Lips moved, but William had no comprehension. His family's words turned to muffled jumbles of nonsense. Occasionally, he could make out speech, but just as quickly as this understanding came, it left, and he was stuck again in a torturous limbo, unable to connect with the family he had so terribly missed.

In.

"He can't stay here. Even in the basement, he can't—"

Out.

In his mind's eye, William held a hand up to the hazed glass separating him from his parents. It had been a lifetime. He barely recognized the family he had been forced to leave just three years ago, but at the same time, they were unmistakably, hauntingly familiar.

"Mother."

He saw his mother turn toward him, and his hopes rose. Maybe she heard him. Maybe his body had managed to call out for her audibly.

But she turned away again, and William banged his fists up against the glass in frustration.

In.

"—should be back any moment. You need to make it clear to her what this means." William looked past his father's anxious pacing to see Gareth sitting cross-legged by the wall.

"We can't do that to her. Besides, her Day is coming, and they'll come looking for her."

"It doesn't matter, Catherine. They'll come looking for her no matter what. She has to—"

Out.

A bench materialized next to William, and he sat down, resting his face in his open palms.

They needed to know.

If they had any idea, they would have left their home a long time ago. It was no longer safe in the Web.

Like it was ever really safe to begin with.

But as much as he ached to tell them, he knew it wasn't an option.

The Lightbringers would find him. There was no doubt. So, if he chose to tell his family of the horrors that waited in the nether regions of the Hub, they would be subject to endless torture at the hands of an operative. Or worse, servitude.

No, they couldn't know. The best William could hope for was to go on the run again. Coming back to Holendast was foolish. Kendall should have sent him in the opposite direction, where no one would think to look for him.

In.

"—can keep him. They're Sympathetics."

"Do you really think we can trust them?"

"They have long been helpful to the cause. During the Uprising, they sheltered many of the rebels."

"But they—"

Out.

They were wasting time.

Helpless and alone, William's mind wandered, imagining the pain that awaited his family if he didn't get away from them as soon as possible.

His mother appeared as his feet, her lifeless body completely soaked in blood, staining her beautiful blonde hair a sickening shade of crimson.

His father lay at his feet, his empty eyes looking up at him, his mouth frozen open in an eternal scream.

The Lyons boy stared in horror, fighting back tears.

"William."

He looked up, seeing his sister smiling back at him.

For the first time, William felt hope, and he smiled, reaching a hand out to Aniya.

But as soon as he touched her fingers, her hand burst into flame, melting the flesh off her bones at an incredible pace.

Aniya's phantom figure stepped back and watched her hand, emotionless, then looked back at her brother as the flame spread up her arm and engulfed her body whole.

Then they were all gone.

William was alone again. If it were possible, even more alone than before.

Unable to even cry in a mass confusion of emotion, he instead stood up from the bench and thrust his fists against the glass harder than ever, growing ever more determined to break through and save his family from a horrible end.

"Please hear me!"

His fists began to bruise, the skin growing darker than the circles under his eyes.

"You have to hear me!"

Blood fell from his hands, but he ignored it.

"They're coming for you! Please, mother!"

The bones in his hands cracked, then shattered.

"Father!"

In.

"Is he okay?"

William halted his barrage against his prison as he saw the girl he had made fun of relentlessly as a child.

It was the girl with the wooden sword he had battled countless times as a youth. Sometimes he won. Sometimes, he intentionally stumbled to the ground, allowing her to claim victory and poke the splintered end of the sword into his back in triumph.

This was no vision. She was here in the room with him, standing just inside the shack. She was leaning up against the door, her face downcast as she looked down at her almost-dead brother.

William fell silent and simply placed his deformed hands on the glass, his heart breaking for the precious girl he had defended from bullies time and time again. The girl who would suddenly need to grow up sooner than he had ever wished.

The bones in his hands reformed again, the skin stitching itself up and the blood evaporating.

"I honestly don't know." His father's voice came from across the room. "We haven't been able to get any response from him. Gareth said he may never wake up."

Aniya's face fell further, and she approached William's body.

His mother spoke up. "It's still possible, of course. I saw worse than this in the war. But if he does wake up, there's no telling how long it could take. In any case, he can't stay out here on the bed. We need to put him in the basement for the night."

William's hopes soared. This was the longest he had been able to hear his family. Maybe there was hope after all.

"Leave him out just a little while longer, Dad. I just want to be with him for a little while."

After rubbing his beard for a moment, their father nodded. "I'll give you a few minutes. Gareth, would you and Catherine join me outside for a moment?"

William heard the front door open and close, but he did not take his eyes off his sister.

They were alone.

"Oh, William. What did you get yourself into?"

He let his hands slide down the glass and hang loosely at his sides. She was the last person he wanted to drag into this. It may have been too late for his parents, given their past, but she was innocent. She knew little about the Uprising, Salvador, or the Chancellor. And if William had his way, she would stay ignorant.

"Is it true? Did you kill the power?"

William looked up in alarm. How could she already know?

"I spoke to Nicholas. He hacked into the government's radios. I heard what you did."

Oh, Nicky. His ingenuity was always going to get him into trouble one day. But William never imagined that it would be his own fault.

Aniya opened her mouth to speak, but she closed it again and shook her head.

In the lifetime he had spent with his sister, he never once witnessed her at a loss for words. A rare sight indeed.

William's right hand grew warm again, but there was no pain. It was a pleasant warmth, the first comforting thing he had felt in a long time.

He looked up and through the glass again. His sister held his right hand in the waking world. He could feel it now, his hand growing warmer with every squeeze of comfort from hers.

Shuddering as heat spread through his lifeless body, William pressed his right hand up against the cold glass.

Almost instantly, the glass radiated the heat from his hand and seemed to pulse, rippling out visible waves along the barrier that separated William's mind from his body.

"Please come back, Will. We all need you." A tear trickled from Aniya's right eye, gently coursing down her cheek and dripping onto their joined hands.

William felt that drop of moisture even in the prison of his mind, and he watched as his hand sizzled, smoke rising from his flesh. The glass surrounding his hand crackled, growing hotter and hotter.

"I need you."

Aniya squeezed his hand tight.

William's right hand exploded in heat and pressure, and it pressed deep into the glass as if it had a mind of its own.

The glass buckled from the pressure, and with one final pulse, the glass shattered into a million pieces.

He opened his eyes.

"Hello, Aniya."

5

A niya woke up early the next morning, thanks to a miniature alarm clock strapped to her skin that vibrated fifteen minutes before the rest of the Web would wake up.

She smiled as she removed the nodules stuck to her chest. An alarm clock powered by her body heat. Nicholas's genius was hard to ignore.

Taking advantage of her extra fifteen minutes, she quietly stood from her mattress on the floor. She was already completely dressed in thermal underwear, leather pants, a cotton sweater, and a long cloak. No power meant no central heating, which made for a cold Hole indeed.

People would begin to wonder today. It wasn't often that the power would go out for more than half a day at a time. The last Black Day was eighty-seven days ago, and the blackout had only lasted for three hours. The longest one had been for fourteen hours, but the Lightbringers later released the same statement they always did: routine maintenance.

But Aniya knew that this one wasn't maintenance.

She tiptoed across the room and lit the kerosene lantern on the table, glancing toward her parents still in bed.

No movement.

After taking the lantern from the table and placing it on the floor, she dragged the rug away from the middle of the floor, folded it up haphazardly, and placed it against the wall.

Aniya opened the trapdoor, and sure enough, there was her brother, his eyes already open.

"William?"

It strained her heart to see his withered face, his shriveled body, his bloody bandages. But the smile that crept over his face at the sound of his name was enough to spark a warmth in her heart that nearly made her forget his injuries.

"Hey, you." She returned his smile, but only for a moment. "I know what you did, William."

An inexplicable expression clouded her brother's face, and Aniya could not tell if it was impatience or anger.

"Nicholas hacked into the government's radios. I heard them chasing you. I heard them—" She halted, her eyes drawn again to the moist, red bandages taped to William's hip. "I heard them shoot you. I heard you take out the power."

William nodded slowly.

"Why?"

No response.

"People need that power, William. They need light. It's the only reason that we live the way we do. That's why I have to choose a husband. That's why Nicholas is wasting his life doing manual labor. That's why you—" Aniya checked her voice, suddenly aware of her increasing volume. She looked up and sighed in relief at the sight of her sleeping parents. "That's why you paid the Citizen Tax, William. Why would you take away the one good thing we've all paid for with our freedom? I thought that you'd get that better than anyone."

William remained silent.

"Do Mom and Dad know?"

He shook his head. "They can't know."

"Would you have told me if I didn't already know?"

"No, Aniya. I wasn't going to tell any of you anything. The less you know, the better. The Silver Guard will be coming for me, and if they think you know anything, they'll take you too."

Aniya bit her lip in frustration. "Are you staying here, then?"

Another shake of the head. "Gareth is coming by later today to help move me. It's not safe here."

"Are you coming back?"

"I really don't know."

Aniya's heart fell. She had gone three years without seeing her brother. To watch him be taken away again so soon seemed cruel. "When is the power going to come back?"

William only stared back at her.

Her heart stopped as she realized his implied response. But she had to hear it for herself. "Is the power going to come back?"

"I don't know. That was the plan."

Aniya muttered a string of curses under her breath, imagining the Web in permanent darkness.

With a look toward the clock in the corner, forgetting for a moment that it had no power, she backed away from the trapdoor and stood up, taking the lantern with her. "I have to go to Assembly soon. Please, if you have any say in the matter, don't leave before I get back. I want to see you again before you leave."

A slow nod.

"Be safe, William."

Aniya closed the trapdoor just as an incredible flash of white light blasted throughout the entire sector, piercing through every crack of the Lyons' shed and blinding her.

Annoyed, she closed her eyes and tried to shield herself with outstretched hands. The only downside to waking up early was witnessing the full power of First Light in all its glory.

Backup generators. With the exception of the oxygen recyclers, the Lightbringers didn't bother to use the backup generators to power the Web during the Black Days, but they wouldn't risk losing another day of work, so the flash of light was deemed important enough to wake everyone up for work and Assembly.

"Aniya, did you wake up early?"

She opened her eyes as the light dissipated, and she turned to face her waking father.

"Just woke up, Dad. Power's still out."

Theodore got out of bed and lit the large torch hanging from the wall. "That's odd. The power went out about thirty-six hours ago. This must be the longest Black Day yet."

Aniya held her tongue. "It'd be nice if they'd let us stay home until the power comes back on. The half-day off was nice."

"Trust me, I wish all work was delayed as well." Theodore looked back at Catherine, who rubbed her eyes and sat up slowly.

"Still out?" she asked.

Theodore nodded. "Go back to sleep, honey. I'll just make something quick before I leave."

"Nonsense," she said, walking to the icebox. "Can you imagine if the Silvers came by and saw you cooking for yourself?"

"Aniya, did you move the rug?"

Her heart skipped a beat, and Aniya spun around to her father's confused stare.

"Yeah, I was just about to wake up William when we got First Light."

Her father quickly grabbed the rug, dragging it back into place. "He needs his rest, Aniya, and you need to be more careful. It's only a matter of time before the Silver Guard comes looking for him, and this place has to look like he never made it here. We're lucky enough that we found him in the middle of the Black."

She nodded absentmindedly.

"I don't want you talking with him before we do anyway."

Aniya put her hands on her hips. "Why?"

Her father ignored her question.

For a moment, she considered telling her parents what she already knew. They would have to listen to her then.

But with a glance toward the rug and what she knew lay beneath, she changed her mind. He had his reasons for not telling them.

"Here you go, Aniya." Catherine handed her a candle and a paper bag. "Be careful on your way to Assembly."

She took the items offered to her, but hesitated. "Can't I eat breakfast here today?"

Her father shook his head. "You always eat on the way to school." Grasping her arms firmly, he looked at her with unblinking eyes. "This is important, Aniya. You must act completely normal. Do nothing different. Say nothing to draw attention to yourself. Besides us, the only people you can trust right now are Gareth, Roland, and Nicholas. No one else."

Aniya raised her eyebrows. "Nicholas?" She never told her parents where she actually went last night.

"Go to Assembly, skip whatever classes you usually do, go to Axel's house, say hello to Violet at her stall in the market, and then come back here at a casual pace. Will you do that for me?"

She nodded.

"Now, here's the most important thing." Her father lowered his voice. "If you come back and there is no candle-light coming from inside, do not enter under any circumstances. Turn around, go find Gareth at the bar, and do not look back. Do you understand me?"

Another nod. "Just wait until I get back to move him," she

said. "I know you're going to hide him again, and I want to see him again before it's too late."

Theodore embraced her and stroked her hair. "My dear Annelise, the light of my life. Everything will be fine. You'll see your brother again, I promise."

After a long moment, Aniya pulled away and moved toward the door, where her mother was waiting with open arms.

"Be safe, Aniya," her mother said as she hugged her daughter. "We'll see you this evening and make sure you have a chance to see your brother as well."

Aniya nodded into her mother's shoulder and backed away. With a hopeful heart and a forced smile, she said goodbye to her parents for the last time.

6

William studied the darkened detail of the wood just inches above his face, counting every knot, divot, and crack for the umpteenth time. It seemed like an entire day had gone by since Aniya had left for Assembly, but it may as well have been just an hour.

As he continued tracing the underside of the trapdoor, he found himself marveling that his parents were able to afford such a material. With no more trees left to create wood, it was a rare commodity indeed. Even the artificial wood the Light-bringers manufactured was uncommon, especially this far out in the Web.

The hidden door above him must have been a late addition to the shack, using materials that he could only assume were stolen. The only other pieces of wood the Lyons owned were the two swords William had made out of scraps Aniya had managed to "find."

He winced as a sharp object pricked his index finger, and he closed his mouth as blood dripped down onto his lips.

Squinting, William brought his hand closer to his eyes. In the dim, orange light that poked through the floorboard above, he spotted a large splinter embedded in his skin.

He took the splinter out and simply stared at his bleeding finger. The initial shock had gone, and he no longer felt any pain from his hand. Whatever pain he should have felt from the small injury was dwarfed by the damage inflicted by the three gunshot wounds across his body.

Though he could barely see, William traced a bloody pattern on the wood above: a four-fingered hand. He smirked. *He probably thinks I'm dead.*

William moved his hand away from his face and let the blood slowly drip onto his bare chest, watching the red droplets course down his atrophied skin and toward the wound on his hip, where they merged with fresh blood oozing from underneath the bandages that had been applied the night before.

Noticing the old bandages for the first time, William sighed and knocked on the wood above him.

He heard feet shuffling along the floor above, and seconds later, the trapdoor opened.

"How are you feeling, Will?" His mother beamed down at him.

He motioned to the now-ruined bandage. "Still not great. I'm bleeding again."

"Let's get your bandages changed," she said, extending a hand to William's good arm and pulling him up and out of the hole with a grunt. "Lie down on the bed. I'll get another cloth."

William slowly took a few steps, wincing, then gently sat on the bed. With another grunt of pain, he leaned back, allowing the blood to collect on the sheets.

"It's a shame Gareth didn't have all of his equipment with him last night," she said, digging in a cupboard. "He could have cauterized it and stopped the bleeding. It would definitely hurt more for now, and the mark would not be very attractive, but you wouldn't lose any more blood."

To be honest, William didn't care. He wasn't entirely

confident he would make it until tomorrow without another injury, or worse. But he wasn't about to tell her that.

"Remind me to give you some jerky before you go back down there. We saved some from the mole last night."

William remembered the days when he would complain about having mole meat for dinner yet again. It seemed like a lifetime ago. But right now, it sounded like a feast.

His mother returned to the bed with a fresh bandage in hand. She carefully peeled off the old, soaked cloth from his hip, wrapping it in a towel.

"In a few days, maybe—"

Her voice came to a halt as a bright, white light pierced through the cracks in the walls.

"The Silver Guard," his mother whispered, terror washing over her face. She pulled William off the bed, helping him to his feet and hurrying him to the hole in the floor. "Stay down."

The trapdoor above him closed but opened again a few seconds later as his mother tossed bloody sheets on top of him, hiding the evidence and her son at the same time.

William slowed his breathing down as best as he could, trying to make his presence unnoticeable as well as calm his racing nerves. He heard his mother blowing several times, and as the sheet over his face grew darker, he realized that she was blowing out the various candles around the house in a desperate effort to guarantee his safety.

A moment later, the door to the shack opened, ignoring a knock of courtesy.

Even though William was covered with a sheet stained with his blood, he could see several bright lights poking through the wood from above, bobbing about the room.

"Catherine Lyons, how are you doing today?" A calm, deep voice spoke pleasantries in an unpleasant tone.

His mother responded, her voice with a slight tremble. "I'm fine, thank you, Alpha. How can I help you?"

This will be over quickly.

"Where is your husband's work assignment?"

"The mill."

"Fetch him, Officer."

The door opened and closed.

"Has your son contacted you?"

"My son? He paid the Citizen Tax three years ago."

"We are well aware of that, Mrs. Lyons. But I can't help but notice that you didn't answer my question. Have you seen or heard from your son?"

"No, of course not. The last time I saw him was the day he left for the Hub. Why are you looking for him?"

His mother's voice grew stronger, its quiver now gone.

Maybe there's hope after all.

"Tell me, why are your lights out? It is a Black Day. Shouldn't your candles be lit?"

"I was about to take a nap."

"With no sheets on the bed? That must be uncomfortable."

"I-I was finishing my laundry."

"You must have remarkable confidence in your skill with a washing board to clean your sheets with no light."

His mother fell silent.

"Refusal to pay the Citizen Tax bears harsh penalties, as does harboring fugitives. Imagine if you and your family were found in breach of such regulations. Not a very pleasant thought, is it?"

"I assure you, Officer, we wouldn't dream of committing such open acts of rebellion against the Glorious Bringers of Light. But now you're the one who hasn't answered my question." Catherine's voice grew stronger. "Why are you looking for my son? I may never get to see him again, but I have a right to know that he is well."

What followed was a silence so still that William could

hear his mother's steady breath quietly whistle through clenched teeth.

When the man spoke again, his words were slowly drawn out, emphasized firmly. "Your rights, Mrs. Lyons, like your electricity, are afforded to you out of the Lightbringers' good graces, and it is within their rights to give them and take them as they please. You would do well to remember that." The man's tone deepened. "And a little respect is in order. I am no officer. As you know, I am an operative sent by the Chancellor himself. Know that rebellion against me is treason of the highest order."

After a few more minutes of back-and-forth that went nowhere, the door creaked open again.

"Ah, Mr. Lyons. So good of you to join us. Please, sit."

A loud thud indicated that William's father indeed sat, but with firm help.

"Theodore Lyons, have you heard from your son?"

"He was assigned to relocative servitude three years ago." His father's words were already much steadier than his wife's testimony.

"That's not what I asked, Mr. Lyons. Your family seems to have a penchant for avoiding my questions. Please be direct, and this will all be over before you know it. Now, have you heard from your son?"

"No."

Another pause.

"I would like to believe you, Mr. Lyons. I really would. My job would be a lot simpler. However, we understand that the farther out we go in the Web, the less . . . forthcoming the citizens are. We honestly don't care. As long as you pay the Tax and do the jobs we assign you, we really don't care. But in matters such as these, the truth, I'm sure you can appreciate, is imperative. Get her on her knees."

Another thud accompanied by a shriek from his mother.

"Don't touch her!"

William's eyes opened wide in panic.

"So long as you answer me honestly. Where is your son?"

Please father, just tell them.

"I haven't seen him, I swear!"

His mother sobbed. "Please, there's no need for this. We haven't seen him."

"One more time, Theodore. Where is your son?"

"He's not—"

Squish.

The sound would haunt William for the rest of his life. The gun, completely silenced, made a quiet clacking noise, but what he realized later to be the sound of the bullet spinning deep into his mother's skull echoed in his ears over and over again.

Squish.

7

"One more time, Mattias."

The teacher's impatient tone perked Aniya's ears, and she looked up from her half-asleep state for the first time since class had begun.

The boy to her right slumped back in his chair and rolled his eyes.

"Up, boy." The elderly man pacing back and forth at the head of the room did not seem to enjoy the class any more than his students.

The boy stood up and shoved his hands in his pockets. "Article X, Section A, Subsection E: If a man is chosen for relocative servitude, he shall report to the Hub immediately for service to the Glorious Bringers of Light."

"You made the same mistake again. *Permanent* service, Mattias."

"Permanent service," the boy mumbled before sitting back down.

"Very good." The professor turned and looked for another student. "Annelise, how about Article I, Section E, Subsection D?"

Just coherent enough to recognize her full first name,

Aniya stood up, shaking her grogginess away. "Article I, Section E, Subsection D: Each family must produce two children for the advancement of the Web, and they are limited to only two children, both of which—"

"That is Subsection B, Annelise. I asked for D."

Aniya racked her brain, then recited, "Article I, Section E, Subsection D: Any additional children born after the first two will be immediately confiscated upon birth and taken for relocative servitude in the Hub."

"Very good, Annelise. You may sit down."

Aniya did so and resumed her subtle slumber.

"Benjamin, why don't you give us Subsection E?"

Another boy stood up and cleared his throat, but before he could speak, the door creaked open and white light flooded the room.

Almost in perfect unison, the entire class rose to their feet and stood with their arms at their side as four men walked into the room. Their metal boots sounded against the wood floor with perfect timing, reminding Aniya of the old-fashioned clocks in a museum she had once been forced to attend. Each of the men wore silver body armor, complete with headpieces equipped with a bright white light that outshone the scarce candles scattered throughout the room. As the men walked toward the teacher, the light sparkled and bounced off their reflective armor, making it difficult, almost painful to look directly at them for longer than a few seconds.

The teacher also dropped his hands to his side and stood straight, holding his head high. "Greetings, officers of the Glorious Bringers of Light. We weren't expecting a visit from the Silver Guard."

"That's the idea," said one. Without another word, the officers stood in a line at the head of the room.

"Well, class. Since we have visitors, why don't we do a little pop quiz? The first three to answer perfectly get to leave class early."

The class stirred, and Aniya looked up. A chance to ditch Regulations Class sounded promising.

"Let's see. Article II, Section A, Subsection B. Anyone?"

Hands shot up all over the room. It was one of the easier regulations, and everyone knew it. Not exactly a good example to show off for the Silvers.

"Antonio?"

A boy sitting toward the front stood up quickly, and rattled off, "Article II, Section A, Subsection B: On their eighteenth birthday, each man must report for their random work assignment and submit their name as a potential suitor to be matched with a female mate."

"Very good, Antonio." The teacher clapped enthusiastically, motioning for the class to do the same.

As a few students clapped softly, the boy grabbed his bag and jogged out the door.

"And now for the next one, Subsection C Revised?"

Dozens of hands shot up in the air, and Aniya rolled her eyes. The Silvers' visit meant a chance for the teacher to show off with some easy regulations and maybe get promoted to a higher grade level, she supposed.

"Lysa?"

A girl to Aniya's right stood up. "Article II, Section A, Subsection C Revised: On their eighteenth birthday, each woman must choose a mate from five potential suitors, each chosen by the Bringers of Light."

The teacher winced as the Silvers looked at each other. "Very close, Lysa."

The girl sat back down.

"Annelise, you should know this one better than most. Your Day is coming up soon, after all. Why don't you give it a try?"

Aniya didn't respond.

At the front of the room, one of the Silvers turned and whispered something to his leader, who nodded curtly.

"Annelise?"

Gritting her teeth, Aniya looked up at the teacher.

She stood up slowly as each of the four lights turned to shine on her directly. She felt naked, exposed, and she raised a hand to block out the blinding light. "Article II, Section A, Subsection C Revised: On their eighteenth birthday, each woman must choose a mate from five potential suitors, each chosen by the . . ." Aniya's skin grew cold, and she dropped her hand to glare at the Silvers standing at the front of the room. She ignored the searing pain in her eyes as her tone hardened. ". . . *Glorious* Bringers of Light."

Apparently ignoring her contempt, the teacher applauded again. "Very good, Annelise. You may collect your things and go."

Aniya snatched her bag, spun on her feet, and left the room amid scarce applause.

Behind her, the leader of the Silvers motioned for his men to stay behind. He switched off his headlamp and stepped into the dark hallway behind her.

Aniya tossed her bag on a bench in the courtyard and sat down, sighing. To hear it constantly from her parents was one thing. To be forced to repeat it in school frustrated her to no end.

If the price to pay for so-called free power was submitting to such strict regulations, was it even worth it?

"Aniya." A hiss came from the shadows to her right.

Aniya looked up and glanced around, but the source of the whisper was unclear.

"Over here."

Still unable to see where the voice was coming from, Aniya got up, leaving her book bag behind, and walked toward the large entrance. As soon as she stepped into the halls of the school, her hand was grabbed, and she was pulled into further darkness.

Aniya opened her mouth to speak but felt a warm hand silencing her.

Roland's face emerged from the shadows, his eyes darting back and forth. He let go of her mouth but kept a tight grip on her hand.

"You need to get out of here."

Aniya pulled her hand away, and she took a step back. "What are you talking about?"

As she backed away, Roland grabbed her again, pulling her further back into the hallway. Without saying a word, he pointed through the window overlooking the courtyard.

Her curiosity won over her frustration, and Aniya looked out the window but saw only black. "What are you—"

"Shh."

Aniya nearly shoved Roland away from her, but she froze as she spotted a dark form moving through the courtyard. She squinted and spotted a tall man in silver armor making his way around the benches, stopping to check every shadow before moving on.

Before she could say anything, Roland pulled her into a nearby classroom.

He closed the door behind them and turned to her, but Aniya spoke before he had the chance. "Is William okay?"

Roland shook his head. "If they haven't found him by now, they're about to. They walked into your house about five minutes ago."

Aniya's skin turned cold. "How do you know? My house is too far away to get here in five minutes."

"Gareth. I don't know how he knows, but he seemed pretty certain. They're going to be coming for you, so you need to leave now. Gareth told me to get you out of the Hole."

Aniya threw her hands up. "Why would they come for me? They're not looking for me. They're looking for William."

"Yeah, but they're going to want to talk to your entire family. Who knows? Given William's condition, they might skip the talking and go straight to shooting. Gareth doesn't want to risk it either way."

Aniya's head spun. *Not again.*

"But my parents . . ."

"It's too late. All we can do is make sure you're safe." Roland shook her shoulders when she didn't respond. "Aniya, we have to get out. Now."

She pictured William, discovered by the Silvers and dragged away. It was hauntingly reminiscent of his departure three years ago. The morning of his eighteenth birthday, just after First Light, a garrison of officers knocked on their door and took him away without giving him a chance to say goodbye.

Now, they were coming to take him again, and Aniya knew that this time, he wouldn't be coming back.

She found herself unable to move, still picturing William's inevitable fate. "I just got him back. I can't lose him again."

Roland slapped her across the face, and Aniya snapped out of her daze.

"I'm sorry, Aniya. I promised Gareth I would get you out, and I can't stand here and watch you get taken, or worse. We need to get moving."

Behind them, the door handle jiggled, and Aniya was grateful that Roland had thought to lock it.

"Okay, let's get out of here."

Roland didn't waste any time. He pulled her to the other side of the room and opened the window that pointed at the main street. "I'm right behind you."

Aniya shook her hand free from Roland and deftly climbed out the window, landing on her feet with grace.

Behind her, Roland's exit from the room was not as smooth, and he tumbled to the ground.

She extended a hand to him, and he gladly took it, muttering, "You made that look so easy. Did you take dance or something?"

Aniya scoffed quietly but did not let her annoyance show.

"I'm a runner. Have been all my life."

Roland let go of her hand. "That's good, because we're going to be doing a lot of that. Right now, we need to get out of the Hole."

"Why do we have to leave Holendast? And what do you mean, we?"

"Just for the time being. They're going to search the sector top to bottom looking for you, and if you're still in the Hole, they will find you." He swiped the dust from his pants. "Besides, it's not like I have a family here that will miss me."

Aniya shook her head. "I can take care of myself. I certainly don't need your help. You're not even as old as I am."

"How old do you think I am?"

Behind them, a loud crash indicated that the officer had succeeded in breaking down the door to the classroom.

Aniya turned around and broke into a light jog. "We can have that conversation another time. Come on!"

Roland caught up, and they broke into a dead run together.

"We need to head to the station. We can take the train tunnel to the next sector," Roland shouted over the sound of their feet on the cobblestone below.

Aniya pointed to the right. "I know a shortcut!" Without waiting, she spun and bolted, leaving Roland behind.

He shouted after her, "What shortcut?"

Aniya took another sharp turn to the right, now heading in the opposite direction of the train station. She heard Roland's footsteps behind her, and she ran faster, knowing that he would soon realize her true destination and try to stop her.

She vaulted over a fence and kept running. That would slow Roland down.

"Aniya!"

She ignored Roland's shout and continued, knowing that every second lost could mean a horrible fate for her family.

The route across the Hole seemed longer than ever, even though she ran now at her fastest. The journey usually took ten minutes at a light jog. Today, Aniya made the trek in a record-breaking seven, though it felt like twenty.

Finally, she could see her house, and her heart sank.

Her home was a glowing beacon in the middle of the Hole. Light escaped from the cracks in the shack, and a foreboding white glow spilled out onto the cobblestone street. Aniya pushed herself harder and sprinted the rest of the way, but she stopped briefly as she stood by the door. She had plenty of time to think while she was running, but she had no idea what she would do once she entered.

She knew one thing for sure. They were not taking her brother again.

Aniya curled her hands into fists and took a deep breath. She reached for the handle but was grabbed from behind and forced to the ground. Her attacker dragged her away as her muffled screams fought against the hand that was clamped over her mouth.

8

William's head spun.

His father's screams came from somewhere in the distance, his anguish drowned out by the awful sound that wouldn't stop echoing in William's ears.

Squish.

After a moment, his father's cries diminished to muffled sobs.

"I won't lie to you, Mr. Lyons. I enjoyed that. I enjoyed it, and I will enjoy killing you if you don't tell me where your son is. Your death has been a long time coming, after all."

Another long pause.

Finally, his father spoke again, his voice quiet but firm. "I haven't seen my son since you took him away from me. Just like you took—"

The sound of metal on bone was sickening, as was his father's cry of pain.

"Your hostility is not appreciated, Theodore. Of all men, it is a mere ten percent that are chosen for relocation to the Hub. You should be proud of your son, willing to serve so that you could be given free energy. Now, please. Do your part and let him serve so you can return to whatever life you have left."

No response.

"Very well. I'm sure we'll find him if we look long enough. It'll go much smoother for us if you aren't around to be a nuisance."

That was enough.

Desperate to avoid another death on his hands, William lashed his fists against the underside of the trapdoor, ignoring the searing pain in his shoulder.

Despite the sudden interruption, the man's tone was even and cool, as if he expected no different. "Imagine that. Sounds like someone has decided to announce his presence."

"No," his father groaned.

"Fetch him."

The trapdoor flew open, and even through the sheet that covered him, William was blinded by several white lights. The sheet was tossed aside, and he was grabbed by both arms and dragged out of the hole, his shoulder and hip burning.

"Stand up."

William clutched his body in pain, slowly writhing on the floor.

"Get him up."

He was grabbed again and made to stand, the pain approaching unbearable levels.

William's eyes adjusted, and his legs buckled again as he took in the sight before him.

The one-room shack was lined with men in silver body armor, each of them standing tall, unmoving, with guns at the ready.

To his right, his father was sitting in a chair against the wall, held down by two men.

Finally, to his left was what broke his heart and stole his little remaining energy. His mother lay on the ground, still and lifeless. A pool of blood had collected under her head, painting the strands of her blonde hair a dark red.

William slowly looked up as his skin flushed, curling his

hands into fists and clenching his teeth. In front of him was a man in a black suit, his arms folded across his chest. William made a weak but determined movement forward, only to be instantly pulled back by two sets of hands.

"It's good to see you again, William." The Operative looked at the bloodied, emaciated boy before him and smirked. "You look well."

His father began pleading. "Please, you've done enough. Don't take any more from us."

"Perhaps if you had been honest and instantly told me where the boy was. You had to learn the hard way, Theodore, that the games you play out here in your beloved Hole will not be tolerated by the Lightbringers." He grabbed another chair and turned it around backwards, sitting in front of William's father. "So, now that you understand that I will settle for nothing less than the truth, I ask that you choose your words carefully. What has he told you?"

His father looked up and stretched forth his hands openly. "Nothing, I swear. He can't even talk. We think he's in shock from the pain."

A ploy William had suggested the night before as a last resort.

"Let me try again. What has he told you? How much do you know?"

"Nothing. You really think I would lie to you after what you just did? You made your point."

The Operative studied his face for a long moment. "Say I believe you. I can't very well let you walk around a free man after what you made me do here. People out here on the edge of the Web are just stupid enough to believe your story. At best, I can take you back with me to the Hub, but you're too old to be of any use to us. Your daughter, on the other hand, in the prime of her life—she could be of some use."

Rage boiled deep inside William, a fury that rivaled the anger he had felt at the sight of his dead mother. The world around him went black, and all he could see was the Operative sitting before him, casually taunting his victims.

"I know she's all set to get married in a few weeks, but I'm sure we can find her a mate somewhere out there. In fact, it's time I settled down, you know. Perhaps—"

"I'll kill you if you touch her," William found himself bursting out helplessly, regretting his words even as they left his mouth.

His father dropped his head in defeat.

The Operative slowly stood and turned toward William, his expression unchanged. "So the boy does speak. This changes things." He smirked again. "In the spirit of cruel irony and poetic justice, William, you should know that I made sure that you were selected for relocative servitude. Payback for this." He turned back around and pulled down his collar to reveal a scar across his throat. "It was your father's fault that we nearly killed you, and because you've just confirmed that I can't trust anything he says, it is now your fault that he has to die."

The room fell silent as William froze in horrified anticipation of what he knew was coming next.

"I'm sorry," his father said.

William turned around to answer, but his father was instead looking at the Operative with sad eyes.

Then, his father moved faster than William had ever seen. He leapt to his feet, fighting his way through the Silvers toward the Operative. He grabbed a gun and opened fire, and one of the officers holding William fell backward into the tiny basement, his headlamp shattering and going dark.

The Operative simply looked on, seemingly amused, until William's father broke through and charged at him.

Then, a knife appeared from somewhere within the man's black clothing, and the Operative made one graceful slice through the air.

William's father stopped his attack, staggering forward as

his eyes widened. Blood seeped out of his neck as his mouth slowly dropped open. The gun slipped from his fingers, and he slowly dropped to his knees as the Operative bent over and whispered in his ear.

"*Now* you know my pain."

William's father clutched at his throat and croaked out his final words. "I'm sorry." He then looked away and inched forward on his knees, pushing past the Operative and slowly making his way toward his son.

But the Operative gave him a gentle push with his shoe, and William's father fell forward limply, crashing to the floor.

William simply stared at his father's dead body, unable to process the many emotions that raged within his heart, fighting for his attention. There was devastation at the murder of his parents. Anger at the Lightbringers for their cruelty. Fear for what was waiting for him back underneath the Citadel now that there was no one to help him.

Yet if he were to single one feeling out as the strongest, it would be a burning hatred. Not for the Operative, though he surely hated the assassin. No, William hated himself more than anyone else. He had seen more death in the last twenty-four hours than he had in his entire life. Five lives ended abruptly and tragically. And it was all for him.

Salvador was right. This wasn't worth it.

The Operative sighed and looked back up at William.

"As for you, well, I can't have you walking around, telling the world what you've seen."

The man gestured toward William, and the Silver Guard surrounding him raised their weapons.

But even as William stared down the barrels of a dozen guns, as self-loathing crashed over him in waves, as he antici-pated being freed from his guilt and surrendering to death, there was something else.

Hope.

It was too late for him, but Aniya still had a chance. She

could still make it out. As long as she kept running, which was what she did best, she could stay alive.

The thought filled him with an odd peace, even as he stood in the blood of his parents. And so, with a deep sigh, William closed his eyes and accepted his fate.

9

Aniya was forced to the ground, now three houses away from her home, back the way she had come. She kicked against her captor, even biting down on the hand over her mouth, but it wouldn't release her.

"Quiet!" A familiar voice hissed.

She calmed at the sound of his voice, recognizing it amid her panic and rage.

Nicholas removed his hand slowly and examined the wound on his hand. "Your teeth are sharper than they look." He sucked blood from his wound and spat it out on the dirt.

"What was that for? They're in my house!"

"And what was your plan? You were just going to run in there and take them all on?"

Aniya glared at him. "I was going to help them."

"You can't help them if you're dead, Aniya."

"They wouldn't," she said, shaking her head. "They might kidnap kids, but they don't kill them."

"I'm not so sure about that. They shot your brother, didn't they?"

"William's not a kid anymore. He's a government employee that sabotaged the power and escaped."

Nicholas held up his hands and stepped back. "Are you defending them?"

"No. I'm just saying, I can see why they shot him, but they wouldn't hurt us. They can't afford to hurt their precious citizens. Now, let me go." Aniya stood up but was tackled to the ground again.

"You don't get it," Nicholas said, pinning her. "The Lightbringers are not very forgiving. If they think you helped your brother, they'll kill you. Or worse."

Aniya struggled against his arms. Nicholas may have hated his work as a bricklayer, but it had made him much stronger than she had realized. She wasn't going anywhere.

"I don't want you to die, Aniya, and neither do your parents. I promised to protect you, so I will. What happens in there now is out of our control. Your parents would agree. It's better that they die and you live than all of you die."

Aniya finally settled down, her energy spent between the run and the struggle. She went limp, and Nicholas slowly let her go.

They stared at each other for several seconds, only interrupted when Roland approached, gasping for air.

"I'm glad you caught her," he said between breaths. "She's too fast for me."

Aniya pointed at Nicholas. "You knew about this?"

Nicholas and Roland looked at each other.

"One of you say something, or I'm going inside."

Finally, Roland spoke. "We promised we would keep you alive."

"You promised who?"

"Gareth," Nicholas said.

"What does Gareth have to do with this?"

But neither of them got the chance to answer before the sound of crying came from Aniya's house.

"Mom," Aniya muttered, standing up.

The crying was suddenly cut short, replaced by a tortured scream.

"Dad!" She ran forward, but Nicholas and Roland stopped her.

As she kicked at them, pushing against their arms, they forced her to the ground again. Aniya thrust her fists against their shoulders as she sobbed, trying but failing not to picture what had just happened.

Roland gently covered her mouth with his shirt, muffling her cries but letting her breathe.

Finally, she quieted.

After several minutes, they let her back up, just in time to watch a procession of Silvers leave her house.

"Quick, hide," Nicholas said.

The trio moved behind a fence for further cover, even though they were three houses away.

Minutes later, long after the last Silver had left, Nicholas spoke again.

"We'd better get going."

He stood up and looked around.

It was enough for Aniya. She took off running, ignoring the protests of the boys behind her and making her way to her home.

Aniya threw open the door, letting it slam against the back wall. She stepped inside the hauntingly dark room and immediately slipped on a puddle of sticky liquid, tumbling to the ground and landing roughly on the uneven floor. Her right hand made contact with a bundle lying next to her, and she felt around, trying to identify the mass.

Rough polyester. Old stitches starting to fall apart. Flesh, still warm, slippery with a thick coating of warm, sticky fluid.

A bearded face.

Father.

Overwhelmed with shock and anger, Aniya shoved herself away from her father's dead body, gasping for air between heavy sobs. She kept backing away until she reached another body lying a few feet away.

Startled, she ran her hands over the other body, her eyes still adjusting.

Mother.

Aniya let herself keel over to the side, falling again on the bloodstained floor, now crying freely, her tears mixing with the blood beneath her.

Unable to even force herself to her knees, Aniya dragged herself along the floor, dreading the worst but desperate to find any sign that William could have made it out alive.

She made her way to the middle of the room, crawling on her hands and knees and reaching around for the trapdoor. The latch should have given its position away, but as Aniya reached toward where it should have been, she toppled forward and nearly fell through the hole in the floor.

Aniya grabbed the surrounding floor to steady herself and keep from falling in, and as she peered in and saw the faint outline of a body, her last spark of hope fizzled out.

William.

She rolled over on the floor and covered her face with her hands, her chest heaving with the weight of her anguish. Her hair lay in a puddle of blood, staining it a sickening red, but she didn't care. Her hands smeared even more blood over her face, but she didn't even notice.

Everything was gone.

She hated Nicholas for holding her back. If only she had gotten there sooner, she may not have been able to stop the bloodbath, but at least she wouldn't be the only one left.

Aniya heard footsteps in the doorway, but she didn't look to see who they belonged to. A dark corner of her mind wished that the Silver Guard had come back to finish the job.

"Aniya," Nicholas whispered, his hand resting on her shoulder.

She didn't look up but cried even heavier. A warm light

flickered near her face, a candle Nicholas had lit when he stepped inside.

"I'm so sorry."

Aniya finally grabbed the hand on her shoulder and squeezed it tight as her anger rose. Her sobs choked her, and her grasp on Nicholas's hand went limp as she heaved into her knees. As her crying became less violent, she squeezed again, this time drawing comfort from the contact.

Nicholas didn't seem to mind Aniya's forceful grip on his hand, and he squeezed back.

Aniya looked up just enough to see Roland fighting back tears of his own as he surveyed the room, taking in the results of the massacre and examining the bodies.

"I'm sorry," Aniya said, spitting out her words in between sobs. "You were right. We shouldn't have come back."

Nicholas said nothing.

Aniya scanned the room, now by the light of Nicholas's candle. Even as her stomach churned at the sight of blood painting the walls of her home, she knew that this would be her last chance to see her family. As her vision adjusted, she let her eyes move from her father, to her mother, and then to the hole in the floor where—

She gasped.

"What is it?"

For the first time, Aniya felt hope.

"It isn't William."

Nicholas brought the candle closer to the makeshift basement, illuminating the dead body that lay inside. It was one of the Silvers, sprawled out in the hole, his helmet cracked into several pieces by the force of a bullet.

"He's still out there."

"Careful, Aniya." Roland said. "William may be alive, but we need to focus on getting you safe. Right now, we have no way to know where your brother is or how to save him."

Even though Aniya knew this, her anger rose again.

William had escaped the clutches of the Lightbringers, just to be taken right back again.

She took a deep breath and steadied herself, ignoring the putrid stench of death that invaded her senses. The thought of her brother still alive stirred hope once more, and her strength returned despite the horrible scene around her.

"Okay."

"Come on," Nicholas said, motioning to the door. "We have to get out of the Hole."

Aniya shook her head. "We? You have a family here, Nicholas. You can't just leave them."

"What family? Trust me, I won't be missed here." Nicholas smiled grimly. "Aniya, we promised Gareth we'd take care of you, and we can't do that from Holendast. Besides, if they can't find you, it won't be long until the Silvers show up at my house anyway. I don't know what they'd do to me, but I don't want to find out."

Roland nodded. "It's safer for all of us if we stick together."

"And if I say no?"

Nicholas shrugged. "We weren't offering. We're coming with you whether you like it or not."

After a moment, Aniya sighed. "Nothing I can say will stop you?"

Roland folded his arms. "Nope. Now, can we get moving?"

Aniya stood up. "Fine. Let's go."

10

"Well, this plan was short lived."

Aniya, Nicholas, and Roland crouched behind a crate, taking cover from the bobbing beams of light that swept the train station.

"Yeah, and the train tunnel is the only way out that I know of." Roland sighed. "Not to say I told you so, but going back to your house only slowed us down."

Aniya bit her lip. "Maybe. At least I know that William is alive."

"That's great," Nicholas said, "but we can't do much about it if we're trapped in the Hole. It's one of the smallest sectors in the Hub. We'd run out of places to hide pretty quickly."

They remained silent for a moment and studied the Silvers' movements. Aniya wasn't sure about Nicholas and Roland, but she couldn't detect any kind of pattern. "Maybe they're not looking for me. Maybe they're waiting."

"If that's the case, then we're wasting time," Nicholas said. He backed away farther into the shadows and stood up, still out of sight. "Let's get out of here and find another way out."

"Where?" Aniya followed his lead. "Roland said that's the only way."

"The only one I know of," Roland said. "There's a few people who would be able to tell us if there are any others. Lucky for us, I'm pretty close to one of them."

"Gareth?"

"Yep. His bar won't be open for another few hours, so we can get in there without being seen. Let's go!"

As Roland took the lead, Nicholas dropped back and took Aniya's hand once again. He hadn't let go much since they had left her house. She hated the feeling at first, when it seemed like he was trying to lead her, but now as he walked evenly with her, she realized it was for emotional support. She found herself not minding so much.

Roland slowed down and led them onto the main street silently. He held up a hand behind him, and Aniya and Nicholas stopped.

After peeking out toward the main street, Roland motioned for them to follow and darted across the street into another alley.

They had just made it into the alley, however, when Aniya saw a white glow from around the corner of the far wall. She snatched Roland's hand and pulled him backward, placing a hand on his mouth.

Roland struggled briefly but stopped as he seemed to spot the light.

Aniya slowly let him go and placed a hand on her chest, her heart racing.

"Please don't let that be coming from the bar," Nicholas muttered.

He stepped around Aniya and Roland, pressing his own body against the wall and peeking around the corner.

After a moment, he turned around and rested against the wall next to Aniya. "They're in the bar now, probably searching the place."

"And Gareth?" Aniya asked.

Roland shrugged. "In there with them, I'd say. My guess is they already searched the clinic, and they're searching the bar for good measure. That's a good sign. Means they're running out of places to look." He peeked around the corner again. "Maybe they'll be gone soon, and you won't have to leave the Hole after all."

"Something tells me they won't give up that easily," Aniya said. She shuddered at the thought of winding up in the hands of the Silvers.

"You really think they'll keep looking for you?" Roland asked. "Surely they'll give up eventually."

Nicholas shook his head. "Not if they think she knows something. It doesn't make sense for them to kill her parents otherwise."

"Something?" Aniya frowned. "Like what?"

"Something worth killing over," Nicholas muttered.

"Get back." Roland grabbed Aniya's shoulder and pulled her back against the wall.

Aniya reached to wrench his hand from her shoulder but froze as bright, white light flooded the street ahead.

From around the corner, she heard heavy boots step out onto the cobblestone. Without so much as a word, the officers marched into the distance, their footsteps fading away gradually.

The trio waited several minutes after the streets went silent, not daring to move.

Finally, Roland released Aniya and stepped away from the wall. "Sorry. That was too close."

Nicholas looked around the corner. "You think it's safe to go in there so soon?"

"No, but we don't have anywhere else to go. It's the only option we have."

They stepped onto the main street, glancing in all directions. Roland beckoned them to follow with a wave of his hand, and he darted into the bar.

Aniya followed and closed the door behind her, slowly turning the knob to avoid making any noise.

"Who's there?" Gareth's voice, while quiet, still resonated across the pitch-black bar.

"It's Roland. Light a candle."

A match was struck from the other end of the tavern, and one small candle soon lit up the room. Almost instantly, Gareth covered it with his hand, only letting a small amount of light through his fingers.

"What is she doing here?" Without giving Roland a chance to respond, he addressed Aniya. "Are you okay?"

"I'm fine," she said and looked at the floor. "But my parents are dead."

The tavern went quiet, and Gareth finally broke the silence with a sigh. "I'm truly sorry, Aniya. I was friends with your parents for a long time, as you know. And your brother?"

"They took him."

"I see. We need to move fast, then." Gareth cracked his fingers open a little more, letting more light illuminate his disappointed gaze. "I told you to get her out of the Hole. If they come back and see her, they'll take her and likely kill us."

Roland took Aniya's other hand and carefully led her and Nicholas through a maze of chairs and tables. "We didn't have a choice, Gareth. They're crawling all over the train station. I was hoping you knew of a second way out of here."

"There is no other way out."

Roland dropped Aniya's hand and moaned. "Of all people, I thought you'd know another way. It's not like we can get into the caves."

"Caves?" Aniya frowned.

Gareth turned to her. "There was once another way out, a series of tunnels throughout the Web, but it was closed during the Uprising. The Lightbringers caved in the tunnels and enforced a no-travel policy on the rebels. The station has been the only way out for a very long time. You're going to have to make it in there and either take the train or walk the tracks."

"It's too well guarded," Nicholas said. "There's no way we're getting in there."

Gareth frowned. "Then you might have to wait."

"Wait a second," Aniya said.

"Then what can we do? She can't stay in the Hole, Gareth. It's only a matter of time until they find her."

"Roland, wait." Aniya tried again.

"Our only hope is to hide her away," Gareth said.

Nicholas scoffed. "Yeah, like that worked for William."

"Guys, shut up!"

The room hushed, leaving only the sound of Aniya's frustrated, rapid breathing.

"How did my brother get back? There's no way they let him anywhere near the stations in the Hub, not with their security."

After a pause, Nicholas spoke up. "She's right. There's no way he could have made it onto the train by the Hub. That has to be one of the most guarded places in the Web. Surely someone would have noticed a nearly dead guy bleeding from a few gunshot wounds."

Another pause.

"I can't explain that, Nicholas. I watched the tunnels cave in myself. I suppose it's possible that there's another way into the caves, but I don't know it, and I'm not sure anyone else could give you a better answer, except for Salvador himself if he were still alive. But it doesn't matter. Even if the tunnel were open, it's too close to the train station to get inside unseen, thanks to the Silvers. I believe that no matter which route you take, you still need to deal with them."

"Are you suggesting we fight?" Roland asked, his pitch escalating. "There's no way we can take them on."

"He's right," Aniya said. "We wouldn't stand a chance."

Gareth smiled. "Your parents were not much older than you when they fought in the Uprising, you know. But no, I'm suggesting no such thing. I say we present them with bait far enough away, and I'm sure you'll have a much easier time leaving the Hole. They can't be everywhere at once."

"A diversion," Aniya said.

"Exactly, young lady. However, I'm not quite sure how to go about this. We have no way of knowing how they will react to a diversion unless you are close enough to see their light, and if you are that close, any diversion you create will be much less effective."

Aniya thought for a moment.

"I think I might know a way."

11

A niya knelt on the floor in the back room, fidgeting as she watched the candlelight flicker.

Eight hours.

Gareth had deemed it unwise to make their move in the middle of the day. Even though the blackout provided constant cover, the Silvers would be far less active during the night, and they needed all the help they could get.

Nicholas had told Gareth about the transmission he had recorded, and Aniya relayed her conversation with William, that the lights weren't coming back on thanks to him. Gareth simply frowned and excused himself to mull over this information.

Now, Aniya sat and stared into the candlelight, ignoring the snores from the boys beside her. A plate of bread lay beside her, untouched. The buzz of customers and music had died away some time ago, leaving her in silence with nothing but her thoughts for company.

She had tried to rest for the busy night ahead, but every time she closed her eyes, she saw her parents lying in a pool of blood, their eyes open but empty. It was all she could do to keep from imagining her body lying next to theirs if she had been at home as well.

Aniya's heart sank as she realized that even though she was safe for now, there was no more future for her, at least not in the way she had imagined. Whatever reason the Lightbringers had for killing her parents, she was sure it could be used against her as well. She would be running from them for the rest of her life, however long that would be.

After dreaming of a life free of the oppressive Lightbringers, no longer subject to their rules and system, she finally got her wish, but at a terrible cost.

And then there was William. If the power was indeed gone for good, surely the Lightbringers had a fate far worse than death planned for him. Who could hope to bring him back alive?

"Wake up."

Gareth stepped into the back room and nudged Roland with his boot. "I hope you got some rest. I'm not sure when it'll be safe enough to close your eyes again."

Aniya couldn't tell which she doubted more, the thought of safety or that it would be enough to make her feel comfortable sleeping.

"It's a good thing I thought to cook our food over fire today, the old-fashioned way. I wouldn't have any for you otherwise."

As Roland rubbed his eyes and shook Nicholas, Gareth laid three open rucksacks on the bar and began stuffing food and drink inside.

"It's late enough that you should be able to carry out your plan with little trouble. I would come with you, but if they notice I'm not inside my shack even a minute after curfew, they'll come looking for me. And given my association with your parents and participation in the Uprising, they would turn their manhunt for a seventeen-year-old girl into a sector-wide lockdown if they aren't planning to already.

"It's imperative that you leave Holendast. I'm not sure when it will be safe for you to return, but I'd imagine it wouldn't be for at least a week. But, Aniya, tantamount to your safety is the recovery of your brother. His act of treason will no doubt mean his death, but I doubt the Lightbringers went to this much trouble to punish a municipal worker. He must have some knowledge, know some secret that threatens their image or status."

Nicholas nodded. "That's what I thought. And if he knows something, we can use it against them."

"Exactly," Gareth said. "And we've waited a long time for an opportunity like this. It should not be ignored."

Aniya scoffed. "What do you want from us? It's not like we can walk into the Hub and take him back."

"Roland and Nicholas, you'll find, are more than capable in many situations, and I've known you long enough to feel confident that you can rise to any occasion. But no, I don't recommend you march into the Hub by yourself. You'll find help if you look hard enough." Gareth turned to Roland. "Look for the Mark of Salvador."

"The Scourge?" Aniya asked.

Gareth nodded. "The grip of the Lightbringers has weakened over the years as unrest and discontent grow stronger. Many Sympathetics are no longer neutral parties. There has been talk of revolution. Your brother may have unwittingly served as the catalyst for a second uprising."

Aniya shook her head. "I just want my brother back. I couldn't care less about your revolution and your wars. You lost your family in the Uprising. Why would you want to fight another battle you can't win?"

"You no longer have a family either, and it wasn't because of any war," Gareth said coolly. "We have a chance and the responsibility to stop that from happening again. As much as I miss my family, they died for a cause I still believe in."

"That might mean something if you had won." Aniya folded her arms.

"Aniya, whether or not you believe in this, you want your brother back," Nicholas said. "We want the same thing, and Gareth has friends who can help us. You don't have to agree with him. Just take the help that he's trying to offer."

After a pause, Aniya nodded. "If it means getting my brother back, I guess I don't have a choice." She looked down at the floor. "I'm sorry."

Gareth placed a hand on her shoulder. "I understand, Aniya. You still have some family left, and I intend to make sure he gets back alive. Now, get going. You won't be safe until you make it to another sector. Nicholas, don't take too long getting your equipment. They can't afford to wait for you."

Nicholas nodded.

"And Aniya, be careful," Gareth said, turning and placing a hand on her shoulder. "It's a good plan, but dangerous. Don't stay there any longer than you need to."

Roland turned to Aniya. "Are you sure you want to do this? I can do it for you, and you can wait for me."

"No, I have to do this." She sighed and clenched her fists. "It's time for me to go home."

12

A house full of occupants, yet devastatingly empty.
A place of love and joy, now darkened by death
forevermore.

A home where Aniya had come to love the smell of mole
as her mother cooked, now soiled by the stench of blood.

Aniya stood in the doorway, not caring for a moment that
anyone walking by would see her. She couldn't bring herself to
step back inside, and yet she couldn't take her eyes off her
parents.

She wasn't a child anymore. She knew what they had been
doing before she came in the night before. They had to have
been so happy. In a world where the government snatched up
their firstborn the second he turned eighteen, they had found
a way to live on, move forward, and even experience bliss.

She resented them and admired them for it at the same
time.

Aniya stepped inside, the fear of the Silvers discovering
her finally outweighing her broken heart.

She knelt beside her parents, placing a hand on each of
their chests. "I'm sorry," she said through her tears, as if her
presence could have prevented this horror.

"I can't give you a proper burial, but you'll get the next-best thing."

She grabbed the kerosene lantern from the counter. After twisting the top off, she turned the lantern over slowly and began spilling the liquid across the small shack, gingerly avoiding her parents.

Once the container was empty, she let both pieces of the lantern fall to the floor, the glass shattering on the ground.

Aniya picked up the matchbook but paused. She knelt next to her parents one last time and kissed their blood-soaked cheeks.

"I'm going to find William, you know. I'm going to find him and bring him back." She stroked her father's hair, which somehow had gone mostly untouched by the blood. "Your Annelise will bring him home, I promise."

With that, she stood up, wiped her eyes, and struck a match.

Then, she let it fall.

Flames sprang up around her instantly and encompassed the room in a large ring. As a solemn afterthought, Aniya walked around the room and lit every candle she could find, stepping over the spreading fire.

After she finished, Aniya stood in the middle of the room between her parents, watching the flames spread, feeling the heat rise, letting the dried blood on their skin moisten again with the touch of her falling tears.

Aniya raised a hand to her face to rub her eyes but stopped and stared at her skin. Her hand caught the light of the surrounding flame and reflected the warm orange glow, blinking and pulsing as the flames around her flickered erratically.

The orange hue of the flame suddenly took on a white glow, and Aniya turned around and looked out the window to see dozens of bright lights in the distance, peeking through the cracks in the walls and spilling into the blazing room.

Aniya took a deep breath.

"Goodbye," she said, banishing the tears from her eyes as she forced herself to stand tall. Then, she turned her back on her home and her parents for the last time and fled.

PART II

ESCAPE

13

Aniya took an alternate route through Holendast to avoid the approaching Silvers, hoping she was far enough away to stay unseen. This indirect path meant an extra five minutes, and she knew Roland and Nicholas must be getting worried.

Sure enough, the boys looked relieved when Aniya finally arrived at the train station and approached their agreed-upon spot, behind a storage container near the front of the trainyard.

"Any problems?" Nicholas asked.

"No. The station?"

"Empty," Roland said. "You should have heard their radios light up when your house, uh . . . lit up. I don't think they knew what to do with themselves."

"Well, let's get out of here before they find out."

They stepped out from behind the storage container and made their way through the trainyard.

However, Roland was almost instantly proved wrong, and they skidded to a stop in the gravel upon seeing a white light flash across the path ahead.

After remaining motionless for several seconds, Aniya

decided they had not yet been spotted. "Come on," she said, waving behind her and taking the lead. She pulled her body close to the storage containers and slowly approached the area where they had last seen the light.

Aniya halted and let Roland bump into her. She ignored him and poked her head around the corner. "There's only one of them."

"Let me see." Nicholas stepped around her and stuck his head out. "It looks like he's guarding something."

After a brief pause, he spun around as Aniya came to the same conclusion.

They spoke in unison. "William."

In her excitement, Aniya spoke louder than intended and was responded by a hail of gunfire.

"Run!"

Aniya obeyed Nicholas's command and took off hard, but she quickly realized that he had run in the opposite direction, leaving Roland with her.

"Where is he going?"

Roland shook his head. "Don't have time for that. Let's go!"

Aniya turned and ran again, bobbing and weaving between storage units, hoping to find an open one. However, they were all securely closed, and each time she stopped to check, the footsteps grew louder. After turning again, she froze. Roland was no longer following her. Her heart began to race, and she took off again, knowing that she couldn't stop for long.

But it had been long enough. She turned a corner and ran directly into a large man in silver armor, bouncing off and landing on her back.

The man opened his mouth to speak, but he disappeared as the light on his helmet blinked out. A second later, he shouted in pain.

In the pitch black, Aniya heard a rough impact and grunts

of exertion. As the light flashed on again, she saw the officer staggering around under the weight of Nicholas.

The light blinked out again, and she heard a heavy punch and a moan of pain.

"Nicholas!" she cried out instinctively, stretching her arms forward in the darkness. The blinding light from the officer's helmet had been enough to keep her eyes from adjusting.

The light came on again to illuminate Nicholas and the officer wrestling on the ground.

Off again.

A sickening crunch.

Silence.

Aniya's heart stopped.

"Are you okay?" Nicholas's voice met her in the darkness, and she fell forward into his arms.

"What do you mean, am I okay? Are you?"

"I'm fine. Gareth's been training me for years."

Aniya's vision finally adjusted again, and she saw the armored man lying in a heap, his head twisted at an awkward and sickening angle.

"To do that?" She swallowed back the hurt of her best friend hiding such an important part of his life.

Nicholas gave a shrug and picked up the officer's gun and radio. "If I need to."

"Nice job." Roland's voice came from behind. Aniya turned to see him running to catch up. His mood changed, however, as he got a closer look at the body. His skin turned ashen, and he bit his lip.

Aniya placed a hand on his shoulder. "What happened to you?"

He looked down. "I tripped," he mumbled.

But Aniya barely heard this, suddenly remembering the more pressing issue.

"William," she said again, running back toward the center of the trainyard.

Sure enough, when she got to the train car the officer had been guarding, she opened the door to find a bloodied mass on the floor staring back at her.

"Aniya," William said weakly, his eyes wide. "What are you doing here?"

She grinned. "Saving you. We need to get you out of here."

"You're not saving me, Aniya," William said, shaking his head. "It's a trap. I hoped you were too smart to fall for it."

Aniya frowned. "We were trying to leave the sector. I didn't even know you were here."

"Besides, their trap didn't work," Roland said in Aniya's defense. "We distracted them. It'll take them plenty of time to get back here."

"What, the fire? Yeah, I heard them talking. But do you really think they'd leave just one man behind to guard their prisoner?" William's frustration faded, replaced by genuine concern. "There's no time to talk, trust me. You have to get out now. They're too smart to risk letting me go like this. They're coming."

As if to confirm William's warning, a voice came from the radio in Nicholas's hand.

"Targets spotted."

William's dark eyes suddenly lit up, reflecting bright lights in the distance.

Aniya spun around to see several bobbing lights approaching from far across the trainyard.

"Get in!" Nicholas shouted.

The trio climbed inside, and Nicholas slammed the sliding door shut as gunfire pelted the metal door.

14

A niya examined her brother's wounds as he spoke.
"I assume you're taking the railroad out of here. If that's closed, which I'm guessing it will be, take the tunnels. I doubt the Silvers would follow you inside."

"The tunnels are caved in," Roland said.

William shook his head. "I've been inside. It was the tunnel by the Hub, but they're all connected."

"But the entrance is closed," Aniya said. "Even if the tunnels are clear, we can't get inside."

The shouts and footsteps grew closer.

"We need to go." With that, Roland opened the opposite door.

"I'm not leaving without William." Aniya grabbed Roland's shoulders and spun him back around.

"You have to," William said. He pointed at his foot, which was securely chained to the wall of the train car.

"I can take care of that." Nicholas took off his pack and placed the radio inside, then knelt and pointed his stolen gun at William's chains. He fired, but the chain link remained firm.

"That's not going to work," William said. "Their weapons

are made to use both bullets and tranquilizer pellets. They want us alive, so it probably doesn't even have bullets. As you can see, their ammo can't even make it through the metal in the door of the train car. Good thing, too."

Nicholas checked the gun and grimaced. "He's right." He dropped the gun and rummaged through his pack, pulling out a black box and setting it on the floor of the train car.

"What's that?" Aniya asked.

"Insurance," Nicholas said. "Just in case."

"Stop wasting time and get out of here, Aniya." William placed a hand on her cheek. "You have to run, and you can't do that while carrying me, even if you managed to free me."

After a long pause, Aniya nodded slowly and stood up, tears beginning to form. "I'm going to find you again, I promise."

But as they turned to leave, the bullet-ridden door between Aniya and her pursuers began to open.

Aniya winced and prepared for the worst, but Nicholas grabbed the handle, pulling the door in the opposite direction. He gritted his teeth. "Guess all that bricklaying paid off after all. Go!"

William looked up and narrowed his eyes. "What are you doing? They'll kill you. Get out of here!"

Aniya stared in horror. "I can't leave you too, Nicholas."

"Too late for that. I'll stay with William and keep him alive. Either that or die with him." Nicholas grunted and dug his feet into the floor. "Of course, if you don't get moving now, it won't matter."

"No, you can't." Aniya held back tears as she tugged on his shoulder. "You have to come with us."

"He's made up his mind, Aniya." William pushed her away. "Stay out of the Hub. Promise me you'll never go near that place." He looked at Roland. "Take care of her."

"What are you waiting for?" Nicholas shouted. "Grab my pack and go!"

Aniya bit her lip and jumped out the open door that Roland held, grabbing Nicholas's rucksack as she went. She quickly found out why the Silvers had not bothered to run around to the other side of the train car as she tumbled down a very steep hill, landing unceremoniously at the bottom on top of a trash heap, Roland crashing down next to her.

She looked up at several beams of light shining down from the top of the hill.

"You might as well come back up, Ms. Lyons."

A voice came from the blinding light, and a man stepped in front, a black form silhouetted by white light.

"You'll save us some time and you some energy. Not to mention I missed dinner for this, and I do hate missing my meals."

Aniya fumed. She turned, but the way up in the opposite direction was equally steep. The trench continued to her left and right, but it was too long of a stretch to run in the open. She would only be target practice for the dozens of officers on the ridge above.

"I'll tell you what. If you come up now, I'll let one of them live. I'll even let you choose. Your brother, your friend, or your lover. It's up to you. Of course, if you choose your brother, I still have to torture him anyway, so you could put him out of his misery and pick your boyfriend. And your friend? Well, you and I both know he's not making the cut either way."

There was no way out.

"Of course, we could just shoot you from here, but then we'd have to come down and get you, and that's too much work. Besides, then we wouldn't be obligated to keep any of you alive, so I wouldn't make us resort to violence if I were you."

He was right. Their escape was over.

"Make your decision, girl. I have nothing to lose, while you, on the other hand . . ." The voice chuckled. "The clock is ticking."

Aniya looked down, resigned. She placed a hand on the rock and dirt in front of her and began to climb.

The man chuckled. "A wise choice."

But then, an ethereal noise sounded from the top of the ridge, then mutated to a boom that vibrated the ground beneath her feet.

At the same time, the world went dark again as the lights on the officers' heads shut off suddenly.

"What just happened?" Aniya asked, too stunned to take advantage of the sudden darkness.

An order came from above. "Find her!"

"Don't know." Roland grabbed her hand. "Let's go!"

Aniya felt her hand being tugged, and the shock faded. She turned and ran as fast as she could, blindly running down the trench.

After a moment, Roland stopped and turned to the side of the trench, crawling up the hill in a spot that seemed to rise on less of an incline than the rest of the steep ditch. Aniya followed close behind, ignoring the dirt and rocks that Roland inadvertently pulled down from above.

Finally, they reached the top, but they had no time to rest. Some of the Silvers had jumped into the trench, but it seemed that most of them had followed their progress from above. They were just a stone's throw away.

Aniya and Roland turned and ran back into the trainyard, vaulting over crates and bowling through empty boxes. The small army chasing them may have been better trained, but their body armor kept them from moving as freely as the two young adults running for their lives.

They reached the train tunnel and stopped. The gate in front of the entrance was locked and wrapped in barbed wire. The chain link gate was several feet tall and spanned all the way to the top of the entrance, leaving no room to climb up and over to the other side.

Their only way out was sealed.

Aniya's hopes fell. The adrenaline, the excitement, the thought that they could have made it out alive slowly deflated.

Next to her, Roland's head began to droop, but only for a moment. He grabbed Aniya's hand and took off running again.

"Where are we going?"

"The caves."

Aniya pulled her hand away from Roland. "Even if parts of the caves are still open like William said, the only entrance we can get to from here is completely caved in. Gareth watched it happen himself."

He grabbed her again. "Shut up and run!"

Frustrated and desperate, Aniya picked up her speed again and followed Roland to a dark corner of the trainyard. With a look back, she noticed that despite their moment of rest at the gate, the Silvers had fallen far behind.

Roland halted in front of a dilapidated, boarded-up passageway. He kicked away rotted wood and continued inside, Aniya close behind.

Only a few seconds later, their progress was halted by a large pile of rubble and debris blocking their way.

Aniya sighed. "There you go. We made it about fifteen feet, and sure enough, the tunnels are closed, just like Gareth said."

"Start digging." Roland seemed to ignore the dejection in her voice and started tearing away at the pile of stone and dirt in front of him.

"Exactly how far do you think you're going to get?" Aniya threw her hands in the air. "You know what's behind that dirt? More dirt."

Roland did not answer, but kept pulling away at the heap in front of them.

"Roland, stop."

He refused, and Aniya could hear the Silvers getting closer.

"Roland—"

Aniya froze. From about six feet above Roland's head, Aniya could see a soft yellow glow. She grabbed Roland's shoulder and pulled him away from the debris.

"Look up."

Roland finally listened and followed her instruction. He looked up but said nothing, instead frantically grabbing at the pile once again. This time, however, rather than pulling the loose stones away, he grabbed at the debris firmly in place, pulling his body up the pile.

Aniya followed suit, climbing up the small hill toward the light at the very top.

Roland reached the top first and poked his head through what looked to be two feet of clearance between the top of the dirt mound and the ceiling of the tunnel. He squeezed through to the other side and reached a hand back over for Aniya.

Aniya reached up to grab his hand, but no sooner did his hand close around hers than another hand gripped her right ankle, this one holding on much tighter.

"Pull me up!"

Roland reached down with his other hand and grabbed Aniya's wrist, now pulling the weight of his friend and the officer that had a tight grip on her ankle.

Aniya swung her free foot around wildly but hit nothing.

Suddenly, the world began to shake violently, and Aniya's cries for help were drowned out by a thundering noise that roared in her ears as the ground vibrated against her chest, bouncing her body against dirt and rock.

It was all Aniya could do to hold on tight to Roland's hand as she shook helplessly. With her free hand, she shielded her face from rocks that shook loose from the cave ceiling, plummeting toward her relentlessly.

Above the din, she heard one of the men below let out a howl of pain as a rock struck an exposed area of flesh.

Aniya let herself hope again as she realized her escape.

Risking a rock to the face, Aniya looked around, desperately searching. Finally, she spotted a large rock near her free hand. She mustered all her strength and pried the rock loose from the pile, throwing it down behind her with a grunt.

The clang of stone on metal rang out, and Aniya's ankle was suddenly free.

"Now, Roland!" She screamed as loud as she could as the thundering noises grew louder.

Aniya's body shot upward toward the gap in the ceiling, hurtling through the gap and past Roland. She fell several feet before her head hit the ground, and she lost consciousness.

15

"Get out of here!"

Aniya's hand radiated warmth as Nicholas held onto it. She looked into his eyes as he begged her to leave him to his death.

But his eyes faded to black, and his face disappeared. All she was left with was the void, though her hand still pulsed gently.

Memories flooded her mind, the escape, the struggle, the fall. But all she could think about was the crushing fact that Nicholas was gone.

Aniya's eyes fluttered open, her head spinning. Thanks to a torch that flickered on the tunnel wall nearby, she could see Roland crouching over her, his face basked in a yellow glow. A glance down revealed that his sweaty hand clutched hers, knuckles white.

The shaking had stopped, and the tunnels were quiet.

"What happened?"

Roland traced his thumb across her forehead and pulled it back so Aniya could see her blood on his skin.

"You fell. I was worried, but the wound didn't look very deep, and your breathing seemed normal." He wiped his thumb on his pants. "Your heart rate is fine, so we can get moving as soon as you're ready."

Aniya sat up slowly, staring past Roland's head at the dozens of lit torches that lit the walls of the tunnel. "How long has it been?"

"A few hours. I tried to wake you up earlier, but you were out. The good news is that no one is following us. The bad news is that it wouldn't have taken long for them to clear a path with their equipment, so my guess is that they're regrouping at another entrance. We've bought some time, but not a lot."

"You know," she said, surveying the tunnel ahead, "for a destroyed tunnel, it seems like it's in pretty good condition."

Roland shrugged. "I guess everyone just assumed that it was a lot worse than it actually was. I'm just happy it's here and we're still alive. But we might not be if we stick around here much longer."

Aniya realized that Roland was still holding her hand. She gently spread her fingers, and he quickly let go.

"I'm glad you're okay," he said with averted eyes.

"Thanks, me too." She looked around. "What happened to my pack?"

"You lost it in the scuffle. We still have Nicholas's pack, though."

"I guess it's better that we have his anyway. He had the radio." Aniya took the pack that Roland offered her and opened it, ignoring the pit inside her heart. Inside the pack were a few packages of mole jerky, a canteen, the radio, and another small device. This item was a black cube enclosed in a glass case. On the cube was a switch with a label that read "prime" and an adjacent button labeled "fire."

"What do you suppose this is?" Aniya turned the device over in her hand.

"A trigger to a bomb?"

Aniya smirked. "Nicholas is a smart guy, but I don't think

he would know how to make a bomb, let alone find the materials for it."

"Gareth would probably know what it is."

"Maybe, but he was pretty clear that we shouldn't go back for a while."

Roland nodded. "Speaking of, we need to get going."

"We can't rest for just a few more minutes?"

"I would love to," Roland said, "but we have no way of knowing how long it will take them to get into the tunnel, whatever route they take."

Aniya placed the device back in Nicholas's old pack. "How will we know where to go? It's not like the Web is easy to navigate, especially in unmarked tunnels."

"I'm not so sure they're unmarked." Roland turned and started walking along the tunnel. "They had to use these caves to hide fighters and move from sector to sector unnoticed. Not to mention these caves didn't always belong to the rebels. There has to be some kind of map or system."

"How do you know so much about these tunnels?"

Roland seemed to ignore her question. "Better question is why are the torches lit?"

Aniya chose to let it slide and looked around at the dirt walls. The hanging torches supplied ample light, a welcome change from the pitch black.

"And who do you think lit them?"

Aniya shrugged. "There's no way anyone could survive in these tunnels very long without food or water."

After a moment, Roland gave a shrug as well. "In any case, the Hole is on the very edge of the Web, so it should be fairly easy to guess which way we need to go. It doesn't look like we've hit the main tunnels yet, but when we do, we're probably directly opposite whatever tunnel will take us to the Hub."

"But if it's so obvious to us, won't the Silvers figure it out?"

"My experience with the so-called Glorious Bringers of

Light is that their minions don't really think for themselves. They'll follow whatever order they're given, even if it means their death, but they aren't trained for strategic thinking."

"What exactly is your experience with the Lightbringers?"

"Shh!" Roland suddenly stopped and pressed himself up against the tunnel wall.

Aniya grabbed the nearest torch and pulled it away from the wall. But it offered resistance, and when Aniya looked closely, she saw a wire attached to the torch and disappearing into the cave wall. She pulled the torch away harshly, snapping the wire, and shoved the lit end of the torch into the dirt, smothering the light. She then joined Roland in what she hoped was a stealthy position.

After what seemed like several minutes had passed, Roland relaxed and stepped away from the wall.

"What did you hear?"

"It sounded like footsteps. It was probably a mole, but it seemed louder. In any case, we're safe for now. If it were the Silvers, we'd be dead by now. They're not exactly subtle." He turned to Aniya. "You didn't hear anything?"

She shook her head. "Blame it on the head injury. Pretty sure there's some dried blood in my ears."

"Attractive." Roland smirked and continued. "If it makes you feel any better, whoever lit those torches is probably not any threat to us. During the Uprising, the Lightbringers tried to avoid the caves at all costs, though I'm sure they'll make an exception for us."

"Why wouldn't they come inside? They have plenty of light."

Roland stopped and pointed toward Aniya's belt. "Turn on the radio."

Aniya grabbed the radio from her belt and turned the dial up. The device immediately screeched and warbled, and she dropped it to the floor, covering her ears and wincing.

The sound subsided as Roland picked the radio up and

turned it off. "Their radios are useless in the caves. When the Lightbringers first ordered the excavation of these tunnels, they installed a communications device that boosted radio signal in the caves. During the Uprising, the rebels altered the device and made it emit a bubble of electromagnetic energy. It interferes with radio frequencies and messes with their lights. As long as they stay in the sectors, the walls of the sky ceiling cuts off the interference, and they're fine. But they can't step foot in the caves without putting themselves in danger."

"You could have just said that instead of making me find out the painful way." Aniya snatched the radio back from Roland.

"I would have tried it anyway. I wasn't sure the technology survived the war. Now we know."

"Is that what happened earlier in the trainyard? How their lights went out?"

Roland shook his head. "I doubt it. This is more like the tech the rebels used during the Uprising, electromagnetic bombs made for a single burst to completely disable electronics. But those were huge devices. I'm not sure who would have any of those, especially since the components used to make those bombs were destroyed after the war."

"Nicholas would know," Aniya said quietly. She had made fun of his technological prowess for as long as she could remember, but she would give anything to have him with her in the caves now, going on and on about the latest developments in microprocessing.

Roland seemed to sense her uneasiness and placed a hand on her shoulder.

Finally, Aniya spoke again, ignoring the pang in her heart. "So these tunnels were actually their idea?"

"These used to be mines," Roland said, as he turned to walk again. "A lot of the equipment the Silvers use is forged from the metals found in these tunnels. When the rebels took over the caves, they became a symbol of rebellion, and that's why their destruction signaled the end of the fight against the Lightbringers. I guess it crushed spirits enough that no one ever got close enough to realize that the apparent cave-in didn't extend past the entrances."

Aniya shook her head. "Where did you learn all this? In Assembly, all they would ever tell us about is a short rebellion and the Lightbringers' victory. My parents wouldn't even explain it. I thought it was strictly forbidden to discuss the Uprising."

"Gareth told me everything he knew. He was convinced that the next generation would have the same idea at some point, and he said we needed to learn from his mistakes. He still thinks we can win."

"Was he one of the rebel leaders?"

"He was a field medic, so he rarely fought, but he was there from the beginning. He knew Salvador personally."

"The Scourge?"

Another nod. "He was close with all the instigators of the Uprising, really. That's why the Silvers pay so many visits to the clinic. They want to make sure he's not corrupting some poor kid with delusions of starting the next Uprising."

"Like you?"

Roland grinned. "Like me."

"But you're not related to him at all? I never understood how you ended up with him. His family died in the war, right?"

"Not quite. Gareth's entire family was executed as punishment for his participation in the Uprising. He took me in shortly afterward. Honestly, if he didn't have me around, I'm not so sure he would still be alive."

"Where is your real family?"

Roland shrugged. "I don't know, and by now, I honestly don't care. If I needed to know, Gareth would have told me by now. He used to tell me that it's safer if I don't know."

"So how do the Lightbringers have you registered?"

"They don't. As far as I know, they don't even know I exist. Like the one under your house, Gareth has a similar bunker under his shack that I hide in during routine checks and visits. There have been a couple close calls, but I've managed to avoid running into the Silvers before today. They can't be too happy that you're running around with someone not in their system."

"I'm putting you in danger, then." Aniya let her head droop in guilt.

"Yes, absolutely. But that's the neat thing about not existing. It doesn't matter as much if you're dead." Roland let loose a wry smile. "Listen, Aniya. Gareth has been more than a father to me. If he says keeping you safe is the most important thing for me to do, then I'm going to make sure that you stay alive. If he says that we need to get your brother back, that's what we're going to do."

Aniya smiled. "Thank you, Roland."

Roland waved his hand. "Don't worry about it. I had nothing better to do. I just hope that if the Silvers catch us, they do so after we get out of these tunnels. I already live underground. Call me crazy, but I don't want to die in a hole in the ground inside another hole in the ground."

"Maybe if—" Aniya was cut short by the torches going out.

"That's weird." Roland's voice sounded unsure.

Aniya edged closer to him. "Roland . . ."

"I wouldn't worry. These tunnels were the Lightbringers'. Maybe they rigged the torches to a timer."

Aniya thought of the wire she had severed from the nearby torch. It made sense. She peered down the path and was surprised to see that despite the sudden extinguishing of the torches, the tunnel was not completely dark. Instead, a strange green glow emanated from the cave walls. The dim light was speckled along the rock with no consistent pattern.

The source of the glow was unclear, but whatever it was seemed to slowly move, just enough to notice.

"Aniya, look."

If Roland was gesturing, she couldn't tell. The green glow gave off a little light, but it was still difficult to make out any details until her eyes adjusted again. She looked around, turning until she saw a distinguishable shape on the tunnel wall behind her.

On the rock wall, in a wet green glow, was smeared a large depiction of a four-fingered hand, almost seeming to reach out at them.

Aniya stared at the crude drawing. "That looks just like the one you—"

That was all she got out before a cold, grimy hand covered her mouth, stifling the scream she would have let out as several more hands grabbed her all over and forced her to the ground, binding her hands and gagging her mouth.

Then a sack was placed over her head and tightened, and she was left helpless.

16

Roland was pushed to the ground. He stumbled over a rock and fell hard on his shoulder, unable to brace his fall. But as much as his shoulder hurt, his feet ached even worse. The walk had already lasted for several hours.

He heard another impact on the ground next to him, accompanied by a grunt. He tried to say Aniya's name, but it came out as a simple "Mmmph?" through the gag in his mouth.

A cold hand undid the sack over his head but did not take it off, only removing the cloth from his mouth before securing the sack around his neck once again. Then, footsteps faded into the distance, and they were alone.

Roland tried again. "Are you okay?"

"Mostly." He heard her scoff. "You said whoever lit the torches wasn't any threat to us. I don't know about you, but I feel pretty threatened."

"At least it's not the Silvers."

"How do you know?"

"We didn't get shot. But whoever it is, they're probably just as dangerous. They came out of nowhere."

"Who do you suppose they are?"

Roland paused. "I have no idea. I can't imagine who would be foolish enough to enter the caves. The tunnels may be dangerous to the Silver Guard, but even more so to defenseless civilians. There's creatures in these caves that don't like their home invaded. It's a crude tunnel system, so there's always risk of a cave-in. Plus, living this close to constant electromagnetic energy is very dangerous for your health. When the radio suppressant was first built, the only reason it wasn't used widespread was because it spread disease among the rebels. If these people live down here, it's likely that their bodies have adjusted and evolved. They are probably quite brutish in size in order to compensate for the energy-sucking nature of severe electromagnetism."

"An interesting theory, young one."

Roland looked up toward the source of the scraggly voice, even though he couldn't see very well.

The sound of flint crackled, echoing throughout the cave.

Through the tiny holes of the sack, Roland saw the spreading glow of a fire illuminating the thin, huddled frame of a person sitting across from them.

"I remember when I was indeed a brute of a man. That was long ago, when there was fire in my heart and strength in my bones."

Aniya scoffed, and Roland couldn't tell if it was directed at the man's strange claim or the fact that he used such flowery language.

In any case, the man seemed to ignore Aniya's reaction and continued, "Now, I must rely on the shadows for my strength, subterfuge my only defense against the tyranny that seeks to bring about my end."

"Enough talk, Daddy. How do you want to do it?"

A new voice, a shrill one, pricked Roland's ears so close that he jumped a little.

"We can flay them, roast them, or just start eating them raw." The girl laughed in a shrieking trill.

"Cannibals?" He heard Aniya say. "I thought that was just a story that the Silvers tell us to keep us from straying too far from our homes."

The girl laughed again, and Roland winced as the high pitch violated his ears.

"Relax, Tami," the male voice spoke again with a chuckle of his own. "These are no Silver Guard. There is no need to scare them yet." His voice turned stern. "However, you did encroach on our territory, and we know by now that the Lightbringers are not beyond sending spies into my camp to destroy us from the inside out. This, young ones, is your trial. I am a fair judge, and you will be allowed to speak your piece. If I am not satisfied with your answers, I will leave you to my daughter, and I cannot promise that she will be as fair. The sacks, please."

With that, the sack around Roland's head was pulled off violently, jerking his neck sideways. He heard Aniya struggle nearby, but he found himself staring at the curious sight in front of him.

On the other side of the small fire sat a man with hair of pure silver, complete with a long beard that seemed immaculately trimmed. His skin was wrinkled and spotted, clinging tightly to visible bones. His eyes were a clouded gray, though they contained a wild spark inside that made Roland shudder. A simple cloth tunic hung loosely on the man's body, tied by a thin rope around his thin waist. On his hands were black gloves, a strange addition to what was otherwise a minimalistic outfit.

A feminine snicker tickled Roland's ear, and he turned around to see a girl dressed in brown leather that was stitched together crudely, draped around her body with no particular sense of fashion to it. A large gun was strapped to her back, a strange addition to her outfit that Roland couldn't help but find amusing.

"I already know what I'm going to do with them. The girl

can die in the fire, but I'm saving the cute one for myself." She grabbed Roland's chin, pulled his face toward hers, and grinned widely, revealing a set of incredibly straight and white teeth, far from the lack of hygiene he expected from cannibalistic cave-dwellers.

"If their trial reveals them guilty, you can have your way with them both. *Que será, será.* But remember that we have these trials for a reason. Let him go, Tamisra."

Pouting, the girl called Tamisra released Roland's chin and pushed his face toward the man across the fire again.

The man lifted a cane from the ground nearby and jabbed it at Aniya, poking her in the chest. "You. Why should we let you live?"

"Well," Aniya said, hesitating. "We're not who you think we are. We're not here on behalf of the Lightbringers, we're not spies, and—"

The man laughed, wheezing. "A weak argument from a weak girl. You should hope your friend does better."

Roland rolled his eyes. "You didn't let her finish. We—"

Without warning, the man leapt across the fire at Roland's chest, forcing him to the ground. "Do not speak out of turn, boy. I will let you know when you may talk."

Roland stared at the man, terrified at the crazed look in the man's eyes. They remained like this for several seconds as the man seemed to study Roland's face, his frenzied eyes darting back and forth.

Finally, the man got up and walked back to his side of the fire, but not before taking a close look at Aniya's face as well.

"Now you may talk."

It wasn't Roland who spoke next, but Aniya. "I know who you are."

The man turned again to Aniya, his eyes blazing. "The only reason you are not on the ground right now is because you are a woman, and I have greater honor than that, but know that my patience is thinning. Speak your piece, and then be silent."

Aniya spoke slowly. "You're Salvador, aren't you? Salvador the Scourge. We're friends."

"The fact that you know my name does not prove that you are a friend. Every spy the Lightbringers send in here knows my name." The man sneered, picking up his stick again and jabbing it toward Aniya's nose. "You and the rest of them, always seeking to take what little we have left. You already took it all, you fiends. What have we more to give? Our lives? We barely have those anymore as it is."

Roland groaned. "I think you've mistaken—"

"You dare interrupt me again, child?" The man spun around, whipping his cane toward Roland and striking him on the cheek. Roland tumbled over as Tamisra clapped her hands and shrieked in excitement. "I will not be silenced. You will let me speak."

Roland got back up, rubbing his cheek. After a long pause, he carefully spoke again. "Gareth never mentioned your willingness to hit children."

The man's expression changed, almost confused, and Roland continued.

"He thought you were dead."

After a moment, the man shook his head. "No. Gareth Tigoro was a known rebel. The Lightbringers know his name very well. You will have to do better than that."

Roland searched his mind for anything that could convince this crazed man. "Wait. *Lumen ad mortem.*"

The man froze. "How do you . . ." Slowly, his expression softened. "Not many of us knew those words. I knew your faces were familiar. There is no doubt. You are Roland," he said, then swinging his cane and pointing at Aniya. "And Annelise Lyons."

17

Aniya stared in wonder at the emaciated man, who now towered over them with a broad smile as his eyes twinkled wildly. She had heard legends of the psychotic rebel leader, but this was nothing like she had imagined.

"How do you know who we are?" Roland asked. "Have you been in contact with Gareth?"

"Sadly, no. He is too well watched by the Lightbringers. I could never have delivered a message without endangering him. I know who you are because I was there when your care was entrusted to my dear, old friend. And you," he said, turning to Aniya, "look just like your mother."

Tamisra frowned. "Does this mean I don't get a new plaything?"

"You are correct, dear. Unbind them."

The girl pouted but obeyed.

"Forgive us. As I said, we are visited by the spies of the Lightbringers on a somewhat frequent basis. Had I any idea who you were, we would never have treated you this way," he said, nodding toward the welt on Roland's cheek.

Aniya smirked. "Maybe we should have led with our names."

"Everyone thought you were dead," Roland said. "The Lightbringers said you were hunted down and killed even before the cave-ins."

"You know as well as I do that their words cannot be believed. Truly, I am disappointed that Gareth believed they could find me in here, let alone defeat me in battle." The gaunt man stood tall and puffed out his chest.

Aniya laughed before realizing that Salvador was not being dramatic. "Sorry."

Salvador simply smiled again. "Alas, I am not the fighter I once was. I have my flock to look after, and my days of battle are over. Yet though our fight has come and gone, the Lightbringers still indirectly oppress us here in the tunnels just as much as they attempt to directly control you in the sectors. The only difference is that you can enjoy a nearly normal life under their rule, while we have been sentenced to a fate worse than death. We eat roots when we cannot find moles. We drink from irradiated pools that collect in dark corners of these tunnels. Most of us have not seen the outside of these caves in nearly eighteen years. What I would give for us to be free again! Unfortunately, the time for war is over."

"Maybe not," Roland said. "You have a chance to help us and hurt the Lightbringers."

"Hurt them? I have heard promises like that before. What could you possibly do to hurt them, little one?"

"They took my brother," Aniya said. "He was chosen for relocative servitude three years ago, but he escaped."

A sad smile spread across Salvador's face. "William. Yes. I am aware of his plight. But I have grave news for you, child. Your brother is dead. He was killed by the Lightbringers in a foolish attempt to attack them a few days ago."

Aniya shook her head. "He's still alive. He was shot, but he made it back to Holendast alive."

"He escaped again?" Salvador raised his eyebrows.

"Again?" Roland asked.

"Yes, again. He came to me and asked for my help, and he was alive and well when we met, at least as well as could be in his condition. Three of our best—well, two of our best and one well-meaning fool—helped him break back inside the Citadel in an attempt to sabotage their power source. I had my reservations about the journey, to say the least. Apparently, they succeeded, but we lost contact until all three of our people showed up just inside the tunnels, all of them missing their heads. We assumed that they delivered your brother back to Holendast in the same condition."

"I think the Lightbringers have a different relationship with the sectors," Roland said. "They would never show such violence to the rest of the Web because they would quickly lose control. For you, though, I don't think the war ever ended."

"Please don't take this the wrong way," Aniya said hesitantly. "But was it the best plan to permanently shut off the power?"

"History is defined by those who recognize their chance to change the world and then take advantage of it. Besides, we lasted for centuries without the help of the so-called Glorious Bringers of Light. We can do it again if it means our freedom. Besides, we did not have time to devise whatever master plan you must have in mind if you dare to venture into the Hub with a single gun."

Aniya looked toward Roland. "About that . . ."

Salvador raised a wispy eyebrow. "You do not have a plan, do you?"

"We haven't exactly had time to think of one," Roland said as he looked away. "We were chased out of the Hole."

"Chased?"

"They came for my brother and killed the rest of my family," Aniya said, dropping her gaze toward the ground. "They took him, and now they're after me."

"Theodore . . . Catherine . . ." Salvador bowed his head

for a moment, and when he finally spoke again, his speech grew rapid as he began pacing. "Your brother must know something. They could have just as easily taken him back. The Lightbringers do not kill lightly, one of their few merits." He looked back up at Aniya with a mysterious stare. "Did your brother communicate anything to you before he was taken?"

Aniya shook her head. "He said the less I know, the better."

Salvador gave a small smile.

"Gareth thinks he knows something big," Roland said. "He's convinced that if we rescue William, we'll have an advantage against the Lightbringers."

"I agree, though rescuing him may prove more difficult than you might imagine. Come, let me show you our home. I do not have men to spare to guide you into the Hub, but I can give you supplies and a warm bed before the dangerous road ahead."

Aniya rose, ignoring Roland's outstretched hand. "We're just grateful you didn't kill us. Honestly, for a second, I was pretty sure your daughter was about to take a bite out of our necks."

"I still might," Tamisra said, again bringing her bared teeth close to Roland's ear.

Salvador laughed. "We may live like animals, but we have not yet resorted to cannibalism, despite Tami's enthusiasm. The roots that grow in these caves sustain us just enough to survive. Occasionally, we come across a mole, which we have come to consider a feast."

"A feast?" Roland frowned. "How many of you are there down here?"

"Though our numbers are many, we have learned to live on very little. But you will find that the moles that roam these tunnels are somewhat larger than the ones you have encountered in the sectors. You were not far off about the radiation,

Roland. At first, the underground rivers sickened us, but our bodies have adapted and learned to rely on the poisoned waters for sustenance. We have found that it gives us more strength than the roots and meat we manage to scavenge, but if we drink too much, it can still kill us. Our bodies do not seem to be as resilient as those of the moles, whose bodies have mutated and grown exponentially after years upon years of exposure to radiation."

Roland cocked his head. "Giant moles?"

"The Great War was ages ago," Aniya said. "The radiation should have died out a long time ago, along with whatever mutations it caused."

"I am sure that is what they told you, what they want you to believe. It is time to open your mind, young one. Tell me, Annelise, who do you think made these tunnels?"

"Not miners?"

Salvador gestured to the tunnel around them. "Look at the walls of these tunnels. Do they look man-made to you?"

"Those are some big moles," Roland muttered, eyeing the twelve-foot ceiling.

"Indeed. It took our fighters several deadly trials to learn how to hunt and slay the beasts. At first, we took shelter and did our best to stay out of their way, but occasionally, one would happen on our camp and wreak havoc. Now, the moles have learned to stay out of our way for fear of death."

"Why haven't we seen the giant moles inside the sectors?" Aniya asked. "Wouldn't they come looking for food?"

Salvador shook his head. "The Lightbringers have installed safety measures for that very reason long ago. If any motion is detected near the exits of any of the tunnels, it triggers a seismic device that generates a small earthquake in the surrounding area."

Aniya looked at Roland, recalling the shaking tunnel during their escape.

"These tremors scare off most of the moles, sending them crawling back into the tunnels. These machines, buried under each entrance, are the same ones used to cause the cave-ins at the end of the war, employed then in a much more damaging manner."

"That's why only the entrances were blocked and not the rest of the tunnels," Roland surmised. "You said most of the moles are scared off. But like Aniya, I've never seen an over-sized mole running around."

"Occasionally, a mole digs a new tunnel and breaks through into the sectors. We never knew what happened after that until one of our patrols witnessed it firsthand a few years ago after the Uprising. A mole had dug straight into Ravelta, at which point all power went off in the sector. The sky was shut off, the streetlights, everything. A few minutes later, the Silver Guard swarmed the mole and took it down. They hauled its carcass back to the new tunnel it made and forced another cave-in using a portable seismic bomb. A few hours later, the power came back on. We have seen a few more of these incidents in various sectors, and the procedure seems to be the same each time."

"Black Days," Aniya muttered. "Whenever there's a perimeter breach, they shut off the power before anyone can see what's going on. I guess the Lightbringers don't want civilians to think about anything but their daily routines. But that shouldn't take them very long. Why do the blackouts last hours?"

Roland shrugged. "Less time for us to figure out what happened, I guess."

"The more they keep you in the dark, the easier it is to control you," Salvador said. "Ironic, really, given that their rule depends on their ability to provide light."

"How do they do it?" Aniya asked. "You must have some idea if you were going to help my brother sabotage them."

"Sadly, no. Our scouts went merely to assist him. I am

afraid the details of the mission were known only to your brother, who refused to give any sensitive information. But if he was able to shut off the power, he clearly knows enough."

"Then it's more important than ever to get him back," Roland said. "If he knows something that can be used against the Lightbringers, we can finish what you started years ago."

Salvador nodded. "That is my hope as well. When the light is still not back in the coming days, hopefully people will be ready to rise up again. My only regret is that I have not the will to join them."

"Come with us now," Aniya pleaded. "We're going to need your help if we want to make it into the Hub and back out alive."

"I cannot, child. My people have learned to survive despite these extreme conditions. We have moved on and found a new way of life. I have an obligation to keep it that way, and I take that responsibility quite seriously. When we lost the war, I had time to reflect on my brash actions, and I made a vow that I would protect my children at all costs. I have lost body parts in the fight against the Lightbringers, but I will not suffer to lose any more of my flock."

Roland nodded toward Salvador's hands. "Speaking of body parts, did they really . . ."

For the first time, Salvador removed his gloves. He brought his right hand into the light, and Aniya noted that his little finger was almost completely gone—reduced to a tiny stump on the end.

"This reminds me of the cost that comes with fighting them. I am not afraid to suffer for my people, but I would never forgive myself if they suffered for me. I have my men train fighters, but they are for defense only, in the event of an emergency. As I said, I am more than happy to give you supplies, what little we have. If, perchance, you succeed, a land of plenty awaits us somewhere in the Web once the Light-bringers are gone. Tamisra, go with Annelise and give her some supplies. Ensure that her pack is retrieved and restored unto her." With that, Salvador's eyes twinkled. "Roland, if you will, I must speak with you alone."

Roland turned, his brow furrowed. "What for?"

"I need to talk with you about your family."

18

Aniya shifted uncomfortably as Tamisra's wild, sparkling eyes examined her from head to toe as if the cave dweller had never seen another girl before.

"A shame," Tamisra said, smirking. "You would have made a tasty treat."

Aniya backed away, her stomach turning.

Tamisra laughed. "Relax. I was never going to eat you. Though I would like to nibble on your friend." She winked and licked her lips. "He is just a friend, right?"

"Yeah, but I don't think you're his type," Aniya said, but then realized that she had no idea what Roland's type actually was.

"Not his type?" Tamisra held a hand to her chest and stuck out her lip. "He doesn't like pretty girls? Or am I too vicious for him?" She bared her teeth and laughed again.

Too uncivilized, maybe.

Aniya didn't say it, but it seemed like Tamisra caught on when she hesitated.

"We can't all be prissy city girls like you, Annelise," she said, sneering and drawing out her name as she rolled her eyes.

Now Aniya laughed with genuine mirth for the first time in days. "We live in the poorest sector in the Web. I wouldn't call myself a city girl just because I wear actual clothes and not . . ." She waved her arm at the girl's strange outfit. "Whatever that is."

"Do you like it? I made it myself." Tamisra twirled.

"I can tell."

To Aniya's surprise, Tamisra smiled warmly.

"I like you."

"Why?"

Tamisra shrugged. "Maybe because you're different. In here, they all wear the same clothes, talk the same way. It doesn't help that they treat me like royalty because of my dad. I can't tell if they respect me or they're scared of me."

"I can't imagine why." Aniya smiled back at her. "You can call me Aniya. I never cared much for Annelise, but that's how your father knows me."

"Aniya it is." Tamisra nodded and waved for her to follow. "Come on, I'll show you to our supplies."

They walked down the tunnel and approached a large steel door with a keypad in the center. Tamisra pressed six buttons, and the door slowly opened.

"How do you have power to operate an automatic door?" Aniya asked.

"We siphon off power from the sectors to a backup generator we have hidden in the tunnels. We can't afford to use the power for much, but this is the only defense we have against the Silvers. There's an early warning system at each tunnel entrance, which is how we knew you were inside, but this is what actually keeps the Lightbringers at bay." Tamisra gestured for Aniya to enter. "Welcome to Refuge."

Aniya stepped through the entry and into a massive cavern, lit floor to ceiling by various candles and torches. On the floor of the cave were hundreds, perhaps thousands of tents, laid out with no discernible pattern other than making room for the dirt roads that curved throughout the cavern. Each tent bore the same symbol, painted in black on the canvas: a four-fingered hand.

In the very center of the cavern was a large shack that stood four stories high, a tower that reached more than halfway to the ceiling of the cavern and stood tall above the rest of the town. The shack seemed to be made entirely of sheet metal, but a few uncovered spots revealed a stone frame underneath.

"How is it so big?" Aniya realized her mouth was hanging open as she surveyed the huge cavern, but she didn't care. The sight was beautiful. Even the uppermost parts of the cavern, where no one could reach to place a torch, were lit with a shimmering green glow.

"When these tunnels were mines, the Lightbringers needed bases to work out of. This was one of them, and for the longest time, their most important one. Taking this cavern was a great victory to the rebels during the Uprising."

Tamisra took Aniya's hand and held on slightly tighter when she tried to pull away. "Trust me."

Aniya hesitated, but surrendered and let Tamisra lead her through the camp. As they walked, she couldn't help but gape at the people stepping out of their tents to watch.

All of them—men, women, and children—were emaciated, but they otherwise seemed perfectly healthy. While the children waved at Aniya, the men and women looked on cautiously. But as they broke Aniya's gaze and noticed her hand joined with Tamisra's, they would look back up again with softened expressions, some of them bearing smiles.

"We don't get many visitors," Tamisra said. "At least not many that don't end up dead before they ever see the camp."

Aniya began to realize the privilege she was being granted, and she smiled, waving back at the children and nodding toward the adults.

"Before we caught on to the Lightbringers' game, we lost

dozens of people to their spies. It took us a long time to let anyone inside Refuge again, and even now—well, you know the trial they have to pass."

"Do many people come here?"

"People have started to figure out that the tunnels never caved in completely. We've sent spies of our own into the sectors to spread rumors so that people can seek shelter here away from the Lightbringers."

"Won't that convince the Lightbringers to come here also? You're stealing away their citizens. They can't be too happy about that."

Tamisra shrugged. "What are they going to do? It's not like they can step foot inside the tunnels. They know how dangerous it is for them. All they can do is send spies and hope that we don't kill them. Even then, they've pretty much stopped bothering. In sectors where it's a bigger problem, they just tighten their grip further. It's not pretty."

"How have I never heard of this? Haven't you sent spies to the Hole?"

"The Hole?" Tamisra frowned.

"Holendast."

"Ah. That's the most dangerous sector, actually."

Aniya laughed. "You wouldn't think so if you've been there. They don't really care about us."

"You'd be surprised. My dad said that after the war, most of the surviving rebels were exiled there. The Lightbringers wanted to keep them all in one place to keep an eye on them. If we went in there now, we'd be picked up by their surveillance immediately. We can't confirm it, but we're pretty sure that a lot of the citizens of Holendast are actually under-cover Lightbringers."

"I don't get it," Aniya said. "Why bother keeping them alive? Why didn't they just kill all the rebels?"

"I really don't know. The only thing that makes sense is that you're still valuable to the Lightbringers somehow. After all, if they had killed all of the rebels, they'd have lost thousands of workers."

"Which means hundreds lost for relocative servitude."

Tamisra nodded.

"Do you have spies in the Hub? Do you know what kind of work they do there?"

"We don't dare go inside the Hub. We have an understanding. This is our territory, and the Hub is theirs. Besides, there's only one tunnel inside that we know of, and they collapsed it right after the incident with your brother."

"Now what?"

Tamisra muttered under her breath, "Now nothing. My father made it sound like he agreed to help your brother. But you should have seen him when he found out about it. I can't remember the last time I've seen him so mad. The team that ran off with your brother did it without telling him because they knew he would never approve such a mission. In the end, he made peace with it only because William said he knew someone inside the Hub willing to help. When our people came back without their heads, he swore up and down that it was the end of his fight with the Lightbringers."

"So that's it?" Aniya scoffed. "He's done just like that?"

"I wouldn't say just like that. He was done a long time ago. Right before the war ended, the Lightbringers executed my mother and brother in front of him. I wasn't even born yet, but I was far enough along that your friend Gareth managed to save me after they killed my mother. But that was the day my father was done with the war. When I heard about William's mission, it felt like we had a chance for a better life, but my father couldn't have been angrier. Then our scouts returned dead, and he was crushed. There's no way he'd try anything now. He's convinced he'll lose me too."

Aniya fell silent for a moment. When she spoke again, her voice was low. "I can't say I blame him for wanting to protect you. I know how he must have felt." She cleared her throat and brushed hair away from her eyes. "And what do you think? I take it you don't agree with him."

"I used to not care. This life is the only one I've ever known. But the more people I see come in from the outside . . . the hurt, the abused, the oppressed—to see them finally smile again after joining us is like nothing I've ever felt. But it only makes me hurt more for those still in the sectors. I'm ready for things to change. My father is as well, don't get me wrong. He's just no longer willing to let his people die to see his dream come true. I don't think he understands that they'll willingly die for him and his dream."

Aniya glanced at Tamisra's face. The girl's eyes were burning again, a fire that blazed with a hunger that Aniya realized went beyond mere bloodthirst.

They arrived at the large building at the center of the cavern, and Tamisra opened the door for Aniya.

The first floor contained dozens of crates and barrels, watched over by one man sitting at a table.

The man looked up, and his eyes opened wide.

"You look like you've seen a ghost, Corrin." Tamisra snickered.

After clearing his throat, Corrin shook his head and replied, his voice bearing a nearly imperceptible shake. "It's nothing. What do you need, Tami?"

"My father asked me to make sure our visitors have supplies before leaving tomorrow. Can you give my friend Aniya the standard three-day package, same for her companion? Use the packs we confiscated and Xander brought to you."

"Aniya?" Corrin picked up two rucksacks from the floor and scanned Aniya's eyes. "Is that short for something?"

"Annelise," Aniya said, frowning. "But I prefer Aniya."

The man only nodded and looked away.

"Let's get you settled, Aniya." Tamisra tugged on Aniya's

arm. "Our cots are not the best, but it's better than sleeping on the floor."

"A moment, Tamisra." Corrin raised a finger, and the girls turned around. "My sons wanted you to stop by when you get a chance. They said that the brisket is ready."

Tamisra laughed loudly, a screech that made Aniya wince. "Malcolm must have said that. I can't imagine Xander being that morbid." She turned to Aniya. "Follow me. We're going to go have some fun."

Her curiosity piqued, Aniya followed Tamisra out of the building, down a different path and out of the camp, stepping into one of the many tunnels that branched off from the cavern.

"Who was that?" Aniya looked back toward the main building.

"That's Corrin. He's my dad's second-in-command, but he also monitors the supplies for the time being because the last guy . . ." Tamisra shook her head. "Besides, there's not much to do around here. Except for—well, you're about to find out."

They walked down a long tunnel, which was lit only by a few scattered torches and the same green glow that Aniya had noticed when she first entered the tunnel with Roland.

She was about to ask about the strange light when a particularly nasty growl came from the distance.

"What was that?"

Tamisra said nothing, but her eyes twinkled as a hint of a smile spread across the girl's face.

The growl grew louder, and a new sound came from down the tunnel, a pattering noise that intensified into a thundering tumult that shook the ground beneath Aniya's feet.

Tamisra stopped, and her smile vanished.

Then, from around a bend in the tunnel came running a large animal at least four feet tall and wide. It bore down on them with an impressive pace, and Aniya instinctively backed away, tripping on a rock and falling backward. She couldn't turn away from the terrifying sight, her eyes drawn to the creature's long nose, then down to its large, gnashing teeth.

The creature pounced into the air directly at the two girls, and Aniya shut her eyes tight.

19

After a few seconds, Aniya opened her eyes again to see the creature pinned to the ground by Tamisra's surprisingly strong arms. One of the girl's hands clutched a large collar around the animal's neck. Still catching her breath, she looked up and spotted several bobbing torches further down the tunnel.

"Who left a cage open?" Tamisra shouted down the tunnel. She was struggling, and Aniya slowly backed away, knowing even this fierce girl couldn't hold the monstrous creature for long.

The beast was huge, much larger than any Aniya had ever seen, but she recognized what it was. She gaped in wonder. "Salvador wasn't exaggerating about the moles."

Tamisra laughed as the mole underneath her squeaked and bucked in frustration. "This is just a little one. His mother made for a good dinner, and this one will make for a good mount."

Two boys about Aniya's age appeared from the shadows and took the mole from Tamisra, attaching two ropes to its collar. While Salvador's daughter had been able to hold the creature down herself with some effort, it took both boys to steady the mole in place.

"Sorry, Tami," one of the boys said. He looked back to the men gathered behind. "One of the trainers didn't secure its cage properly, and you know this one will get out the first chance it gets."

"It's a he, Xander, and his name is Brisket." Tamisra folded her arms. "And maybe he'd behave better if you treated him with respect."

The other boy smirked. "He bucked you clear across the arena yesterday. Respect hasn't gotten you very far."

"We'll see about that, Malcolm. There's always today."

Aniya gaped. "You ride these things?"

She received a sharp elbow in her side from Tamisra. "Things?"

"Who's this?" Xander turned toward Aniya.

Tamisra put an arm around her. "This is Aniya, our newest rider."

"Oh, no," Aniya said, distancing herself from the creature. "I'm not getting on one of those things."

Another jab from Tamisra.

"You look like you just came in from the sectors," Xander said. "You're definitely in for quite a ride."

"Doubt it," Malcolm said. His cold eyes narrowed as he gave Aniya a once-over. "The city girl won't last five seconds."

"I don't think you've made it five seconds on Brisket yet, Malcolm," Xander said, nudging his brother with an elbow. "I'll bet you a half-ration that she can make it longer than you."

"You're on."

Xander handed the rope in his hands to a man behind him and shook Aniya's hand. "I'm happy to meet the girl who's going to best my brother. It's good that he's put in his place every now and then."

"We'll see," Malcolm scoffed.

Tamisra grabbed Aniya's other hand and pulled her along. "Come on!"

The trainers took the mole from Malcolm, and the group continued down the tunnel and came to another cavern, this one nowhere near as large as Refuge's main camp, but still quite sizable.

"This is what we call our stable," Tamisra said, her hands on her hips.

In the middle of the cavern was a large, roped-in area. Along the walls of the cavern were several metal cages, and in the glow of the torchlight, Aniya could make out the glowing eyes of animals contained in each one.

"You'll need this."

Aniya turned to see Xander presenting her with a torch.

"If they're not too angry, the moles are attracted to the light," he said. "Ironic, really, considering they like to burrow into the ground."

Tamisra took her own torch and waved it slowly in front of the mole she called Brisket. The animal quieted down and stared into the light, its nose following the flame as it wavered and flickered. "We think it's part of the mutation. It seems to almost hypnotize them."

With that, she vaulted onto the animal and grabbed the back of its neck. She placed her hands on her hips triumphantly.

"See? Just like that."

The mole, however, seemed to wake up from its trance and began to stir. Sensing the load on its back, it began to thrash, launching Tamisra into the air and several feet away, where she landed with a moan.

Malcolm laughed scornfully as he grabbed the ropes and waved another torch in front of Brisket, calming the creature down again. "Just like that, huh? I don't think this one can be tamed."

"Let me try."

Aniya turned to see Roland leaning up against the wall of the cavern next to Salvador and another man.

"How long have you been here, cutie?" Tamisra jumped to her feet and smiled.

Roland seemed to ignore the term of endearment. "Long enough to see you fall on your face."

Tamisra's smile grew larger. "Feisty, aren't you?"

As Roland approached Brisket, Xander placed a hand on his shoulder. "I wouldn't recommend starting on this one. We just brought him in a few days ago. Hasn't had any training yet."

"Neither have I," he said. "Should be fun."

Roland took the torch from Aniya but stopped as she placed a hand on his arm.

"Where have you been?"

He looked at her with a gaze she could not interpret. "Later."

"Careful, pet," Tamisra said. "I don't want Brisket to hurt you before I've had my way with you."

Aniya rolled her eyes. Just when she was starting to like her.

Malcolm glared at Roland. "So, you're Tami's new plaything?"

"You had your chance," Tamisra said, waving her hand dismissively.

Roland waved the torch in front of Brisket's eyes slowly, and the creature drooped its head, bobbing in time with the torch. With considerably less agility, he grabbed the mole's neck and jumped on its back.

The instant Roland landed, the creature's eyes flew open, and it bucked again, sending Roland tumbling into the dirt not far from Tamisra's landing place.

It bucked again and rammed Xander's chest with its snout, sending him tumbling to the ground.

The mole was now free, and it snarled at the rest of the

trainers that began to approach, keeping them at bay. It growled louder and hissed, and even Tamisra's eyes widened as she pulled Roland away from the agitated creature.

Meanwhile, the man standing next to Salvador had burst into action, and he strode toward the arena, shouting at the trainers. "Tie it down, men. It can't overpower all of us together."

"Yes, Lieutenant!" One of the trainers tossed a rope toward the mole, and a noose settled around its neck.

The man known as the lieutenant turned to the other trainers. "Not one at a time. All together!"

But it was too late. Brisket spun around and charged, tackling the rope-wielder and biting into his neck.

Over the trainer's screams, Aniya heard the lieutenant shout, "Bring it down!"

"No!" Tamisra shrieked. She lunged forward and knocked a gun from the lieutenant's hands.

The trainer next to Aniya launched a spear toward the mole, driving the tip into Brisket's side. The mole shrieked, its agonizing cries echoing throughout the cavern. It turned and charged again, this time directly toward Aniya.

As the beast bore down on her, Aniya found herself rooted to the ground in terror. As a desperate last resort, she held up her hand in front of her face and closed her eyes, preparing for the worst.

But it never came.

The mole's footsteps slowed, and it came to a halt inches from her hand.

After a second, Aniya opened her eyes slowly to see the mole staring back at her, its eyes wide. Her every instinct told her to pull her hand back before it was bitten off, but she found herself stretching out her hand, gently laying a finger on the tip of the mole's snout.

Brisket sniffed her finger, then withdrew sharply. After a

moment, it cocked its head, then pushed its nose forward again, placing its snout into Aniya's hand again.

Slowly, Aniya stood up, carefully stroking the mole. She removed the noose from around its neck and tossed it to the ground. Then, as her left hand massaged its nose, her right explored the mole's body, caressing its head and neck. As her hand reached its back, the mole whined and flinched, and the spear in its side quivered.

Keeping one hand on its nose, Aniya held her breath and wrapped her hand around the spear's base.

"I wouldn't do that if I were you," a voice came from behind Aniya, and she turned to see the man who had been shouting orders.

"Lieutenant Haskill is right," Malcolm said. "You're just going to enrage it."

Aniya ignored them and pulled the spear out quickly, wincing as Brisket shrieked again. The mole swayed as blood trickled from its side. She stroked the animal and examined the wound. It didn't seem very damaging. Just deep enough to hurt.

"They're quite resilient creatures."

Aniya turned to see Tamisra, the only one bold enough to join her side.

"The larger ones have even thicker skin, almost like armor. He probably doesn't even feel it now that the spear is out." A spark lit up Tamisra's eyes as she nudged Aniya. "Want to go for a ride?"

"I don't think he'd let me."

"For some reason, he likes you more than any of us. If anyone has a chance of staying on, it's you."

Aniya looked at Brisket again. Sure enough, the mole seemed docile now, even uttering a low, peaceful sound that was quite unlike a growl. She grabbed its neck, and it seemed to crouch to the ground slightly, as if inviting her up. Without giving herself or the animal a chance to change their minds,

Aniya leapt onto its back and steadied herself as the mole raised up to its normal height again.

"Okay, I was just saying that," Tamisra said, her eyes wide. "I didn't really think it'd be that easy."

Xander approached and handed her the two ropes. "Here. Use these to direct its movement, pull to stop, and whip up and down to make it go faster."

Aniya took the ropes hesitantly. "Can you repeat that?"

"You'll figure it out," Tamisra said before Xander could respond. With that, she smacked the mole on its hindquarters, and it reared slightly before dashing forward.

Aniya was unprepared for the start, and she almost fell off immediately, but she managed to hold on to Brisket's neck with one hand. After a few seconds, she pulled herself back up to a seated position as they took off down a tunnel.

Brisket's body shook back and forth with every pump of his legs, and Aniya had to continually pull on the ropes in a desperate attempt to keep from falling. Maintaining her balance proved harder than Aniya imagined, and she was sure she would fall off at any second as the mole ran faster and faster.

The torches on the wall flew by, and as Aniya grew more accustomed to the creature's movements beneath her, her only concern was the very real possibility of getting lost in the labyrinth of tunnels that ran throughout the Web.

So before Brisket had a chance to turn down another fork in the tunnels and disorient Aniya for good, she pulled the reins backward gently, slowing her mount. She then pulled the right rope only, directing Brisket to turn around in the tunnel and go back the way they had come.

Within a few minutes, Aniya was back inside the cavern, greeted by several applauding trainers. Tamisra jumped up and down gleefully, clapping her hands. Malcolm stood next to her, folding his arms while Xander elbowed him in the side and grinned. Lieutenant Haskill gave her a nod of approval.

Only the trainer that Brisket had bitten seemed to be in a sour mood, and he glared at the mole as another trainer bandaged his neck.

Aniya dismounted and handed the ropes to Xander and Malcolm, who guided Brisket into one of the cages by the wall, but not before the mole nuzzled Aniya's cheek in farewell.

"You did it!" Tamisra slapped Aniya's back, making her stumble forward. "I'm glad we decided not to kill you after all."

Roland approached and stuck a tongue out at her. "Show off." He hugged her, whispering in her ear. "I thought that thing was going to kill you."

Aniya smiled and hugged him back. "You worry too much."

"Hey now, hands off my pet!" Tamisra pulled Roland away and wrapped an arm around his neck as she smiled at Aniya. "I hope you had fun, but you two need to get some rest if you still plan on leaving tomorrow."

Aniya had forgotten for a moment that their stay in Refuge would be a short one.

"Well done, young one."

The trio turned to see Salvador, who had approached them silently.

"Few of our riders have such natural talent. I daresay you may even rival my daughter."

"I wouldn't go that far," Tamisra said, elbowing Aniya for the third time.

"Then you do not give her much credit, Tami." Salvador approached and placed a hand on Aniya's shoulder. "Your father would be proud, Annelise."

Words caught in Aniya's throat as her eyes grew wet.

"She likes 'Aniya,' Father." Tamisra spoke up after a moment of silence with a forced laugh.

Salvador kept his eyes on Aniya. "I like her given name

better. It suits her."

Before the following silence could stretch on once more, Tamisra piped up again. "Well, we need to get going and let them get some rest." She tugged on Aniya's hand and led her away from Salvador.

With one last look at Brisket, then Salvador, Aniya followed Roland and Tamisra back to the main camp.

When they approached the central building, Tamisra gave them back their rucksacks. "There's two cots on the fourth floor where my father sleeps. Take those, get some rest, and I'll take you to Ravelta as soon as you wake up."

"Ravelta?"

Tamisra nodded toward Roland. "He'll fill you in."

Aniya and Roland made their way upstairs, set their rucksacks aside, and made themselves comfortable on the two cots.

After several moments of silence, Aniya rolled over to face Roland. "You haven't said anything in a while. What's up?"

Roland shook his head. "Nothing. Just thinking about the way ahead. We still have to make it through Ravelta somehow, the sector right next to the Hub. Whatever tunnels that may have once led to the Hub have been too well covered by the Lightbringers, according to Salvador. We're not getting in there through the back door."

"Tamisra said the same thing," Aniya said. "Does he have any ideas for getting into the Hub itself?"

"He said he'd explain in person before we leave."

"What did he want to talk to you about?"

"Plenty."

"Like?"

"Like how much we need to get rest for a long trip ahead. We'll talk tomorrow, okay? We'll have plenty of time with nothing else to do but walk."

Aniya frowned as Roland blew out the candle, but she rolled over and eventually gave herself over to sleep.

The night passed uneventfully, and they woke up a few

hours later, silently gathered their things, and made their way downstairs.

"Finally!"

Tamisra stood up from the table, where Corrin remained sitting. He glanced at Aniya, then quickly looked away as Tamisra continued.

"You know you slept for fourteen hours?"

Aniya wasn't surprised. After her last few days, she could have slept longer.

"Come on," Tamisra said. "My father is waiting for us."

They stepped out into the camp but halted as a loud bell sounded from somewhere in the cave.

Tamisra's eyes flew wide open, and she took off running.

Aniya and Roland followed until they stood near the entrance of another tunnel, where Salvador stood waiting.

"What is it?" Tamisra asked, breathing heavily.

"The Ravelta tunnel," Salvador said. "It could be a mole. Could be the Silver Guard. But our tripwires in the main tunnels usually go undisturbed. The moles have adapted to our ways, and the Silver Guard have learned their lesson. We have sent out a few scouts, but I think I already know the answer."

Aniya knew as well, but she asked anyway. "What is it?"

"The only thing that's changed is your presence. The Lightbringers know that the fastest way to the Hub is through Ravelta." Salvador narrowed his eyes. "Annelise, they are coming for you."

20

Aniya walked down the tunnel with a silence brought on not just by the impending danger, but also by her guilt.

As she walked with Roland, both of them surrounded by two dozen men, she hung her head in shame. After incredible loss, Refuge had learned to thrive again, at least as much as they could in the irradiated caves. Salvador had built a city where people could live free of the threat of the Lightbringers.

And she had brought an army to their front door.

As if he sensed her shame, Roland clutched her right hand. She slipped away, feeling undeserving of his touch.

"Don't feel too bad," Tamisra said, walking on her other side.

Am I that transparent?

"It's been a long time since I got my hands on one of those shiny spooks," Tamisra said. "It's about time for a fight."

Malcolm spoke up from behind. "Please. Giggling at them during the trial doesn't count as fighting one of them. And trust me, it's a lot different from sparring with us in the arena."

"Clearly you haven't wrestled with Tamisra since you

broke up," Xander said. "She's tough when she's not going easy on you."

"We can settle that when we get back," Malcolm muttered.

"Silence, boys," Corrin said from directly in front of Aniya.

Xander bowed his head. "Sorry, Father."

The plan had changed. Rather than going to Ravelta, they would be going to Basradur, its neighboring sector. It was still close to the Hub, but not the first place the Lightbringers would suspect her.

The trip would be a long one. According to Salvador, they hadn't even made it to the Basradur tunnel yet. The caves stretched on much farther than Aniya thought, and the trip seemed even longer as she couldn't help but dwell on her unfortunate circumstances.

Minutes later, she heard footsteps in the distance, but it didn't sound like the thundering steps of the Silvers. Nevertheless, Salvador ordered the group to extinguish their lights and remain still.

Soon, they were joined by three men carrying torches, led by Lieutenant Haskill.

"We're clear," the lieutenant said. "It's a mother. A squad waits in the Ravelta tunnel when you're ready. We've already disabled the torches."

Salvador softened and smiled. "Good. Then our guests will be privileged to see an amazing sight before their departure. I guess we shall be taking the Ravelta tunnel after all." He turned around. "Don't bother lighting your torches. We're almost to the epicenter."

Lieutenant Haskill led the group for a few minutes until they reached a large cavern about half the size of Refuge. The cave was lit by several torches, revealing dozens of smaller tunnels branching off from this central location.

"This is our epicenter, made from the remains of a nest of

moles. It took us a long time to clear this place out." The lieu-tenant guided the group through the cavern. "Much like the Lightbringers' Hub is the core of the Web, this cavern is the center of this network of tunnels. From this point, we can reach most of this quadrant of the Web."

After a few minutes, they reached one of the tunnels, and Salvador raised a finger to his lips. "From here, we must be very quiet. Keep your lights out."

They walked into the tunnel and continued on until the light from the epicenter faded. Aniya could make out several torches lining the walls of this tunnel, but they had been extinguished. In the dark, she smelled a faint odor, a putrid one that made her stomach churn.

The group halted, and seconds later, a soft, green glow appeared in Salvador's hand, just enough to light their way through the tunnels.

"What is that?" Aniya whispered as she peered at the mass in Salvador's hands and noted that it seemed to be slowly moving. "I've been seeing them all over."

"Earthworms," Corrin said quietly, "exposed to centuries of radiation. We've affectionately come to know them as glow-worms. They're quite handy in the most desperate of situations, and we've found that they give off just enough light without giving our positions away."

Roland poked at the clump of critters. "To the Silvers?"

"Among others," Lieutenant Haskill said. "You've probably never seen them before because they're neutralized by artificial light, including luminescence from the sky ceilings. But here in the caves, where we use nothing but fire, they thrive and absorb energy from the natural light."

Salvador held a finger to his lips and turned, leading the group down the tunnel, his figure a dark silhouette against the soft green glow emanating from his hand.

"What is that smell?" Roland plugged his nose. He turned to Aniya, who also covered her nose with her hands.

Though Roland had tried to speak quietly, Salvador hushed him and spoke even lower. "You shall see soon enough."

But despite Salvador's quick dismissal of Roland's comment, the Scourge paused. After a moment, he shook his head, and they continued.

Finally, they approached several other people waiting in the tunnel, most of them with spears in their hands. Two of them carried guns.

Wordlessly, the two groups merged and continued.

The large group continued through the tunnel, led by Salvador and his handful of green light, and followed by the unarmed Aniya and Roland in back.

"I think the boy was onto something," Aniya heard Lieutenant Haskill whisper to Salvador. "It's not just the mother. Do you smell that?"

Salvador nodded but said nothing. The Lieutenant turned around, frowning, and whispered something to Corrin.

Aniya sniffed again, and the putrid smell overcame her senses, nearly causing her to retch. But another smell lingered below, a faint one that she couldn't quite place.

She relegated the smell to the back of her mind, and as a splash came from below, Aniya looked down and noticed that her left foot was immersed in a thin stream of liquid. The Ravelta tunnel, it seemed, was close to an underground river. She took a step to the right and continued.

A few more steps, and the group stopped.

"Let's wake her up," Salvador said quietly.

Malcolm stepped out in front and pointed a large rifle down the tunnel. He peered down a sight and fired one shot.

A piercing shriek rang out and echoed through the tunnels. After a moment of silence, a menacing growl came from the tunnel ahead, slowly turning into a deafening roar.

Salvador took a spear from Xander as Lieutenant Haskill raised his voice. "Ready!"

The ground shook beneath Aniya's feet as the roar intensified.

"Now!"

The group raised their weapons and braced themselves.

A massive creature appeared in the green glow, its eyes narrowed and teeth bared in rage.

Aniya had seen and killed many moles in her time, most of them standing just under a foot tall. But this monster was easily ten times the size of the largest mole she had ever encountered before Brisket. And unlike the smaller ones, this beast had flesh that seemed to be covered in thick, scaly armor, except for a large, soft spot on the animal's belly. Its eyes were wide open, a tiny red glow in the very middle of its massive, black pupils. But its massive teeth caught Aniya's attention the most, and her mouth dropped open as they gnashed wildly with every step.

As those with guns fired at the mole, the beast rushed the group and was pierced by dozens of spears, each of them digging deep into the animal's belly, its seemingly only vulnerable spot. The monster let loose another howl of pain and retreated a few steps, pulling itself free from the spears.

"Again!" Lieutenant Haskill shouted, shoving a new clip into his gun.

The creature dug its hind legs into the ground, preparing another assault.

"Now!"

But this shout didn't come from the lieutenant.

The group froze as the command echoed from beyond the mole, much farther down the tunnel.

Aniya glanced at Salvador, who dropped the spear and drew a gun from a holster at his side, his eyes wide.

"We're not alone."

In the distance, past the mole, another faint glow appeared. It raced toward them, a bright orange light approaching the group faster than the beast had.

Suddenly, the mole burst into flames, a ten-foot, blazing abomination.

The fire continued past the mole and raced past the group as they dove to the side and out of the way. The tunnel, around eight feet wide, now had a two-foot strip of fire running down the middle.

Aniya's shock broke as Roland grabbed her arm.

"Your foot, Aniya!"

She looked down to see her left pant leg catching fire, the flames beginning to spread up her calf. As she dropped to the ground to extinguish the fire in the dirt, she realized that rather than an underground river, she had been stepping in fuel.

Aniya stood again and was met with a terrifying sight: the mole, still a writhing mass of flesh and flame, seemed to dance in the blaze, kicking out wildly as it screamed with a guttural cry.

Then, from behind the burning monster, came a new threat.

In the distance, white lights flashed on and backlit the giant, fiery mole, casting a dark shadow on the group and shielding them from the blinding light.

The tunnel exploded in noise as several small explosions rang out from further down the tunnel.

Bullets bounced off the mole's armored epidermis, causing no harm, but the animal shrieked in pain as the fire ate away through its tough outer layer and reached sensitive flesh.

With a roar, the mole rushed toward the group in a frenzied run, but collapsed after just a few steps and writhed on the cave floor just in front of the group.

Now that the mole lay down in a smoldering heap, the white light burst through and blinded Aniya, and she stumbled backward. She fell to the ground and held her hands in front of her eyes.

"The lights, Salvador!" Corrin knelt by Aniya's side, placing his body between her and the armed intruders. "The electromagnetic device must be down."

"Then radio Refuge!" Salvador's voice came from the group. "If their communications work, so do ours. Lieutenant, get the engineers on the emergency channel and tell them to turn it back on, now!"

A bullet whizzed by Aniya's ear, and one of Salvador's men fell in the small strip of flame, his motionless body quickly catching fire.

Corrin stretched his arms wide, blocking Aniya's body further, but he fell over on top of her with a grunt of pain as blood spurted from his shoulder.

Salvador turned to Aniya and Roland. "You must leave, now! Tamisra, take them to the Basradur tunnel, but go no further. Then, go back to Refuge and rally our troops. Go, now!" He threw his glowworms to the ground, their bodies now black and lifeless.

Roland grabbed Aniya's hand and pulled her out from underneath Corrin's body. She offered no resistance, instead running with him as fast as she could, careful not to step into the fire.

Behind them, the gunfire continued, accompanied by screams of pain. A few bullets made their way past the main group, barely missing the fleeing trio.

That is, until Aniya's hand was suddenly yanked, forcing her to stumble to the tunnel floor, dangerously close to the thin wall of fire. She turned around to see Roland sprawled out on the ground.

"Roland!" Aniya screamed and jumped over the fire to kneel next to her friend.

"Is he okay?" Tamisra knelt next to Aniya, her voice escalating even higher than her normal shrill pitch.

"I don't know," Aniya said. "Help me."

The two girls carefully rolled Roland onto his back.

Roland's eyes were shut tight, a low moan escaping his pursed lips. He sat up slowly, clutching his left leg. Aniya looked down and saw a steady stream of blood flow from Roland's calf, slowly coursing off his body and into the nearby fire.

"You've gotta go, Aniya. You need to make it to the Hub and get William back." Roland spoke through clenched teeth. "Promise me you'll get him back."

"Come on, pet." Tamisra pulled at his arm and began to drag him back up. "You're not done yet."

Aniya wrapped her right arm around Roland's other side, forcing him back up again. "Come on, we can make it!"

Roland continued to protest, but the girls hoisted him up and continued on.

They kept moving at a slow pace until Roland suddenly gave way and crumpled to the ground. Another bullet had managed to find his hip.

Roland squirmed in pain. "Gotta keep going, Aniya. Get out while you still can."

Aniya clutched his hand. "I can't just leave you!"

"You have to. This is more important than me. Remember," he said wrily. "That's the neat thing about not existing. It doesn't matter as much if you're dead."

"Roland, come on. It matters to me." Aniya fought back tears. "I care."

"Then make this worth it. Find your brother and Nicholas and bring them home. Trust no one but Kendall. Get her out of here, Tamisra."

Tamisra nodded. "I'm coming back for you."

Aniya opened her mouth but was cut short by the sound of more gunfire, louder now.

"We've got to go, Aniya." Tamisra pulled on her arm.

"No. You stay with him." Aniya pushed her away. "You take care of him. When I come back, he has to be alive. I can't lose anyone else."

Tamisra hesitated but nodded. "Take the third tunnel to your right. Don't come back until someone comes to get you. There may be nothing to come back to."

"I understand," Aniya said, standing.

"Go."

She turned and ran, faster now that she was on her own.

Behind her, more gunfire rang out, and she heard no more from Roland. The tunnel curved before her, and Aniya turned, leaving the fire behind her and running into the darkness, completely and utterly alone.

21

Aniya ran.

She ran through the pitch-black tunnel, not stopping to grab a torch from her pack, even though she could no longer hear gunfire.

She ran through her tears, which now flowed freely and heavily.

She ran with all her might, growing weary in her legs and in her heart.

The darkness surrounding her provided no sight of her destination, so Aniya ran blindly, stretching her arms forward to keep from running into the walls of the tunnel.

Her mind drifted and gave way to her imagination. In the black ahead, Aniya saw Roland's dead body, riddled with bullets. She pushed the image out of her mind, but it came back a second later, this time showing Tamisra sprawled out on the cave floor next to Roland, their blood mixing on the dirt between their bodies.

With a pained shout, Aniya banished the thoughts from her mind, embracing the dark instead and running even harder.

Finally, through her tears, she saw a tiny glow in the distance.

The epicenter.

With renewed strength, Aniya pumped her legs harder and raced against the fear and anger that brimmed inside her. She pushed aside the faces and focused on only the light.

At last, she came out on the other side of the tunnel and into the cavern of light, and Aniya let her tired legs give way, willingly falling to the ground with reckless abandon. Her mind urged her to get up and run, but she did not hear any noise from the tunnel behind her, at least not over her heaving breath.

After a moment sprawled on the dirt floor, Aniya pushed herself to a seated position and backed up against the opposite wall, still keeping an eye on the tunnel from which she had just emerged.

She only let herself rest until her breathing steadied and some energy returned. If the Silvers made it past the Scourge and his men, their next stop would be the epicenter, where she would be an easy target. But if she were in one of the many tunnels that branched off from this central location, the chances of them finding and catching up to her were very slim.

So as soon as her strength returned, Aniya stood.

"Third tunnel on the right," she muttered to herself. It made no sense, really. If Ravelta was the closest sector to the Hub and Basradur was the second closest, wouldn't their tunnels be adjacent? But then again, the tunnels were made by moles. They moved in whatever random direction seemed best at the time.

Knowing she didn't have much time left before the Light-bringers would catch up, Aniya reached into her rucksack and quickly drank some water and took a bite of mole jerky. As she put her supplies back, she noticed a small pouch tied to the top of her pack.

Aniya took the pouch and opened it to find several glow-worms packed together. She took the worms out of the pouch and held them to her face, examining the creatures with fascination. Her skin tickled as their thick bodies slowly intermingled, seemingly content to rest in a stranger's palms.

After a moment, she put her rucksack back on, leaving the worms in her hand, and headed down the third tunnel to the right.

The way was easier now that she had some light, and it helped that she traveled at a light jog rather than a dead run, allowing her to travel with more care.

She had been jogging for several minutes when she was blinded once again.

The tunnel lit up as bright as day thanks to several flashlights strapped to the heads of men in silver armor, standing not a hundred feet from her.

The Lightbringers had guessed her next move and were waiting for her.

"Now!"

A command echoed from down the tunnel, and Aniya instinctively dropped to the dirt floor as bullets whizzed overhead. At least she thought they were bullets. As she listened to them hitting the tunnel walls, she realized they were tranquilizer pellets.

Something crunchy tickled her palm, and she looked down to see the blackened corpses of the glowworms clutched in her hand. She let go, and they rolled away and onto the dirt.

This time, the Silvers' lights were strobing wildly. A tiny spark of hope ignited in Aniya. Refuge must have turned back on the jammer, and it was emitting a signal that interfered with the Lightbringers' communications and lights. She had a real chance of escaping now, thanks to the added confusion.

She took a deep breath and readied herself. Aniya didn't know how their guns worked, how long it took to reload them, or if they needed to be reloaded at all, but she knew that if she stuck around much longer, it wouldn't matter.

The strobe of the lights slowed, and she jumped to her feet, turned, and ran, thankful that the Basradur tunnel had more twists and curves than the tunnel to Ravelta. The flashing light quickly turned to a faint, flickering glow behind her, and she vanished into the darkness.

As she neared the epicenter, Aniya pictured the Silvers emerging from the Ravelta tunnel victorious, holding Roland's decapitated head in front of her, mocking her as they sedated her and took her away. After all, she had been in the Basradur tunnel long enough that it was a very real possibility.

However, as she stumbled into the epicenter, she was relieved to see that the Silvers had not made it to the cavern yet.

Aniya paused briefly to catch her breath. She tried to focus on her options and not the hopelessness that nagged at her mind. If she went down a tunnel that she thought might be close to the Hub, the Silvers might be there waiting as well. If she moved farther away from the Hub, she knew it would be much harder to find her way to her brother.

But it didn't seem to matter. The tunnels' paths seemed to be completely random and could go anywhere. All she knew was that three tunnels to the left was the tunnel to Ravelta, to the Lightbringers, to Roland's wounded—maybe dead—body.

She didn't even know which tunnel led back to Refuge. All tunnels were completely dark now. She guessed it was intentionally done by Salvador's men as a safeguard against intruders, just like when they first captured Aniya and Roland.

Though it wouldn't hold up well against the Silvers, with flashlights mounted on their helmets.

She had only one choice.

Aniya steadied herself, chose a tunnel at random, and began running.

22

Hours later, Aniya finally broke through a pile of rocks and debris and stumbled into the fresh air—at least as fresh as it could be now that the oxygen generators had been offline for three days and they were running off recycled air. Still, it was better than the caves.

The tunnel entrance remained still. No quake like the one she had experienced when leaving Holendast. Was the device broken? She remembered Salvador saying that the Ravelta quakes were not triggered, but the Silvers had made it inside after all, so maybe all the devices were intentionally turned off? Aniya could only guess.

The sector, as she expected, was without any artificial light coming from the sky ceiling, but it was dimly lit with the natural, warm glow of hundreds of candles scattered throughout.

As she stepped away from the cave, Aniya looked around and noted that unlike the Hole, the caves began nowhere near the trainyard, but rather on the opposite end of the sector, at the bottom of a hill near the marketplace.

Aniya surveyed the rest of the sector. From what she could see by the candlelight, this part of the Web didn't seem to be struggling to get by, and the sector seemed almost furnished, though by no means luxurious. There were still some smaller shacks scattered throughout the sector, but for the most part, the sector seemed to be filled with modern buildings and modest houses. Aniya sighed in relief. She may not have made it to Ravelta as planned, but it appeared as though she was getting closer to the Hub.

With one final look at the tunnel behind her to make sure that it looked undisturbed, she secured her pack and hiked up the hill and into the market.

As if the perpetual darkness in the Web didn't make it hard enough to keep track of time, the nearly two days she had spent in the tunnels left her completely disoriented, so it was confusing at first to see local vendors advertising and selling their goods in what may have very well been the dead of night.

Her most pressing question was where she had ended up. She was safe for now, and the Lightbringers may not have known where she was, but she didn't have any idea either. And not that she was excited at the prospect of venturing into the Hub, but any time not spent heading that way seemed like a waste of time.

She very nearly approached one of the vendors and asked what sector she was in, but she realized how suspicious that might sound. Those loyal to the Lightbringers would be quick to bring such peculiar circumstances to the authorities' attention.

Aniya rubbed the back of her neck as she took a deep breath. She didn't know how far out into the Web the Lightbringers' search for her had spread. Obviously, the Silvers were to be avoided at all costs, but had her picture been circulated among the citizens in other sectors? It wouldn't take much. All they had to do was say that she was wanted in connection with the sabotage of the power, and the entire Web would turn against her.

Then again, the Lightbringers seemed to rely upon a thorough control of the Web. If they issued a widespread warning about anything, they would run the risk of inciting panic, which would quickly eat away at their tight grip of the sectors.

Just before her racing thoughts could overwhelm her, a flash of inspiration inspired her to grab the radio from her belt and turn it on carefully. Sure enough, a crackle of life came from the device. The radio was no longer suppressed by the technology in the caves. Grinning, Aniya turned off the radio and shoved it in her pack. She looked around and gratefully noted that the busy town square masked the noise from the radio.

This presented her with a new option. Find a quiet area where she could listen to the radio. She might eventually hear clues as to where she was and whether the Silvers were alerted to her presence.

Of course, that was the real trick. The entire Web, as far as Aniya knew, was overpopulated in most sectors. It would be difficult to find a quiet moment alone no matter where she went.

In any case, it wasn't wise to remain in the marketplace any longer than necessary. Aniya didn't see any Silvers lurking around, but their appearance was inevitable here in the busiest part of the sector if she waited much longer.

She glanced around, but all visible paths seemed equally unattractive. With the exception of the hill behind her that lead back toward the caves, the commerce district of the sector stretched on in every direction. Her frustration rose, and her heart rate sped into a mild panic as she fumed in indecision. She became aware that she was drawing attention to herself, and that only made her even more anxious.

"Stop that child!"

Aniya's eyes flew open in alarm, her panic escalating to an all-time high.

She was spotted.

Aniya spun her head around wildly, looking for the source of the shout.

A small but rough blow knocked her over, sending her tumbling back down the hill. After she finally rolled to a stop, she got up and spotted a small figure running away from where she had been standing. A large man followed close behind, his fist in the air.

"Stop her!"

Aniya sighed in relief as she realized that she was not the child in question. She deftly climbed back to the top of the hill and watched the chase continue. The feeling of safety did not last long, however, as she saw several beams of light in the distance, pointed in her direction and bobbing up and down. She turned and walked briskly toward the commotion, blending in with the growing throng.

As she neared the front of the mob, Aniya saw that the chase had ended. The large man was standing nearby, resting with his hands on his knees as he heaved in exertion. A young girl stood a few feet away from him, wriggling in the hands of another man.

Though her body seemed to be one of a younger child, the girl's face revealed an older age, and Aniya guessed that she was in her early teens, the discrepancy likely caused by malnutrition. The thief's long, brown hair hung below her waist, and a thin layer of dirt seemed to cover her entire face, making her wide eyes look even brighter. She wore a dull brown shirt that hung loosely over her thin frame and covered half of her ragged denim pants. While the outfit was nothing impressive, what drew Aniya's attention was a large, clear crystal that hung by a leather cord around the girl's neck. It had popped out from underneath the girl's shirt as she struggled, and now it bobbed and swayed loosely.

"Do you know what the penalty for thievery is, child?" The large man stood up tall and approached the waif, wagging his finger. He picked up a small leather bag by the girl's feet and withdrew a loaf of bread and an apple.

Aniya turned her nose up at the sight of the artificial fruit.

"You're lucky the Silvers didn't see you. I have a little more mercy than they do." After a moment's consideration, the man's face softened slightly, and he placed the apple back in the leather bag, handing it back to the girl. "Go now. And don't let me catch you near my stand again."

The child nodded and took the bag, and the man holding her released her wrists.

"What's going on here?"

It was too late.

Aniya felt the crowd move around her, making way for five armored men.

The girl was on full display now and stood in the spotlight created by the lights mounted on the helmets of the Silver Guard. The crystal around the girl's neck blinked and sparkled as it swayed and caught the light at different angles.

"Nothing, officers." The large man turned and stepped between the Silvers and the girl. "Just a misunderstanding."

A sixth man stepped forward and scoffed. He wore a plain, gray uniform with red stripes. "An awfully large crowd for a misunderstanding." He pushed past the man and stepped toward the child, who stood frozen in terror. "We heard talk of a thief. Is this the culprit?"

The girl shook her head, displaying her empty hands.

"Then you won't mind if I look in your bag." The officer snatched the satchel from the girl, twisting her arm from the sheer force of the pull.

The girl grasped her arm, wincing and uttering a pitiful whimper.

An apple, the merciful gift from the wronged vendor, fell to the ground, condemning the hungry child.

"That's hers, Officer. I've never seen it!" The large man

pleaded from behind the officer, placing a hand on the officer's shoulder.

The officer grabbed the man's hand and spun around, forcing the vendor to his knees as a cracking sound came from his shoulder. "I didn't ask you, did I? Though I should be thanking you because your early defense of the girl proved her guilt to me. Think before you speak next time." He released the man and turned to the thief.

"I'm sure you're aware of the punishment that theft carries," the officer said, reaching to his side and unfastening a metal clip on his belt that secured a large whip. He nodded to the surrounding officers, two of whom marched forward, each grabbing the girl's hands. "But I'm sure something can be arranged if you'd rather not suffer the consequences of your actions." The officer approached the girl and used the whip to pull the dangling crystal closer to him, staring at it with wide eyes. "That sure is a nice trinket you have."

The girl, however, yanked her head back sharply, letting the crystal bounce off the whip and fly directly into the officer's face, hitting him square between the eyes.

With a hiss of pain, the officer recoiled. He swiped his bleeding forehead with his palm and looked down at his hand.

"So be it," the officer growled. He gestured to the two men holding the girl, and one of them reached for the front of the girl's shirt and started to pull roughly, tearing the fabric.

"What's wrong with you?" The vendor shouted. "She's a child."

Everyone froze as the lead officer turned around and glared at the large man, who was still on the ground and holding his arm in pain.

After a moment that seemed to stretch on forever, the officer turned around again.

"Let the girl keep her shirt."

The man nodded and released her shirt. He and his partner turned the girl around and pulled in opposite directions, stretching the thief's body and nearly suspending her in the air.

A tail of leather fell to the ground as a whip uncoiled at the lead officer's side. He smirked. "It'll probably come off all by itself anyway."

Without hesitation, the officer reared back and snapped his wrist forward, letting the whip fly.

The tip of the whip cracked and licked the girl's back, creating a thin, diagonal tear in her shirt from shoulder to waist. Red flesh peeked out from underneath the torn, brown shirt.

Aniya admired the thief. The girl's body trembled, but she did not cry out.

Another snap from the whip and another lash on the girl's back as her legs began to shake.

Yet another strike, and her legs gave out completely.

Now, with no support coming from their victim, the officers pulled harder on the girl's arms, fully suspending her.

The lead officer pulled his arm back farther and swung the whip with an incredible speed, now unleashing the full extent of the girl's punishment.

The sound of the whip echoed throughout the sector, as did a howl of pain as the girl finally succumbed to the pain.

"There it is." The lead officer grinned widely. With renewed vigor, he began to whip his victim in fluid, repeated attacks, an unrelenting assault on the girl's back.

What remained of the thief's shirt fell away from her torso. Thin, red stripes covered her bare back, and what little untouched flesh there was took on a dark purple tint, contrasting starkly against the girl's pale side.

The girl's cries turned from howls to screams to wails as the stripes on her back began to split open, blood dripping to the stone below.

Finally, the lead officer fastened the whip back to his belt and motioned toward his men.

The thief unceremoniously fell to the ground as she was released. Heavy sobs shook her body as she writhed in pain on the cobblestone.

"Remember the much harsher penalty for anyone who dares to help her." The lead officer turned around and waved his hand, pushing past the crowd and marching away without another word.

23

The girl curled up in a ball on the ground, wailing into her knees as her hands clutched her ankles.

Time stood still for a moment as the crowd, unable to do anything out of fear, watched the half-naked girl rock back and forth in agony.

Then, without a word, the crowd dispersed, each man and woman returning to their business and letting themselves forget about the sobbing girl in the middle of the street.

Aniya looked for the discarded apple, but it had been kicked aside long ago. With another look at the thief, she turned away and walked back the way to the marketplace.

She approached the same vendor that had been robbed, just now returning to his stall and resuming business. "How much for your apples?" she asked, picking up two in one hand, one in the other. Without waiting for an answer, she began to juggle the fruits, not taking her eyes off the vendor.

"Two coppers," the man said quietly, refusing to look Aniya in the eye.

Aniya feigned disgust. "No wonder she robbed you." She let two of the apples fall back toward the man's baskets, one of them missing the mark and rolling a few feet on the cobblestone. The third apple, which Aniya had thrown much higher than usual, finally came down, which she caught and quickly let fall into the large sleeve of her cloak, trapping it inside with her elbow.

The vendor, his attention on the rolling apple, missed this and reached toward the fruit as Aniya turned away.

Aniya marched back to the girl on the ground, but when she was mere feet away, a hand landed on her shoulder. She spun around, her heart racing as she prepared to fight whoever stopped her, but she paused as she was met with gentle eyes.

It was an aged man with a beard that nearly reached his belt.

"I saw you take from the fruit stall," the man said quietly. "I assume for the poor girl."

Aniya opened her mouth to defend herself, but the man stretched forth his hand, presenting her with a sizable burlap package.

"Mole meat," the man said. "Take care of her."

Without another word, the man turned and left, leaving Aniya in shock at the stranger's kindness. After a moment, she let the apple fall out of her sleeve and into her hand, then placed it in her rucksack along with the package of meat.

Aniya made her way back to the girl, who was still crying in the street. Without breaking stride, she took her cloak off and wrapped it around the girl. Careful to avoid as much of the girl's back as possible, she picked up the girl with some effort and carried her off the street and toward a cluster of shacks. As she walked, she looked from side to side, positive someone would eventually spot her, but she went unnoticed by dozens of bystanders who refused to look in the thief's direction.

Once away from the crowd, Aniya gently placed the girl down in an alley overlooking the marketplace, leaving the cloak wrapped around her. She took the apple from her sack and presented it to the girl, whose cries had finally died away.

"My name's Aniya. I brought you a present."

The girl's eyes widened, and she took the apple, munching down excitedly. Between bites, she managed to offer one word: "Kira."

"I don't get it, Kira. Why didn't you just give them the crystal? It's not worth that kind of a beating."

The girl paused mid-chew and looked up at Aniya. "It is to me." With that, she turned her attention again to the apple.

Aniya watched the girl eat but frowned when she left the apple half-eaten in her hands without another bite. "Is something wrong?"

"It's for my papa," Kira said, placing the remainder of the apple in the pocket of the cloak.

"Finish it." Aniya pulled the package of meat out of her rucksack just long enough for Kira to see. "I have more that he can have."

The girl smiled as her eyes began to water. "Thank you, Aniya. Though I will save the apple for him. It's his favorite."

"Doesn't he have food?"

"Hard to get food without money," Kira said. "He hasn't worked in years."

"I thought the Lightbringers make everyone work."

"He can't." Wincing, Kira stood up. "Thanks for helping me, but you should go. If the Silvers find out . . ." She shuddered.

"Maybe you can help me. Where am I?"

"Are you lost? It's not like Shyvale's a big sector."

Shyvale.

Aniya's hopes fell. She never cared much for the geography of the Web, but if she remembered her lessons correctly, she had run in the opposite direction of Ravelta and the Hub, winding up in a sector not too far from Holendast.

"Never mind. Do you have room for one more person in your home? I just need a bed for the night."

Kira scrunched her nose in confusion. "You don't have a home?"

"Not one that I want to be in tonight," Aniya said after thinking quickly. "I would really appreciate it. If not, that's okay."

"Of course you can stay with us. No one else tried to help me. It's only fair that I do the same for you."

Kira turned and guided Aniya out of the commerce district and into what looked like one of Shyvale's poorer districts, where smaller shacks seemed to be the only housing.

"So if your father doesn't work, how do you get food? You don't steal every day, do you?"

"I don't get caught every day," Kira mumbled.

"Do you have a sibling old enough to work?"

Kira shook her head. "My father filed for disability, so he only had to have one child. My mother was forced to work, even though it's not usually allowed. But she died a few years ago. It's just been me and Papa."

They stopped at one of the shacks, and Kira opened the door. Aniya followed her inside and closed the door as Kira lit a candle.

The light illuminated a man who had been sitting down at a table in the pitch black.

"Kira, you're home!" The man stood up and slowly approached as a small red light crept across the floor. "And you've brought a visitor. Who's this?" He looked in Aniya's direction, but slightly over her head.

"This is Aniya, Papa."

Aniya stretched forth a hand, but the man didn't take it. "It's nice to meet you," she said, withdrawing her hand.

The man smiled. "Glad to have you here, young lady. My name is Urich, and you are welcome to join us for supper." He turned to Kira. "I don't suppose you brought bread?"

"Sorry, Papa. The man with the bread didn't come today. But I did bring you a present." Kira grabbed her father's hands and placed the leftover half of the apple in his palms, ignoring Aniya's questioning glance.

"What luck! It's very difficult to make these treasures grow down here." Urich took a large bite from the apple and took his time enjoying the snack. "Don't worry about the bread, Kira. We can try again tomorrow."

Aniya pulled the package from her rucksack. "Actually, we brought something better."

"If my nose does not deceive me, that is mole meat!" Urich clapped his hands. "A rich dinner tonight indeed. Kira, would you start a fire?"

Kira handed Aniya's cloak back to her and walked across the room to a fire pit, grabbing a new shirt from a closet and clothing herself as she moved.

Urich's excitement over the mole meat was almost amusing to Aniya. Back in Holendast, it was the most readily available food, one that Aniya had grown accustomed to years ago. It was far from tasty, and the meat was difficult to cook without making it too tough to eat comfortably.

But to a family that had next to nothing, it must have been rare to have the opportunity to enjoy mole meat for dinner.

Aniya continued. "If you'll accept this as payment, I was hoping to stay the night tonight."

Urich's smile doubled in size. "A guest! Our luck is good today, Kira. You are most welcome to stay here as long as you need, child."

"And I would be happy to help in any way I can."

"Don't worry about that, dear girl. Between me and Kira, we manage." Urich took another bite of the apple, and Aniya couldn't help but smile when juices slipped from his mouth as he tried to chew and grin at the same time.

"Anything interesting happen today?" Urich turned and walked toward a small table as Kira stepped away from the fire and lit more candles.

As he walked, Aniya again noticed the red light that flashed near the floor. In the candlelight, Aniya could now see the source of the red flash.

Urich walked with a cane, but not for support. On the tip of the cane was a small light that flashed whenever the cane tapped the ground.

She realized what his disability was, the reason he couldn't work anymore. She realized that the light wasn't for himself, but for other people—he couldn't see it anyway.

"No, just the usual." Kira turned to Aniya, shaking her head.

"Good. I heard a whipping all the way from here, and I feared the worst. I haven't had to listen to that in months." He turned back toward the girls. "Aniya, you are welcome to rest on my bed while I prepare supper. It will take some time, and if I'm not mistaken, given your breathing, you are quite tired."

Urich was right. Aniya's legs ached from her earlier run, and the rest of her body was beginning to shut down as well, now that the adrenaline was wearing off. She carefully hugged her new friend and lay down on the bed Urich had indicated. Within seconds, she drifted into a deep sleep.

24

"Wake up, sleepyhead."

Aniya's eyes slowly opened, revealing Kira standing above her.

"How long did I sleep?" Aniya sat up in the bed and rubbed her eyes.

"Just a few hours," Urich said from across the room, sitting on the other bed and fumbling with his shoes. "I asked Kira to wake you because I didn't think you wanted your food to go cold. I'm sure you're hungry by now, and it's your food anyway."

Aniya smiled. "I'm happy to share with you. It's the least I can do to repay you for the bed."

"Enjoy, and take care of Kira while I'm gone." Urich stood up and shuffled toward the door.

Kira frowned and left Aniya's side. "Where are you going, Papa?"

"We need food before morning, sweetheart. I doubt our friend's stay is a permanent one, and her food will be leaving with her, I'm sure."

"But I can get what we need," Kira said, pulling on his arm. "You don't have to beg for us."

"I don't like you doing it either, Kira, especially since it usually turns into you stealing. We both know how dangerous it is. I couldn't bear for you to be whipped by the Silvers."

Kira bit her lip and hugged her father tightly, wincing as he returned the embrace.

"I'll be back later," Urich said as he kissed Kira's forehead.

With that, he turned and left the shack, letting his daughter close the door behind him.

When she was sure that the blind man was out of earshot, Aniya spoke. "I see why you didn't tell him what happened earlier today, but I'm not so sure you should have hidden it from him."

"It would hurt him more than it hurt me."

Aniya stood up and approached the table where Urich had left her food. "He's your father. I just think it's something he should know."

"What's your father like?" Kira asked quickly, turning away.

"He's dead," Aniya said, lowering her voice. She sat down and began stuffing her mouth so she wouldn't have to elaborate.

"Oh." Kira sat down on her bed. "I'm sorry. When did it happen?"

Aniya swallowed, horrible images racing through her mind. "Not long ago, actually. My mother died around the same time. I lost our home shortly after that, so that's why I asked to stay the night. I've been wandering around, looking for a new place to call home."

She continued eating, somewhat impressed with her own improvisation, but her stomach churned as she recalled finding her parents dead just a few days earlier. The food was good, but her appetite was waning.

"I'm very sorry," Kira whispered. Then she perked up. "Well, I'll have to ask Papa, but I'm sure he'd be more than happy to have you stay as long as you'd like. He really likes you, you know."

"You think so?"

"He said you remind him of me, and I'm pretty sure he likes me a lot. So that's something, right?" Kira beamed.

"Well, I really like him too." She finished eating, and she rose to wash her plate. "I would love to stay with you, but there's things I need to do." She took a jug of water from the counter and poured a small amount into her dirty bowl, letting the contents rinse out into a hole in the counter and onto the ground beneath the house. She then picked up a rag and wiped the bowl. "Do you know anything about the Hub?"

"Where the Lightbringers come from?"

"That's the one. I need to go there."

"What in the Web for?" Kira's eyes widened.

Aniya grimaced. "I have friends there, and I need to bring them back."

"No one ever comes back from the Hub." Kira grabbed Aniya's arm. "Please don't go there. You'll get caught."

"I have to. If it makes you feel any better, I wasn't planning on taking the train. Too heavily guarded by the Silvers. But I was hoping maybe there's another way?"

It was a tough ask, especially of a child, but transportation was very restricted in Holendast. Maybe things were different here in Shyvale.

"Well, there's the caves, but they collapsed a long time ago."

That was out of the question. There was no way to know if any tunnel was safe now.

Kira shrugged. "That's the only way I know of besides the train tunnel."

"Yeah," Aniya said, sighing. "I thought so too."

She was trapped.

There was no way she could make it on the train and out

of Shyvale unseen. The only way into the Hub was back through the caves. Back past the Silver Guard.

Even if Salvador had managed to defeat the Lightbringer invaders, Aniya would have no way of knowing. Besides, as soon as she stepped inside the tunnels, she would probably trigger the earthquakes near the entrance, which would undoubtedly warn the Silvers, whether or not they had taken over the caves. The quake devices may have been turned off temporarily to allow the Guard to sneak into the caves, but surely they would be turned back on to help them find her.

She would have to wait until someone came looking for her.

According to Tamisra, Salvador's scouts would travel to the sectors every so often, so it wasn't out of the question.

Of course, that was assuming there was anyone left alive in the caves.

So, her choices were either wait to be rescued or wait to be found by the Lightbringers.

Aniya looked at Kira, who still seemed to be deep in thought about another way into the Hub. Aniya smiled. At least she had a friend in this new place.

Let the waiting begin.

PART III

CONFRONTATION

25

Two Weeks Later

In the top floor of the Citadel, the Chancellor stood in front of a massive window, staring out at the Hub below.

Thanks to the glow of the fires within, he could see smoke rising from countless factories in neat columns and rows on the valley floor. If there was any consolation amid these troubling times, it was that production would not cease. It didn't take electricity to maintain most of the factories. Simple fire would do the trick.

The Chancellor craned his neck, hearing a pop come from his spine. He licked his dry lips and sighed. Between the power outage and the saboteur's sister, there seemed to be no end to the stress.

He touched a device on the side of his head and activated his earpiece.

"Add a session with Malena this week."

A female voice responded. "You already have a weekly appointment with the masseuse, sir. Are you sure you—"

"Put it down. In fact, until things improve, schedule an additional one every week."

"Yes, sir."

The Chancellor licked his lips again and went back to quietly surveying the Hub.

"Your Excellency?"

With a sigh, the Chancellor turned back toward the room for the first time in nearly ten minutes.

A dozen men sat at the long table in the center of the room, most of them avoiding eye contact with the Chancellor. The one exception was one of his engineers looking back at him timidly, pointing his finger in the air.

"We were discussing the power situation?" The man's finger shook slightly as the Chancellor glared at him. After a moment, the man dropped his finger and looked down at the table. "I was just wondering if we were finished, sir."

The Chancellor remained silent and folded his arms.

"But we can start again whenever you're ready, sir. Sorry, sir."

At the far end of the table, a man in a gray cloak sighed and let his forehead fall into his palm, shaking his head slowly.

After several more minutes of awkward silence, the Chancellor finally spoke.

"Come here, Mr. Stroud." He laced his words with a sweet, disarming tone, and he beckoned with a finger gently.

The man who had interrupted the Chancellor froze.

"Come now, I don't bite."

Slowly, the engineer stood up and joined the Chancellor at the window.

The Chancellor threw an arm around Stroud, grinning as the man flinched. With his other hand, he waved grandiosely at the window.

"This is the best view in the whole Web. Thanks to this massive window, I get to enjoy an inspiring panorama that excites and calms the spirit all at once. From here, I can see the entire Hub, working in perfect synchronization to maintain and improve our beloved world. I see the scanners zipping through the air, guarding our borders and protecting our assets. And when we have power, that glorious power which two weeks ago you assured me would only take days to fix, I see the ceiling gently turning, painting the sky with a magnificent spectacle to die for."

The Chancellor turned to face the engineer. "Surely, you can understand why I am so entranced by the sight of it all. Can you not?"

Stroud nodded as sweat dripped from his head. "Yes, your Excellency. I mean, no, your Excellency. Wait. I mean—"

The Chancellor laughed. "I know what you meant. I know you're new to your position—congratulations on the promotion, by the way—and if you do well, I just might have a similar window installed in your office a few floors down. Be careful, though. These things are rather fragile. Mine actually broke just a couple weeks ago." He shook his head slowly. "The most tragic incident. Not long after he failed me and the Web was plunged into darkness, your old boss stumbled and broke my window."

As the engineer's eyes grew wide, the Chancellor nodded.

"That's right. I couldn't believe it myself. Ceiling to floor, the whole thing shattered. The poor man fell all the way to the base of the Citadel. It took the janitors hours to clean the mess up. A true tragedy, I know—these windows are quite expensive. What a waste."

Stroud's lip quivered. "I won't fail you, your Excellency."

"Tsk, tsk, don't say that. The power should be restored by now, no? You already have failed me. You're turning out to be just like your predecessor." The Chancellor gasped as his eyes widened. "Believe it or not, he liked to interrupt me during board meetings as well. I'll tell you what, Stroud. The similarities between the two of you are quite striking."

"I'm sorry, your Excellency." Stroud backed away from the

172 | DAVID WEBB

Chancellor. "I'm sorry. I'm so sorry. Please forgive me, your Excellency."

The Chancellor's grin grew broader as the engineer stumbled back toward the table and sank into his seat. He turned back to the window, licked his lips, and took a deep breath.

"There appears to be no lasting damage to the reactor, you've bypassed the corrupted pillar, you improved the failsafe on the reactor, system strain is down to twenty-five percent, you should have the power back on tomorrow, and this will never happen again."

He turned back around to the table and glared at Stroud. "Am I missing anything?"

Stroud shook his head rapidly.

"Good. Then we are ready to continue."

An audible sigh escaped Stroud's lips as the rest of the table stirred.

After stalling for one more moment, the Chancellor waved his hand as he forced down a smirk. "Dismissed."

Without a word, the men stood up from the table and left the room, leaving behind only the Chancellor and the man in the gray cloak on the other end of the table.

"I'm glad they know better than to complain by now," the Chancellor said, his smirk breaking through.

The man in the gray cloak stood up and gathered the notes he had spread out on the table. "I'm surprised it's taken them this long." He paused and frowned. "Did you really throw Peterson out the window?"

"Of course not," the Chancellor said. "I took him out to the balcony and pushed him over the edge. You think I'd destroy this window? Who knows how long it would take for them to make another?"

"Good point," the man said. "Can I offer you some advice?"

"That's your job, isn't it?"

"Indeed. Maybe you should lay off the killing in times like

these. For all we know, Peterson could have restarted the reactor by now."

"You think I like killing?" The Chancellor grimaced. "My dear Adviser, you should know by now that I only do it when necessary. I barely have the stomach for such acts of violence. You know how I feel about the horrible work we do. You weren't around then, but I suggested another way a long time ago."

"So I've been told."

"But people understand violence. They understand fear." The Chancellor turned back to the window. "It's the only way to lead people like this."

His Adviser joined him at the window. "It didn't have to be. You didn't have to do this the hard way. If you hadn't turned off the suppressants—"

The Chancellor waved his hand, and his Adviser closed his mouth.

"Anyone can lead a Web full of mindless robots. I must understand opposition, embrace it, and overcome it if I am to be a true leader." The Chancellor nodded solemnly. "It's what the Web deserves."

"Yes, your Excellency."

A muffled beep came from the Adviser's belt, and he raised a finger.

"A moment, sir. That would be your operative."

The Chancellor laughed. "My operative? Given the liberties he's been taking with my orders, I wonder if my claim on him hasn't expired."

"Tell me about it." His Adviser stepped aside and pulled his communicator from his pocket. "Go."

The Chancellor ignored the discussion behind him and continued surveying the sector below.

His Adviser could never understand. The intricacies of leadership had taken years for the Chancellor to learn, a lifetime to master. The sacrifices he had made were inconceivable to those who had not been forced to make them.

To lead is to be misunderstood, the Chancellor recited in his head. It was the mantra by which he had lived for decades. This had turned out to be the case time and time again, and by now, the Chancellor expected no less.

Such was the curse of leadership, and it was a burden that he bore with pride in times like these. He knew that few others would have the strength to make the impossible decisions that faced him every day.

But in the end, they would all thank him. They would one day understand and praise his courage to lead in the face of such challenging circumstances.

One day.

"There's been a development, your Excellency."

The Chancellor turned to his Adviser, who had rejoined him by the window.

"Yes?"

"We've found her, sir. She's in Shyvale."

"She didn't get very far at all, did she?" The Chancellor smiled. "What are you waiting on me for?"

"Your permission, sir. She's proven to be a slippery one. I believe it will be much easier to catch her if we deploy the asset."

"Yes, that's why you've kept him alive, isn't it?"

"Yes, sir."

"And I have your assurance that he will acquiesce to all of your commands?"

His Adviser nodded. "Safeguards are already in place."

"Good. Send in the asset. Bring the girl in alive."

"Yes, sir."

26

"Remember. If you get caught, you die."

The Shyvale marketplace went about its normal business: throngs of people bartering at various stalls, vendors arguing with them, and the normal flow of people walking in the busy street.

In the midst of the hustle and bustle, no one took notice of the two cloaked girls crouched in a nearby alley.

The Silvers were nowhere to be seen. Maybe the Guard was spread throughout the Web, hunting for Aniya. Maybe they were gathered in the tunnels to trap her in case she came back. Maybe they knew where she was, and they were just waiting for her to show her face.

Aniya didn't want to think about it.

But the last two weeks had gone by without incident. Kira had proved a trustworthy friend, and with her father's permission, she had told Aniya she could stay in their home as long as necessary. Even when the Silvers came by a few days after Aniya's arrival, Kira had helped her hide in the makeshift basement they had constructed, similar to the one in Aniya's old home, and told the officers that she hadn't seen their fugitive. Even Urich played along and said he would be happy to help the Lightbringers in any way.

After that, there was no more lying to Kira or her father. Aniya came clean with them both and explained her plight in detail to Urich. He didn't seem surprised. In fact, he called himself a Sympathetic. During the war, he had both supplied and sheltered rebel forces without actually taking a stand in the war. And now that Aniya was on the run, Urich said he felt duty-bound to help her as well.

But although he encouraged her to stay in the house, Aniya had been getting uncomfortable. A few days ago, she finally convinced Urich to let her roam about the sector, so long as she remain in disguise and keep a low profile.

For Aniya, that meant wearing a cloak with the hood pulled up at all times. Not much of a disguise, but she blended in because most people donned cloaks on the cold Black Days.

However, she found it hard to fully comply with Urich's second condition, that she keep a low profile. It wasn't long before Aniya's boredom drove her to entertain herself with her favorite pastime: stealing.

Though the punishment would be severe if she were caught, Aniya knew the risk was minimal. She had mastered the art in Holendast, a smaller sector with fewer people. Now, in the crowded streets of a more populated sector, she would be undetectable.

Aniya did not feel guilty about breaking Urich's rule. Besides the rush of adrenaline she got when picking a pocket or pilfering a vendor's stall, she wanted to teach Kira to steal in a more effective manner. No more whippings for her.

"Really? I get caught, I die? That's a little drastic." Kira smirked. "I already know the punishment, and those wounds have pretty much healed by now anyway. It wasn't my first, you know."

"Yeah, but with my help, it will be your last. Besides, if you think about a more permanent punishment, you'll force your-self to be more careful. That's what I always do, and I've never been caught."

"Guess it's worth a try. And you'll show me first?"

Aniya nodded. She poked her head out from the alley, then stepped into the street, sliding past the crowd and letting it move around her. She wanted to make sure Kira could see her actions plainly, so Aniya picked the closest vendor as her target and approached.

It was not the same general vendor that Kira had stolen from two weeks ago. This stand specialized in fruits and sported a collection of apples, oranges, and grapes.

Aniya had not had any fruit in years. With a distaste of the Lightbringers came a distrust of their technology. Such vege-tation should have been impossible to produce even if they lived on the surface, thanks to the dead sun. Here, miles underground, it was possible but unnatural to grow such plants and foster them under radioactive lights. At first, she wondered how the vendors still had fruit now that the power had been out for two weeks, but she now realized that no new fruit was actually growing. This fruit had been sitting out the entire time. Her stomach churned as she looked at the synthetic fruit, two weeks old but looking as good as new.

Despite her personal preference, however, the fruit would make a good example for Kira, so Aniya mentally picked out an apple and an orange, knowing that the grapes would be too awkward to steal. It would take only one grape falling loose of the bunch to give her away.

Aniya put her open rucksack on the ground in front of her and continued to stare at the fruit.

"Can I interest you in some produce, little lady, or are you just looking today?" The vendor peered across his stand at her, obviously wary of the girl who had been staring for just a little too long.

Aniya picked up two apples with her hands, letting her large cloak sleeves cover the fact that she had managed to trap a third apple between her elbows. She raised her arms up and pretended to compare the two apples in her hands. "Just making sure they're fresh."

The vendor laughed. "You don't have to worry about that. These things will last for several more weeks before going bad. A miracle, these things are. Though the price has gone up because I have not been able to grow any more since the power's gone out. Three coppers each."

Aniya frowned and placed the two apples back, letting the third fall into her open rucksack below. She then reached for an orange near the middle of the stand with her right hand while her left hand stretched farther out, picking an orange in the back. Her left arm masked the motion of her right elbow knocking an orange off the stand and into her rucksack as her right hand pulled back with its orange.

She weighed the two oranges in her hand, tossed them briefly, then put them back.

"I think I'll just wait until the lights come back on."

The vendor shrugged. "Suit yourself."

Aniya picked up her rucksack and made her way back to the alley, where a clapping Kira was waiting for her.

"That was impressive!"

"And that's just one method. An even easier way is distraction, misdirection. Get them thinking about anything besides what's in front of them, and you can get away with murder. Now you try. Just be careful."

Kira moved to leave but hesitated. She turned again and pulled her necklace out from under her shirt, handing it to Aniya, who took it by the large crystal dangling on the end.

"Take care of this for me," Kira said before turning and leaving the alley.

Aniya sat and made herself comfortable. Her stomach growled, but she couldn't bring herself to eat the fruit she had stolen. She made a mental note to steal some meat before going back to the house.

Her attention turned to the necklace in her hand. The crystal was nearly the length of her longest finger and twice as wide. It was crudely cut but polished to a brilliant shine, revealing a beautiful, complex interior that was completely clear, though distorting the image of her palm below.

Aniya realized that she had been staring at the crystal for several seconds, and she looked up to find Kira.

The girl had disappeared in the crowd, but before Aniya could grow anxious, Kira reappeared in front of a meat vendor.

Or maybe she'll grab some meat for me.

Aniya watched as Kira stood in front of the stand. She didn't appear to be taking any action, and Aniya wondered for a moment if Kira had either lost her nerve or didn't know what to do next.

But a second later, the meat vendor flinched and grabbed at his lower body, squeezing his eyes closed.

In the instant that the man closed his eyes, Kira snatched a bundle of meat and disappeared into the crowd. Within seconds, Kira was back in the alley.

"What did you do?"

"I kicked his leg underneath the stand."

Aniya laughed. She had never taken such a direct approach before. "Well, I guess that's one way to do it."

"Whatever works, right?"

"As long as you don't get caught!" Aniya rubbed her hand on Kira's head affectionately, tousling her hair. "Here's your necklace back, by the way." She handed the crystal over to Kira, who gratefully took it back and slipped it over her neck.

"Thank you," Kira said. "I didn't want to risk the Silvers taking it from me. It was too close the last time."

"What is it?"

Kira hesitated. She dropped her gaze and fiddled with the trinket around her neck, lowering her voice slightly. "It was my mother's."

She paused again, and Aniya waited patiently.

"The Lightbringers use crystals for their technology. Computer chips, medical equipment, the skydome . . . When my father stopped working, my mother took a job refining them and sorting them. She said this one reminded her of me, so she took it. I don't know how she got it out without them noticing, but she gave it to me for my birthday. Just a month later, she died of radiation poisoning. Apparently, crystals have all sorts of different properties, and some of them retain radiation just as strong as it would have been centuries ago when the bombs fell in the Overworld."

Aniya bowed her head, unable to think of anything to say that seemed appropriate.

"They took her body and studied it. We never got her back, so this is all I have left of her." Kira looked up again, tears moistening her eyes.

Aniya embraced Kira and gently stroked her hair. "I'm sorry. I'm glad you have the crystal, and I hope the Light-bringers never get their hands on it. All I have left of my parents are memories. Maybe my brother, but I don't know if he's even still alive." She released Kira and stepped back. "Let's get back to the house and cook that meat. I'm starving."

Kira nodded.

But before they could leave, white lights appeared as if from nowhere.

As they drew further back into the alley, Aniya watched dozens of officers flood the marketplace and form a line in the middle of the street as the crowd backed away from them. The last of the Silvers settled into place and stood silently.

The marketplace went silent, and the entire sector seemed to come to a halt.

"Good afternoon, citizens of Shyvale."

A booming voice came from the square as a man in a black suit stepped into the road, pacing in front of the line of Silvers.

"And good afternoon, Annelise Lyons."

A niya froze.

  Even in the dark alleyway, she felt incredibly exposed, as if the Silvers' lights were all pointing directly at her. In reality, Aniya was safe, several hundred feet away from the Lightbringers. But as the Operative turned around slowly, surveying the market, she could have sworn that he made eye contact with her.

  Kira looked at her and whispered, "How did they find you?"

  "I don't know," she said.

  "Your presence is requested in the town square, Ms. Lyons," the voice boomed again, the volume amplified by a megaphone in the Operative's hand. "We know you're here. I will grant you that you hid yourself well. We searched each sector top to bottom, but we now have it on good authority that you're here in Shyvale."

  How? It wasn't like she had spent much time out in public. Only a few people saw her on the first day, and she had stayed inside for most of the last two weeks.

  "You'll make it much easier on all of us if you turn yourself in. There are people who would love to see you again. Your brother. Your boyfriend."

Aniya's heart ached. She knew she couldn't trust the Operative, but she wanted to believe William and Nicholas were both alive.

And Roland? What happened in the tunnels?

"If it makes you feel better, I have very strict orders to bring you in alive. You will be unharmed, untouched. I can promise you that."

It didn't make her feel any better.

"If you won't do it for your family, do it for these poor people. You know better than most the punishment that awaits those who harbor enemies of the Lightbringers."

The Operative waited.

"Fine."

The volume increased.

"I now speak to the citizens of Shyvale. In case you've forgotten, sheltering fugitives carries the penalty of death. If any of you have information of this girl's whereabouts, speak now and you will be forgiven."

Aniya's face suddenly appeared on the sky ceiling. For a moment, it seemed like the power had been restored, but she looked down and saw that the image was being projected from a device the Operative held.

She looked back up and clenched her fists as she realized the image, taken from her Assembly identification, had been altered drastically. Her eyes were narrowed, accompanied by eyebrows that had been thickened and tilted, giving the impression that she was angry. Her skin was tinted a pale, sickly color. Her cracked lips were spread open in a spiteful grin, revealing yellowed, slightly pointed teeth.

"She is an enemy of the Lightbringers, and she is an enemy to you as well. She and her family are directly responsible for the power outage. They are the reason you have no light, no heat, no power."

The crowd lit up for the first time, a buzz arising from Shyvale as people began to whisper to each other and grumble in anger.

"With your help, we can restore order and electricity. But we must have the girl before that's possible. So, I ask you—not as a superior, but as a friend who wants the power back as much as you do—please, help us find the girl."

The buzz from the crowd grew louder, but no one singled themselves out.

"Help us so we do not have to resort to unpleasant methods."

The crowd remained steady, and Aniya smiled. If anyone knew anything, they were not willing to give her up.

But her smile faded as the Operative reached into the crowd and dragged a person back toward the line of Silvers.

Aniya looked closely. It was an older man with a beard so long that she first thought it was a design on his shirt.

Her breath stopped as she recognized him as the man who had given her mole meat for Kira after her whipping.

The Operative pulled a gun from his belt and forced the man to his knees, placing the barrel of the gun against the back of his head.

"Annelise Lyons, step forward or watch this man die."

Kira tugged on Aniya's cloak. "Are they really going to kill him?"

"No, Kira. The Lightbringers rely on us just like we rely on them. There's no way they would publicly kill someone. The last time the public got angry, they started a war that cost the Lightbringers a lot of resources."

"I don't know, Aniya. They might get mad at the Lightbringers, but I think they'd be even more mad at you."

Aniya turned around. "Would you turn me in?"

Kira paused. After a moment, she shook her head. "No. I would never do that."

"Let's hope the rest of them feel that way." Aniya turned back around.

The Operative no longer had his gun to the man's head. Rather, he was pacing back and forth once again.

Aniya smiled as she realized she was right. He was bluffing.

"Make no mistake, Ms. Lyons. He will die, and then for every day that you fail to turn yourself in, another person will die."

"Aniya . . ." Kira's voice grew uneasy.

Aniya spun around. "Do you want me to turn myself in?"

Kira didn't answer. She simply looked down at the ground, clutching the crystal hanging around her neck.

Aniya's heart sank as she realized what Kira's answer had to be. Shyvale was her home. Aniya was a friend, yes, but one that she had known for only two weeks. She had helped Kira, but it was a small act of kindness. Maybe it would have been different if she had stepped in and stopped the Silver from beating her.

This was her sector. These were her friends. Aniya had forced Kira into a position to choose between a stranger and her kinsmen.

She was right.

Aniya stood up but couldn't bring herself to take a step forward. Her legs turned to jelly, quivering, almost buckling underneath her body.

The Lightbringers mutilated her brother. They killed her family. If she turned herself in, who knew what her fate would be?

Aniya turned around and grabbed Kira's shoulders.

"Look at me. They're not going to kill him. I promise. There's no way they would risk another uprising by killing someone in public. Besides, Shyvale's not that small. For all their operative knows, I can't even hear him. Please trust me.

That man is going to be safe. You're going to be safe. I promise."

Kira stared back at her with an expression that alternated between fear and anger. Finally, she sighed and nodded.

"Okay."

Aniya hugged her tightly.

"We're going to be safe."

Then, a gunshot echoed throughout Shyvale.

Aniya turned around in shock and watched the bearded man fall to the ground, dead.

28

Aniya lay in bed, watching Kira enjoy her last bit of sleep before First Light.

They were alone in the shack. Urich had left the house at some point in the night. Kira had not spoken a word to Aniya since they returned home the evening before, but her father had at least remained pleasant toward her. Apparently, he had not heard the news. Like the rest of the Web's tech, the public announcement system was down, so the Operative's ultimatum had been heard only by those within earshot of the marketplace.

Maybe it was better that he didn't know.

The night before, Aniya had finally promised Kira that she would leave the sector today, one way or another, before the Operative could kill someone else. Kira had simply nodded. Her gaze remained empty, and Aniya couldn't tell if she was in shock or angry.

Even now as the girl slept, her expression was pained, twisted. Aniya knew that Kira would never be the same, and she knew that she had lost a friend.

Aniya sat on her cot, watching Kira's unsteady breathing. The weight of the man's death the day before hung over her head, the image of his lifeless body fresh in her mind. Someone else would die today if Aniya didn't do something. And if anyone found out where she had found shelter, Urich would die too.

She had to get out. Away from Kira, away from Shyvale, away from everyone. Death seemed to follow her wherever she went. No one seemed to be safe as long as they were close to her.

Unfortunately, the only way for Aniya to ensure Shyvale's safety was to make her departure as obvious to the Lightbringers as possible. That meant causing a commotion by the tunnels. It meant that by the end of the day, she would either be running for her life again or in the hands of her pursuers.

But to Aniya, there wasn't a choice. She couldn't stand to see another person killed because of her.

She rose and packed her things quietly. Her original plan was to leave at midday, but as Aniya watched yesterday's execution play out in her mind over and over, she knew that every second she stayed meant danger for Kira and her father.

She had almost finished packing when the backup generators kicked on and blasted First Light throughout the sector.

"Where are you going?"

Aniya winced. As the blast of light faded away to darkness again, she turned to see Kira rubbing her eyes.

"I'm leaving. It's not safe here for me or you."

"You still have a few hours."

Aniya shook her head. "I don't want to risk it any longer. I've stayed way too long as it is."

"At least stay for breakfast. Please." Kira's eyes welled up as she looked at Aniya pitifully, her sadness the first intelligible emotion the girl had expressed since the day before. "My father will want to say goodbye to you anyway."

"Okay," Aniya said, trying to hide her shock. She had expected the silent treatment to continue. "But just breakfast."

Kira made some cold oatmeal for Aniya, who accepted

the food gratefully, even though she had supplies in her ruck-sack. She had tried to convince Kira to let her eat from her own stash of food, but Kira insisted. Food was a valuable commodity in the poorer sectors, and Aniya knew she should feel honored to accept what was apparently a farewell gift from the girl.

Instead, she ate every bite with a pit in her stomach, avoiding eye contact.

"Are you still going to the Hub?" Kira asked as Aniya ate.

Aniya nodded.

"I hope you find your brother."

"I just hope I make it out of Shyvale alive. If I had tried to leave before they found out I was here, I would have stood a better chance."

"I thought you said you would have triggered some sort of . . . earthquake alarm?" Kira scrunched her nose.

"Probably, but they still would have had to come get me. Now that they're already here, it'll be that much easier for them."

"Well, you can at least try."

Aniya shrugged. "It's the only option I have left. I have to go that way anyway, or they won't know I've left." She continued to eat in silence.

Several minutes passed. Aniya wanted to finish quickly and get out, but her appetite wouldn't let her eat more than one small bite at a time.

"Uh-oh." Kira's voice trembled. "Aniya, they're coming."

Aniya snapped her head up in alarm.

Kira was standing by the window, pointing outside. "They look like they're in a hurry."

"Get back." Aniya leapt to her feet and rushed to the window.

Sure enough, several beams of light bobbed in the distance, but they seemed to be moving off to Aniya's left. Then, as if they sensed her gaze, they all simultaneously turned and pointed directly at the house, nearly blinding her even though they were still several hundred feet away.

"Do they know we're here?" Kira's voice trembled.

Aniya quickly stepped back from the window and reached for her pack. After rummaging for a moment, she pulled out the radio. This wasn't right. Surely, she would have heard something if they had discovered her.

But as she gazed at the lifeless device, she remembered that she had shut if off again the day before when they went to the market. With trembling fingers, she turned on the radio and cranked up the volume.

"Approaching the house now."

"Affirmative. Alert the asset and prepare for forced entry."

Aniya turned the radio off and stuffed it in her bag. She had heard enough.

"We need to leave now. What's the fastest way to the tunnel I showed you without using the main road?" Aniya's hand grazed something else inside the bag.

"They're coming from the way you need to go," Kira said. "You'd have to circle around them."

"Well, it looks like that's my only option." She pulled out the other device Nicholas had given her.

"Your only option? What about me?"

Aniya pried open the glass case and tucked the device under her belt behind her, careful not to flip the switch or press the button. "You need to get as far away from me as possible. That's the only way you'll be safe." After pulling her shirt over her belt and hiding the device, she stepped toward the window again, and her eyes widened as a bright red light washed over the approaching officers. "Change of plans. Don't move, and don't panic."

"I thought you said we were going to run?" Kira's voice raised in pitch and volume.

"They have scanners out there. And if they're anything like Nicholas described, there's no way we'd make it past them unless we lure them inside first." Aniya rushed around the room, extinguishing each candle until the room was dark. "If it makes you feel any better, if we had left any sooner, they would have seen us anyway."

Kira began to whimper.

Aniya placed a hand on her shoulder. "Trust me."

Even though tears were streaking down her cheeks, Kira nodded.

The sound of heavy boots closed in on them like a thunderstorm, and the mechanical hum of the scanners surrounded the shack, creating a cacophony that carried the threat of death.

The footsteps stopped, and silence fell over the house.

"Aniya—"

The door flew open with a loud bang.

Bright light flooded the doorway, and Aniya raised a hand in front of her eyes, trying to make out any shapes.

Several men marched inside and lined the walls of the shack. By the time they all settled into place, there were at least fifteen armored men pointing guns at the two girls, and the shack was completely illuminated by the lights on the men's helmets.

Then the Operative walked in.

"Annelise Lyons. You're a hard girl to find."

Aniya dropped her hand to her side and stood face-to-face with the man in the black suit. Rather than speaking, she glared at the man with steely eyes.

"You should be proud of yourself. This is by far the most effort we've put into finding someone since the war. Even your brother was exactly where we expected him to be." The Operative seemed to be in no hurry, but instead dragged a chair away from the table and sat in the middle of the shack. "You, on the other hand, have had us scrambling all around the Web. I will admit that it's been nothing short of fun trying to predict where you would pop up after you disappeared into the tunnels. You even put up quite the fight. I advised my superiors against venturing into the caves after you, but they just couldn't wait. Sure enough, that proved fruitless, and all we did was lose a squadron to a giant rat and tunnel trash."

Aniya's heart filled with hope. Roland could still be alive.

"However, all fun must come to an end, and it seems that we have come to just that time."

Her heart sank again as she realized that though Roland may be alive, she would never see him again. But she still refused to speak.

"Don't fret," the Operative said, as if reading her thoughts. "It's not your end. I don't have the authority to kill you, and even if I did, I could not do that without compromising the Lightbringers. Your mother and father didn't really have the chance to pass on any information your brother had obtained, but you . . . You have been running around the Web saying who knows what to who knows whom. We will be having many discussions in the near future regarding exactly what you've told those sympathetic to your cause. And I can personally promise you that they will not be fun discussions."

Aniya's eyes remained steady, but her hands began to tremble. She placed them behind her back.

"Surely you have something to say now. If not you, then maybe your friend here." The Operative turned to Kira and grinned. "After all, we don't plan on killing you, but we have no use for her. That is, unless my superiors are willing to bend the rules and place her in relocative servitude. We always have room for more."

Kira began to whimper again. Aniya took the girl's hand and clutched it in her own sweaty palm, but she kept her other hand behind her back.

"Might as well take her. We can dispose of her father on the way out of town, so no one would miss her anyway."

With this, Kira broke into tears.

"No sense in staying here any longer. This sector is depressing."

The Operative stood up and tossed the chair aside. He turned to his men and gave a curt nod.

"Stun them and tie them up."

With her left hand, Aniya squeezed Kira's hand one more time. With her right hand, she flipped the switch on the device that stuck out from underneath her belt.

Fifteen guns raised as one.

Aniya closed her eyes and pressed the button.

29

A deafening whine shook the walls of the shack, and the room was plunged into darkness as the Silvers' lights all blinked off simultaneously.

Without waiting for the Silvers to respond, Aniya lunged forward and rammed her shoulder into the Operative's unarmored chest, sending him reeling to the ground and clearing a path to the door.

With Kira's hand still clutched tightly in hers, Aniya ran over the Operative's supine body, forcing the door open and spilling out onto the walkway outside. Wasting no time, she let her momentum push her into a dead run, yanking Kira's hand and forcing her forward. There was no time to be gentle.

Several large metal orbs littered the roads of Shyvale. They were now dark, powerless, thanks to the strange device that Nicholas had left for Aniya.

Aniya shuddered and ran past the debris, not sure how long it would be before the scanners would come back to life. She set her sights on the road ahead and led Kira into the center of town, hoping to lose the officers in the crowd.

As people stopped and stared, one man in particular took a special interest in the two girls. Aniya recognized him as the

198 | DAVID WEBB

same man that had chased Kira through the streets two weeks earlier. As they passed him by, he calmly walked back to his stall and pushed it over into the street.

Dozens of apples rolled across the street behind the running girls, creating several small obstacles for any pursuers.

Aniya turned just long enough to gratefully wave to the man.

The man nodded at her and raised a hand, pointing four fingers in the air.

Maybe not everyone here wants me dead.

Seconds later, the first officer arrived in the square. It wasn't long before his foot landed on an apple instead of cobblestone, and Aniya smiled as she heard his armor crash to the ground.

A shot rang out, and Aniya's skin crawled as she was forced to wonder whether it was a desperate shot at the running girls or a punishment for the man who had helped them.

Leaving the town square behind, the girls continued and crossed into the industrial district.

Shyvale, while not much larger than Holendast, seemed much more successful than Aniya's modest home sector. Businesses seemed to be prospering, and the sector was expanding with what little room it had left.

Here in the industrial district, more buildings stood in various stages of construction but forced to halt in the dark of the Black Days.

To the rest of the Web, it was a sign of progress, the badge of a successful sector.

To Aniya, it was the perfect hiding place.

She chose one construction site that was already five stories tall, knowing there would be plenty of places to find shelter inside. The Lightbringers would be forced to slow down their chase and spread out, perhaps even giving Aniya and Kira opportunity to escape and leave their pursuers behind.

This particular building had completed framework, and the first floor sported finished walls and a locked door, discouraging any intruders. But if anyone happened to scale the wall of the first floor, they would be free to move about the building by way of the open second floor.

Aniya approached the building and climbed the wall effortlessly. Kira attempted to follow, but she apparently was not agile enough to grasp the ledge, and she slipped and fell back down.

"Help me!"

Aniya lay down on the floor and extended her arm over the edge, reaching her hand down as far down as she could. "Do you see my hand?"

"No!"

She waved her hand around wildly, hoping Kira would see the movement even in the dark. From below, she could hear Kira grunting and jumping.

Finally, Aniya felt fingers graze her palm.

"Right there! Just keep trying. I won't move my hand."

Kira jumped again and grabbed her hand but slipped away. Heavy footsteps grew close.

"Again!"

"Aniya!"

Kira's scream gripped Aniya's heart as the footsteps suddenly halted. Aniya pushed herself farther over the edge, dangerously teetering on the edge of the building. With one last grunt, she swung her hand wildly, reaching for something, anything.

Aniya's hand finally made contact, and she closed her fingers tightly.

But all Aniya held was a crystal attached to a leather cord.

From below came a dull thud.

Aniya froze.

"Kira?"

Silence.

Then, a loud bang as the locked door below burst open.

Aniya's heart raced as she crawled away from the edge. She stood up and immediately hit her head on a piece of rebar sticking out of the wall. She put her free hand to her head and felt warm liquid coursing down the side of her face. Ignoring it, she swiped her hand on her pants and ran deeper into the construction site, dodging discarded materials and boxes as best as she could in the dark.

The footsteps grew louder.

She managed to find a set of stairs in the corner, but apparently, so did her pursuer on the floor below as heavy footsteps echoed throughout the stairwell. As quietly as she could, Aniya climbed the stairs to the third floor, hoping that whoever was chasing her would stop at the second level.

Aniya reached the third floor, and she ducked into a corner behind the stairwell, dragging a large box in front of her.

Then the footsteps stopped, and everything went silent.

The deadly game of hide-and-seek paused, and Aniya held her breath.

For what seemed like an eternity, Aniya crouched in her corner as her pursuer remained still. Neither made a sound.

Then, finally, the footsteps resumed, slowly advancing.

Aniya breathed slowly and carefully as she listened. Her pursuer was definitely still on the floor below.

But a few minutes later, the footsteps shifted, and her breath caught in her lungs. They now echoed in the stairwell around the corner once again, growing louder with every step as they ascended to Aniya's level.

With every step, her breath quickened, and when her pursuer reached the third floor, she was nearly hyperventilating.

Aniya pulled the box closer and held a hand over her

mouth. She became very aware of her heart, pounding against her rib cage at an incredible pace. The hand over her mouth began to drip sweat that slipped through the cracks between her fingers, slowly seeping into her mouth. The salty tang lingered on her tongue as she trembled.

Her other hand still gripped Kira's crystal, squeezing so tightly that the edges of the rock cut into her skin. But the pain distracted her from her panic, and her breaths began to slow.

The footsteps slowly began to move across the room. She thought she heard her pursuer say something, but she couldn't make it out.

And then Aniya realized her escape.

As the footsteps continued deeper into the room, Aniya stood up. She took a deep, slow breath and carefully stepped out from behind the box, walking around it and peering into the darkness. In the pitch black, she would be nearly invisible, even if her adversary were facing her.

She slipped the necklace over her head, tucked the crystal under her shirt, and slowly made her way toward the stairs.

Aniya's escape was inevitable. The Silvers, spoiled by the light their headlamps provided, were all but useless in the complete darkness. She moved quietly toward the stairs, her steps silent compared to her pursuer's much louder footfalls, which echoed throughout the construction site. There was simply no way she could be caught now.

But as she silently celebrated her escape, her hopes soaring, the lights came back on.

Shyvale lit up in an explosive glow as the sky ceiling powered up, the artificial sun blinking on and flooding the sector with light.

As Aniya's eyes adjusted to the light, she found herself standing ten feet away from a man in white armor, a powerless light built into his helmet.

He was looking right at her.

Aniya took a deep breath and looked the man in the eye, doing her best to stare him down with whatever dignity she had left. As the spots in her eyes began to fade, she realized it wasn't a man, but a teenage boy. The last of the spots disappeared, and she saw the details in his face—the last face she would ever imagine underneath one of those helmets. The face of her oldest and closest friend.

"Nicholas?"

30

"I'm so glad you're okay." Aniya wanted to run into Nicholas's arms, but heavy news bore down on her, and she looked at the floor. "They took Roland."

No response. She looked up at him again.

"I guess they told you. What happened to you? Did they force you to join the Silvers?"

Aniya stepped toward Nicholas but halted abruptly as he raised his gun.

"Nicholas, what's going on? It's just us. If we hurry, we can leave now and save William. I don't think I can do it alone."

She stepped toward him again, but Nicholas also took a step backward.

"Better yet, you can sneak me inside if they think you're on their side. I've been trying to figure out how to make it into the Hub, but if you're on the inside, then maybe—"

Nicholas cut her off by pulling something from the back of his belt and tossing it toward her, all while keeping the gun pointed at her head.

A pair of handcuffs landed at her feet.

"Put them on."

204 I DAVID WEBB

Aniya stared.

"Nicky—"

"Now."

After a moment, Aniya bent over and picked up the handcuffs. She looked again at Nicholas for any hint of a gesture or look that might indicate he was acting against his own will.

Nothing.

In desperation, she threw the handcuffs at her old friend in an effort to distract him, and she turned to run.

A deafening shot rang out, and Aniya felt a sharp pain in her shoulder. She froze and looked down at a small rip in her shirt, bleeding skin beneath, torn by the graze of a bullet.

The damage to her shoulder was minimal, but her heart was irreparable.

She started to turn, tears in her eyes, but she was tackled to the ground from behind.

Nicholas wrenched her hands behind her back and pressed her cheek into the concrete. She felt cold metal slap down on her wrists, and then she was forced to her feet.

"Let's go."

She was paraded to the train station, escorted by four other officers that had finally caught up to her and Nicholas.

The Operative and ten more Silvers stood over Urich and Kira, who were both on their knees and bound.

"No," Aniya whispered as she looked at Kira, whose cheeks were wet with tears.

The Operative stretched his arms wide. "Ms. Lyons, so good of you to join us again. I'm sure you know Urich, the man who betrayed you."

Urich bowed his head. "I'm so sorry, Aniya. I couldn't let them hurt my daughter."

The Operative shook his head and smirked. "You must be frustrated at this betrayal, considering the lengths you've gone to in order to stay hidden. I was planning on killing the girl's father myself, but if it would make you feel better, you're more than welcome to pull the trigger."

"No, you promised us protection!" Urich shouted. "You said we would be spared if we turned her in."

"Oh, I wish I had the authority to make good on such a promise. But I have no way of knowing what the girl has told you."

"They have nothing to do with this," Aniya pleaded, resorting to lies. "I didn't even tell them who I was, so they couldn't have possibly known that I was on the run from you."

Nicholas forced Aniya to her knees next to Kira, and she jerked her shoulder back into his hand as he let go.

"Even so, they're here now, so even if you're telling the truth, it doesn't make a difference." The Operative withdrew his gun and fastened the silencer. "We have peace to maintain, and we can't very well do that if they're running around and telling the population about how the big, bad Silvers kidnapped their houseguest."

"But whipping them in the street is okay?" Kira muttered.

"Oh yes, they told me about that. It's a shame that had to be done to a girl as young and pretty as yourself, but an example had to be set."

Kira turned to her father. "I'm sorry I didn't tell you, Papa."

Urich just nodded slowly, his head pointed to the ground. "I didn't want to believe it, but I knew it had to be you."

"Please let them go." Aniya tried again. "Move them to another sector if you have to. Put them in relocative servitude. Just let them live."

"Oh, we fully intend on milking young Kira here for all she's worth. In the past, we have only allowed males the great honor of serving the Lightbringers directly, but I'm confident she'll make a fine addition to our team. However, we have no need for a blind man." The Operative pointed his gun at Urich's head, lightly resting the barrel on his temple.

Urich bowed his head, pressing against the gun. "Go ahead. I have dishonored my name and forsaken the cause I once stood for, all for nothing."

"Papa, no!" Kira now sobbed heavily.

Urich shouted, "Don't look, Kira!"

Kira turned and cried into Aniya's shoulder.

The Operative let the moment drag on, tapping the barrel of the gun against Urich's forehead as he smiled.

"But then, it's not fair to shoot a cripple."

He turned and fired.

Kira's head snapped backward, and she fell to the ground and rolled over once before lying still.

The scream that emanated from Urich's lungs chilled Aniya to the bone, and she became numb with shock and rage. She opened her mouth to protest, curse, anything, but she couldn't find strength to speak or the words to say.

Urich's scream turned into miserable sobs. He crawled over on his knees, his hands still bound, to where he last heard Kira's voice. When his knee touched her side, he let himself fall forward, resting his head on his daughter's chest, crying into her clothes.

The Operative put his gun away. "Dispose of the body, tranquilize the girl, and leave the old man. Be on the train in five minutes."

One of the officers piped up. "I thought we were going to kill him."

"Do you really think anyone would believe an old, blind man? He's inconsequential. Now, follow your orders." The Operative turned and walked toward the train.

Silvers pulled Urich away from Kira as the crying man shouted through his tears.

"Don't touch her! You stay away from her!"

Aniya watched the officer pick Kira up as a gun cocked behind her.

Then, everything went black.

31

In the front passenger car of the train, the Operative slouched back in his booth and allowed himself to relax for the first time in weeks. He had been studying maps, analyzing escape routes, and barking orders nonstop ever since the first Lyons brat had escaped the Hub.

But now everything was as it should be.

The lights were back on, everyone was back in their pods, the peace was kept, and the Web could continue on as normal. Of course, there was still the old, blind man back in Shyvale, but he would soon be dubbed the village lunatic thanks to his crazed rants.

The Lyons girl and her brother had caused quite a stir. It seemed they had inherited the troublemaker gene from their parents. All things considered, the Operative felt he deserved a raise. In fact, he decided that as soon as he got back to the Hub, that would be his first order of business.

If nothing else, at least he got a small bonus. The crystal that had hung around the girl's neck now lay on the table, wobbling with every vibration of the train. The Operative flicked the crystal and watched it spin, sparkling as it caught the glow of the interior lights.

How a girl like that could get her hands on a rock like this, he had no idea. He was no scientist, but he knew enough to recognize that this was not a common crystal. This looked like the kind the Lightbringers used under the Citadel, perfect for storing energy. They were quite valuable, and he could surely trade it for just about anything. If nothing else, it made for a nice trinket.

His reverie was disturbed by an officer's entry into his cabin.

"She's secured, sir."

The Operative shook away his annoyance at the interruption and sat up in his seat as he shoved the crystal in his pocket. "Thank you, officer."

The Silver turned to leave.

"You know, I doubted that you would remain loyal to our cause."

The officer stopped and turned.

"Why's that, sir?"

"I seem to recall dragging you kicking and screaming from Holendast just weeks ago. Weren't you and the girl close?"

Nicholas shrugged. "The Chancellor made some very good points. Besides, it's not like he gave me a choice."

"He never does, does he? Still, you could have betrayed us."

"I would never do that. The Chancellor was right. The power and the peace it provides are more important than any one person." Nicholas looked at the ground. "I loved her, but she endangered our way of life. We could have lost the entire Web to darkness. She had to be taken care of."

"Quite right." The Operative pulled a bottle from the side compartment and placed it on the table. "Come, sit with me."

Nicholas hesitated but obeyed.

The Operative pulled two glasses from a tray on the edge of the table. "The Adviser was right about you. I don't agree with him on much, but he made a good call with you."

He poured a small amount of liquid from the bottle into both glasses and passed one of them to Nicholas. "If it had been anyone else that cornered her in Shyvale, she would have gotten away. You were a risky move, to be sure, but a good one."

He raised a glass and motioned to Nicholas, who picked up the drink and eyed its contents briefly.

"Relax," the Operative said, laughing. "You're no good to me dead. Besides, poison is a woman's game."

Nicholas tapped his glass against the Operative's, then downed its contents with one swig.

The Operative smiled. *A boy after my own heart.* He drank from his glass as well and set the cup back down by the bottle.

"Now, listen to me closely, boy."

His smile vanished, and he drew his gun, placing it on the table with the barrel pointed at Nicholas.

"It may not have been poison, but it was a chemical designed for one purpose: to truly test your loyalty." He smirked again as Nicholas's face turned ashen. "You can calm down, boy. I'm not going to make you kill your girl-friend or anything, as amusing as that would be to watch. This is a truth serum. Very effective during the war, and something we didn't anticipate needing again. I'll admit that much bloodshed could have been avoided if I had used this earlier. The girl's family may not have needed to die after all. But then, that wouldn't have been nearly as fun. Besides, I had to finish something that they started a very long time ago."

Nicholas's expression turned sour, and the Operative laughed again. "Just be glad that while my superiors give me carte blanche to act as I will, I unfortunately have to proceed with caution when it comes to the Lightbringers' assets. Sweet Annelise, for example, is not in any immediate danger. Neither are you if your answers to my questions are acceptable. And because I just drank from the same bottle, you can be sure that

I am telling you the truth when I say that I will kill you if I don't like any of your answers."

Nicholas nodded slowly.

"Let's begin." The Operative relaxed his gun hand and set his weapon on the table. "I understand the arrangement you have with the Chancellor, but did you say anything to the girl when you arrested her?"

"I told her nothing except to restrain herself."

"Good. Now, we are all aware of your passion for technology. Somehow, the girl obtained a short-range electronic pulse bomb that wiped out our electronics, similar to the one you used back in Holendast. Do you know how she acquired the device?"

"She got it from me."

The Operative snarled and picked up his gun.

Nicholas held up a hand. "It was before you took me from Holendast and brought me to the Hub. It was in my pack when we got separated."

The Operative slowly brought his hand back down, but he did not release the gun.

"Next question. Will you follow my every order to the letter, no matter what I say?"

Nicholas shut his mouth.

"You may want to answer before I take your silence as a negative response."

"I get my orders from the Adviser."

The Operative narrowed his eyes. "You answer to me."

Nicholas shook his head. "I was deployed at the request of the Chancellor. He left the details in the hands of the Adviser, whose explicit instructions were that I answer to him and no one else."

"Then let me be as clear as possible." The Operative raised the gun and pressed the barrel against Nicholas's chin, pointing up. "The Adviser gave me very explicit instructions as well, and if you act against my wishes, you directly disobey the Adviser. If I, as an emissary of the Chancellor and of the Glorious Bringers of Light, give you an order, will you follow it?"

Nicholas looked the Operative in the eye. Then, with an unfaltering voice, he responded.

"Yes."

The menace vanished from the Operative's face, replaced by a large smile.

"Good. Then bring me the girl."

Nicholas left, and the Operative poured another drink, setting it across the table.

The boy knew enough that if he chose his childhood crush over his new leaders, he could bring this operation to a swift end. His newfound dedication to the Lightbringers was more than a little suspicious, but it seemed that there was no cause for worry after all.

Of course, it was still worth keeping a close eye on him.

Now, all that was left was to find out what the girl knew. It's not like she was going anywhere, but if she did know something and had managed to tell anyone else, there could be a problem.

But that's what I do best. Fix the Lightbringers' problems.

He looked at the drink on the table that he had saved for the girl.

Eh, what's the harm?

He grabbed the drink and downed it with pleasure, then poured another glass. Whatever chemicals the geeks from the lab put in the liquor somehow made it even tastier.

"Here you go, sir." Nicholas entered the train car with their captive in tow.

The Operative didn't turn but instead gestured at the booth across from himself with a wave. "Have a seat, Annelise. I hope the journey has been pleasant so far."

Nicholas forced the girl down across from him, then sat across the aisle.

Aniya slumped forward slightly, her eyes rolling.

"Wake up, girl." The Operative snapped his fingers under her eyes. "I know the tranquilizers we use are quite strong, but I need your full attention."

Aniya slowly sat back up, shaking her head.

"Good morning. I gather this is your first time on one of our trains. Quite different from the tunnels you're used to, I'm sure. How does it measure up?"

She didn't respond as she wiped her eyes with her shackled hands.

"I apologize. That's quite rude of us." The Operative snapped his fingers again, this time in the direction of Nicholas. "Free her hands."

Aniya glared at Nicholas as he unlocked her handcuffs, but he wouldn't return her gaze.

"There, that's better. Now, please, enjoy a drink," he said, gesturing toward the glass on the table. "You must be thirsty."

"No, thank you."

The Operative gestured toward Nicholas. "Would you mind, Officer?"

Nicholas hesitated.

"It seems our guest needs assistance, Mr. Kent," the Operative said, snarling. "I suggest you help your friend."

With a glance toward the Operative, Nicholas marched across the car and took the glass in one hand and Aniya's hair in the other. He pulled her head back and forced the drink into her mouth before she had a chance to close it.

"Swallow," Nicholas said.

Aniya refused, trying to spit the liquid out but only gagging on it.

The Operative shrugged. "You can either drown in it or drink it. Your choice."

Finally, she swallowed, and Nicholas released her.

"Good. Let's begin."

32

"Aim higher."

The arrow thudded into the dirt wall behind the target, and Roland laughed.

"Not that high."

Tamisra threw the bow to the ground and put her hands on her hips. "I didn't even aim any higher. I've been ignoring you this whole time."

"Well, that's probably why you still haven't hit anything," Roland said, rolling his eyes.

"Says the guy who couldn't hit the broad side of a mole with a spear two weeks ago."

Roland smirked. "Yeah, but I got better. You still can't hit anything with a bow."

"What do I need a bow for? We do have guns, you know. It's not like we get to use them that often, but we do have them."

"Oh, yeah?" Roland put a hand on his hip. "What are you going to do when you run out of ammunition? Besides, if you can't aim with a bow, I'm sure your aim with a gun is questionable at best."

Tamisra jumped on Roland's back and wrestled him to the

ground. He went down easy, and she vaulted him and pinned him to the dirt floor.

Roland winced as his leg and hip pulsed with pain. His injuries had significantly healed, but he was still recovering.

"What are you going to do now, boy?"

"Judging by the state we're in, I'd say that's entirely up to you."

Tamisra smiled and let go of his arms. She didn't get off, but instead folded her arms and thrust her head in the air in triumph. "You bet it is."

However, her victory was short lived.

Roland grabbed her as she dropped her guard, throwing her to the side and letting her momentum roll her over and carry him with her, doing his best to ignore the pain. Now, he sat atop Tamisra, but he didn't make her same mistake of letting go, instead pushing her shoulders down firmly.

"What are you going to do now, girl?"

"I do what I want." Tamisra reached up as far as she could with pinned shoulders. She grabbed Roland by his neck, pulling him down and kissing him fiercely.

After several seconds, she let him go, and he sat up, his head spinning. "We should do what you want more often."

Tamisra smirked and pushed Roland off her. "You would be so lucky."

Roland grinned. Tamisra was the strangest girl he had ever met, and he couldn't help but be utterly fascinated by her. He had spent a week trying to figure her out, but he happily gave up the lost cause when she kissed him without warning one day when he was resting in the clinic, recovering from his gunshot wounds.

He had spent the next week training with her, mostly target practice and sparring. He taught her techniques that Gareth had passed on to him and Nicholas. It was a more strategic way to fight, using an enemy's strength against them.

Tamisra was able to learn with some difficulty, and in return she taught him a more brutal fighting style.

Their practices were exhausting, but they were always broken up with kisses when no one was watching. These pleasurable distractions made the sessions significantly less painful, despite Roland's injuries from the Lightbringers' attack.

"Tell you what," Roland said, picking up the bow again. "You hit the target, and we can do what you want some more."

"And if I miss?"

"Then I kiss you some more."

Tamisra laughed. "What's the difference?"

"You'll have taken one step closer toward mastering a useful life skill. Plus, you get to win, and I know how much you like winning."

"You got that right." Tamisra took careful aim at the target once again.

"Tamisra! Roland!"

A voice from a nearby tunnel startled Tamisra, and the arrow flew even farther off course than before. She turned and growled at Xander, who jogged into the cavern, his breathing ragged.

"You'd better have a good reason for interrupting us."

Xander came to a stop, and he leaned over, catching his breath.

"Any day now," she said.

Finally, Xander straightened up, only to turn to run again, motioning for them to follow. "We found Aniya."

Roland's heart sped up, and he took off after Xander, ignoring the pain in his leg and accidentally leaving Tamisra behind to catch up. It didn't take long since Roland's stride was severely impaired by his wound.

The trio made their way back to the main camp and into the central building. Xander opened a trapdoor in the corner, ushering Roland down into Salvador's basement war room.

Roland stepped inside to see Salvador, Corrin, and Lieutenant Haskill poring over a large map on the table. Malcolm sat in the corner, his left arm in a sling.

"I assume you've heard?" Corrin looked up. He wore a matching sling on his right arm, and his shoulder was thickly bandaged.

Roland nodded. Behind him, he heard the trapdoor close.

"Where is she?" Tamisra asked.

"She's on a train to the Hub," Lieutenant Haskill said grimly. "Scouts from Shyvale report that her capture was six hours ago. The Silvers left with her immediately afterward, and they're probably halfway to the Hub by now."

Roland sat by the table, stunned. He could only imagine the horrors that awaited her. "I can't believe it. I promised to protect her."

"It's not your fault you were shot." Tamisra petted the back of his head.

Roland ignored her. "What can we do?"

"Nothing," Salvador said. "We are simply not equipped to pick a fight with the Lightbringers."

Lieutenant Haskill shrugged. "That's debatable. We have moles and numbers on our side. We even still have guns and ammunition, thanks to our decision to limit their use over the years. But I agree that for now, we do nothing. We would need to prepare for such a battle, and even then, the losses we would suffer may not be worth it."

"You suggest leaving Aniya to die?" Corrin shook his head, biting his lip. "In the war, we never would have left a man behind."

"But we did, Corrin." Salvador placed a hand on his general's good shoulder. "We had to make some hard choices then. You know this better than most. It is no different now. We must continue on with what we have left, which means not risking our men in open battle. I am afraid I cannot agree to yet another foolish mission."

"I don't want to fight them," Roland said, clutching the edge of the table. "I just want to get Aniya back."

Tamisra looked at him strangely, but Roland ignored this.

"I got shot the last time I tried to help your girlfriend," Malcolm said, nodding toward his sling. "We've already suffered enough for her. I say we cut our losses and move on. We don't owe her anything, and she's not worth getting ourselves killed over."

"Why are you even here?" Xander asked. "If you're not going to offer anything helpful, you might as well leave."

"Quiet," Corrin said, glaring at his sons.

"Look, the tunnels run in a different route than the train, right?" Roland leaned over the table and examined the map. "According to this, the railroad goes through every sector, forcing the train along a twisted path throughout the Web. Our mole-made tunnel to the Hub goes straight there, more or less."

Lieutenant Haskill shook his head. "Even if we were to use that tunnel, we still wouldn't be able to catch up. The walk would take days."

"So we start now," Corrin said. "We can't just do nothing."

Salvador sighed. "Nothing is exactly what we must do, Corrin. You would waste time walking there just to turn around and come back when it is too late?"

"We've got moles," Xander said.

"Not many that could make that journey," Malcolm said. "The girl's brother took the two best ones."

Roland gritted his teeth. "Then we'll ride them until they die and then walk the rest of the way." He straightened and stood nose-to-nose with Salvador. "I'm getting her back, one way or another. I'm not leaving her to die."

Salvador and Roland remained in a staring match for several moments until a soft voice came from the corner.

"You love her, don't you?"

Roland turned toward Tamisra. He wasn't sure what to say to that. Finally, he approached her and gently laid his hands on her shoulder.

"Of course I do."

Tamisra looked down.

"But not like that. I've never loved her like that, and I never will."

She looked up again, her eyes wet. "Promise?"

Tamisra was the fiercest girl Roland had ever met. Other men looked at her with a mix of admiration and fear. Even looking at her himself, he felt strange, like everything about her excited him and scared him to death all at the same time. But now, she seemed no more than a scared girl, terrified of losing the most important thing in her life.

"Promise."

As she embraced him, Lieutenant Haskill spoke up again.

"Even if you could get there in time, the tunnel to the Hub has been sealed. You might get close, but there's about fifty feet of rock and dirt between you and the Hub."

Tamisra pulled away from Roland. "You and I both know that's not a problem."

"What, you want to blow the exit?" The lieutenant shook his head. "Unless the charges were placed on the other side of the cave-in, it's not safe enough. And even if you could convince the moles to dig your way out, there's no guarantee that they would dig straight into the Hub. Besides, doing either would attract unwanted attention instantly and make us a target. We'd be practically welcoming them inside."

"They're already welcoming themselves inside!" Tamisra threw her hands in the air. "And something tells me that the Ravelta incident won't be the last one."

"They got what they came for," Salvador said. "They will not be bothering us again."

"What they came for is Aniya," Roland said, his hands curling into fists. "You know what she means to me. I'm going to go get her with or without your help. If you don't help, our blood is on your hands."

Tamisra looked down. "Please, Father."

Salvador stared at the two for a moment. "If you succeed, they'll only come for her again."

"Then we'll leave," Roland said quietly.

Tamisra's eyes widened. "Roland . . ."

He forced himself to ignore Tamisra and continued, "Even if we manage to save her, William would still be trapped inside the Hub. We left Holendast to protect Aniya and to find some way to save William. I don't think we're going to get that kind of help from you, so we'll go somewhere else. Luckily, there's people in the sectors who still believe in the Scourge, even if you no longer do."

"Careful, boy," Malcolm hissed, his eyes narrowing. "You wouldn't speak to him like this if you knew what he was capable of."

"I wouldn't know. He hasn't shown me any sign of the so-called great warrior I've heard stories about." Roland glared at the aged warlord. "It's time to fight. We can end this now. We can finish what you started."

Corrin turned to Salvador. "Consider this. Even if we fight them in open battle, victory isn't too far-fetched. This could be the turning point for Refuge. It could mean our salvation at last."

Salvador bowed his head, and for a moment, Roland thought maybe they had managed to convince him.

But the Scourge finally shook his head.

"No. I cannot let you go, and I will not waste our resources and men on another suicide mission that will only draw attention to ourselves. My word is final."

With that, Salvador walked upstairs.

Tamisra looked down. "I'm sorry, Roland. He—"

But Roland didn't want to hear it. He left the basement

and went back upstairs, slamming the trapdoor behind him and ignoring Salvador as he limped out into the camp.

He didn't make it very far before Tamisra caught up to him.

"You're going anyway, aren't you?"

He didn't look back. "Guessed that, did you?"

"Roland—" She placed a hand on his arm, and Roland jerked away.

"Are you going to try to stop me?"

"No."

"Then stay out of my way."

Roland marched on but fell flat on his face as he was tripped in the darkness. He rolled over, ready to fight, but Tamisra grabbed his wrists.

"I'm coming with you."

33

"I must say, you have certainly made my job easier," the Operative said, leaning back in his seat once again.

Across from him, the girl slumped in her seat, leaning forward. She rested her cheek on the table, sweat running down her pale forehead.

"If you don't know anything, then you certainly couldn't have told anyone else. Good thing, too. It's a waste of resources to send more men into the caves to track down your tunnel rat friends."

Nicholas stood back up, but the Operative held up a finger.

"Just a moment, boy." He leaned over the table and folded his hands, grinning at the girl. "Out of curiosity, why didn't you just turn yourself in back in Holendast? The Lightbringers want nothing more than peace, and you would have helped us secure it. You would have been well rewarded for your prompt integrity."

Aniya sat back up and glared at him. "You really expect me to believe that? You thought I knew something, so you brainwashed Nicholas and killed an innocent girl, all after killing my parents. I'm pretty sure you wouldn't have let me off that easy if I turned myself in."

He laughed again. "Surely you didn't think that your actions would not have consequences? Ms. Lyons, your government works because it has rules, and it is very good at enforcing them. If you steal something, you're whipped in the streets. If you betray our generosity, you suffer execution. We don't enjoy it—well, I say 'we' on behalf of the Light-bringers. I myself have different proclivities. But it must be done. The last time they turned a blind eye, the Uprising happened. And with war come many more casualties than just a few. In any case, Nicholas wasn't brainwashed, as you put it. We offered him a choice, and he chose to listen to reason. As a matter of fact, I offered him the very same drink I gave you, and he proved to me that he would obey my every command."

Aniya looked up at Nicholas, her lips quivering.

"Would you like to see?" The Operative nodded at Nicholas. "Hit her."

Aniya turned back to the Operative in alarm.

Nicholas stood up slowly. "You said you wouldn't make me hurt her."

"Wrong. I said I wouldn't make you kill her. Now, hit her."

"Nicholas, you—"

Aniya was interrupted as Nicholas's open hand struck her across the face.

The Operative smiled. "He's mine now."

Nicholas bowed his head and muttered, "He's right, I—"

"Save it," Aniya said, holding a hand to her red cheek. "I don't know you anymore."

"You can take her back to her quarters now, Officer. Don't bother with the handcuffs. I think she knows she's not going anywhere."

Nicholas pulled Aniya up and exited the train car.

When the Operative was sure they were out of earshot, he

pressed a button on the side of the table, and a digital display slowly descended from above until it rested at his eye level.

The screen lit up. The Operative pressed three buttons, then waited.

After a moment, the display fizzled into a video feed, showing a man dressed in gray.

The Operative cleared his throat. "Checking in, sir. She doesn't know anything. Apparently, the boy never got a chance to tell anyone about the reactor."

"Good. No harm done, then."

The Operative paused. "We may have a minor problem."

"Yes?"

"Sir, the Scourge is still alive."

The Adviser nodded. "I see."

"I anticipated you may want to use this information to track him down, but the girl doesn't know the tunnels well enough to lead us back to him."

"No matter," the Adviser said, waving his hand. "He's an old man by now, not in any position to finish what he started. Forget the Scourge and bring the girl in."

"For what purpose? She doesn't know anything. We can dispose of her and just move on already."

"The girl will live. Our reasons are our own."

The Operative frowned. "I want to speak to the Chancellor."

"Is my word not good enough for you, assassin?" The Adviser snarled. "As far as you're concerned, what comes out of my mouth are the Chancellor's words, so you will not question me or those sent on my behalf. And the next time you dump your vile mixture of alcohol and chemicals down a government asset's throat, you'll find yourself in a pod next to the girl's brother. Are we clear?"

"Yes, sir." The Operative narrowed his eyes. "But while we're being transparent with each other, let me as well make one thing very clear. You may be the Chancellor's right hand, but I am his left. If I suspect that you are not acting in his interests, if I believe you are working against him in any fashion, I have the right and obligation to investigate and report my findings to him. If I find that you are guilty of treason, I'll kill you and your precious assets myself."

After a very long pause, the man spoke again. "Bring the girl in. We'll continue this conversation when you arrive."

The screen went black.

The Operative growled and poured another drink. *He doesn't know. He couldn't know. He's sitting pretty in the Citadel while we get our hands dirty.*

He downed the drink.

What is he not telling me?

He only had a few minutes until they would arrive in the Hub, at which point it would be too late to interrogate the boy again. He stood up, pulling his gun from its holster.

Time to find out.

34

Aniya lurched forward. She had tripped on the entry to the next train car, but she caught herself on the railing before completely losing her balance.

"Are you okay?"

She scowled. "What do you care?"

"I serve the Lightbringers now, but I never stopped caring for you."

She felt a hand on the back of her shoulder, and she spun around, shoving a finger in Nicholas's face.

"Don't touch me again."

He looked down. "Please, Aniya. Don't make this hard on yourself and harder on me."

Aniya scoffed. "You didn't seem to think twice when you hit me, when you shot me. You're their puppet. That's clear now."

They passed into another car, this one full of electrical equipment.

"I have my orders, Aniya. If I disobey them, I die. If I follow along, you stay alive. That was one of my conditions, that you live."

"Gee, Nicky. What a sacrifice on your part. I can't believe

you would do that for me." She rolled her eyes. "What did they say to you to get you to abandon everything you believed in? What happened to you?"

Nicholas remained silent.

"I get nothing? Eighteen years of friendship and you don't have the decency to explain why you threw it all away?" She turned away again and kept walking. "You really are one of them now."

Aniya opened the door to the next train car and stepped over the gap, eyeing the rocks below. Not hearing the door close behind her, she turned around to see Nicholas, still in the previous car.

"You coming?"

Nicholas didn't move. He held up a finger and cocked his head.

She jumped back over into the car she had just left and closed the door. "What are you waiting for? Don't you have more girls to kidnap?"

He shook his head, his finger still in the air.

"Whatever. You can stay if you want. Who knows? If I reach the last car, I could just jump off. I'd die at these speeds, but I don't see a bright future ahead of me anyway."

Still nothing.

Aniya rolled her eyes and turned around. "Suit yourself."

"Wait."

She felt a gloved hand around her wrist.

In a flurry, Aniya twisted around and punched Nicholas in the nose.

"I said don't touch me," she said as he fell to the floor.

Nicholas held a hand to his nose as blood seeped between his fingers. "I deserved that."

Aniya folded her arms across her chest, her eyes watering.

"I probably deserve a lot worse than that." He stood up, wiping his bloody hands on his silver armor.

"I'm sure you'll get what's coming to you."

Nicholas looked over his shoulder, then back at her. "I don't blame you. You've been through a lot. I know your parents—"

"Don't talk about my parents," she said, her hands curling into fists again.

"I didn't kill them."

"You may as well have."

Nicholas didn't answer.

"If you really do feel anything for me, answer me this. Why did they kill my parents? Why didn't they just take them like they took my brother?"

Nicholas looked away. "I doubt they were supposed to die. After the Uprising, most of the rebels were executed, but influential people like your parents were kept alive and under the government's thumb to show that even after the war, the Lightbringers were still in control. But after your parents sheltered your brother and hid him from the Operative, they committed treason. Even then, they should have been brought before the Chancellor for a trial."

"Then why did your friend kill them?"

"The Operative, who is not my friend, doesn't always represent the interest of the Lightbringers. He's more or less given free rein to work as he sees fit, and he goes a little too far sometimes. If it's any consolation, whatever punishment the Chancellor would have given your parents would have been worse than a bullet to the head."

Aniya squeezed her eyes shut and tried to block out the images that Nicholas's graphic words prompted. "How can you say such a thing? At least they'd be alive."

"I'm not so sure about that."

Aniya opened her eyes. "And what about me? The Operative could have killed me after he found out that I don't know anything. What's going to happen to me?"

"You will be punished," Nicholas said, grimacing.

She couldn't believe this was the same Nicholas she had

grown up with. The one that played tag with her and William. The one who taught her how to pick locks. The one she had once stolen a kiss from during one Black Day.

"What kind of punishment?"

Nicholas didn't answer but cocked his head again. After a moment, he nodded. "We need to move."

Without waiting for her to respond, he placed a hand on her shoulder and pushed her forward.

Aniya exploded with rage and grabbed his hand. She spun around, wrenching his arm awkwardly, and prepared to punch him again, but she found herself trapped as he latched on to both her hands.

He twisted her back around and shoved her up against the wall. A second later, handcuffs bound her wrists once again.

"Let's go."

Nicholas pushed her again, and she stumbled forward helplessly, struggling to maintain her balance.

They stepped into the next train car, and Nicholas closed the door behind them.

"Stay here."

He continued into the car and approached a group of monitors. After pressing a few buttons, he studied the screens, ignoring Aniya.

Curious, Aniya approached, but careful not to make any sudden movements.

The screens showed footage of various train cars, all of them seemingly empty. But motion drew Aniya's eye to a screen that revealed a man advancing through a train car, his weapon drawn.

The man disappeared, reappearing within seconds on another monitor.

Aniya backed away from the screen, her eyes wide. "Why is he—"

Nicholas hushed her and held up a finger, cocking his head again.

After a moment, he pointed back the way they came. "We need to go back."

"Why? I thought he—"

"Move!"

He pushed her again, and the urgency in his voice made her think twice before protesting again.

They stepped back into the previous car, one that contained various mechanisms and control panels. Nicholas scanned the car, his eyes darting back and forth.

"Close the door," he said to Aniya.

"What are we—"

Nicholas held up his finger yet again.

"Stop shushing me."

He ignored her and approached a large yellow lever affixed to the floor. "Find something to hold on to."

"Why? We—"

"Now."

Confused, Aniya searched the room, finally settling on a railing that guarded a window. She placed a hand on the rails, but Nicholas shook his head.

"Not there. Too close to the glass."

"Will you please tell me what's going on?"

But then, the opposite door opened, and the Operative stepped inside, his gun drawn and pointed at Aniya.

"I can't help but notice that this is not where I asked you to take the girl, boy."

Nicholas stepped in front of the lever. "I was on my way, sir."

"Then why is the next door already open?"

Nicholas turned around. Sure enough, the door was still open. "I told you to close the door, Aniya."

She rolled her eyes. "Why would I listen to you?"

"You've always been like this, you know. You have to do things your own way. God forbid you follow an order."

"You shot me!"

"Enough." The Operative cocked his gun and looked at Nicholas. "It's clear to me now that your loyalty is not as unwavering as it seemed. Surely you understand if I proceed to the Hub without you, boy."

He turned and pointed his gun at Nicholas, who backed away, pressing his body up against the lever.

"After all, you're no longer needed."

Nicholas glared at the assassin. "The Adviser will have something to say about that. I'm here under his orders."

"The Adviser believed that you would comply with our mission. You did help capture the girl, but I think your cooperation is beginning to wane. Personally, I don't want to risk it."

With that, the Operative fired, and Nicholas's body fell backward, his full weight landing on the lever.

An earsplitting grinding noise split the air, and the train car shifted sideways. For an instant, Aniya found herself inches off the ground as the floor dropped out from underneath her.

Then, the car lurched sideways. The Operative flew into the wall and hit his head, dropping his gun. Aniya was thrown to the side, her back colliding with the wall, and she lost consciousness as the train exploded around them.

35

A niya woke up amid flame and wreckage.

Smoke and putrid fumes ravaged the air, making it almost impossible to breathe.

Above the ringing in her ears, she could hear the harsh screech of metal as the remains of the train slowly collapsed around her.

Still handcuffed, she pushed against the large steel beam clamping down on her leg, but she was helpless against the incredible weight. She took a deep breath to prepare for exertion and choked on the polluted air.

She was trapped.

"Help!"

There was no telling where she was. The train had broken apart, and she was outside, but she couldn't see past the black smoke that surrounded her. She could be calling out in the middle of a random sector. She could be in the train tunnels, with miles to go until civilization. She could be in the middle of the Hub, surrounded by a dozen Silvers.

It didn't matter. If she didn't escape soon, she would die anyway.

"Help!" she called again, fruitlessly trying to push the metal off her leg.

A figure stepped out of the smoke and knelt at her side.

"Hold on, I've got you." It was a man's muffled voice.

The steel beam on her leg began to move, and Aniya pushed as her rescuer pulled.

Finally, she was free. She backed away from the immediate debris and, exhausted, let herself fall backward, her head coming to rest on dirt. Above, she could see a tiny spot of blue light past the smoke.

She was in a sector.

Aniya felt herself lifted off the ground.

"We've got to get out of here before the Silvers arrive."

The ringing in her ears subsided just enough for Aniya to recognize the voice. She tilted her head to the side and bit Nicholas's hand.

Nicholas yelped and dropped her. "What was that for?"

She didn't answer, instead climbing to her feet and running away.

"Aniya, wait!"

Still wading through smoke, she walked right into the arms of another armored man.

"Gotcha."

Aniya lost her balance as she was dragged away from Nicholas and out of the smoke. She looked up to see a man in silver armor gripping her shoulders tightly.

The man threw her to the ground, stepped on her stomach, and reached for his radio.

"Attention, squad leader, I—"

That was as far as he got before Nicholas leapt out of the smoke and onto the soldier's back. The two men staggered back and forth for a moment before Nicholas managed to get a firm grip on the sides of the man's head. He twisted violently, a sickening crack emanating from the man's neck as he crumpled to the ground.

Nicholas stood up and brushed himself off. His armor was gone, and he was now clothed in gray compression clothing. He picked up the man's gun and pulled out the magazine, counting the ammunition.

Aniya put her anger and bitterness aside for a moment, making way for confusion. "Why are you helping me?"

"Change of plans." He grabbed Aniya's hand and pulled her up. He withdrew a key from a pocket and undid her handcuffs. "We need to get moving before more of them show up. Here, I found this for you." With his other hand, he presented Aniya's rucksack, which she took.

"What about the Operative?"

"He's dead. Looked like he hit his head pretty hard." Nicholas reached underneath his shirt and pulled out Kira's crystal. "I think this belongs to you."

Aniya took the necklace cautiously and slipped it over her head. "I thought he shot you. How are you still alive?"

"The Silvers wear pretty thick armor."

"So why don't you keep it on?"

Nicholas shook his head. "The Lightbringers were tracking me with it, making sure I held up my end of the bargain. Sucks because there was a radio built into my helmet, and that's the only way my contact could reach me."

"Your contact? What are you talking about?"

"It's better that you don't know. We're still in danger, and too much is at stake."

Aniya refused to accept this response. "No. You owe me some ans—" She stumbled suddenly as her head felt light. Before she could say anything, Nicholas picked her up and started carrying her. "Absolutely not. Put me down."

Nicholas kept walking. "I was pretty well protected thanks to my armor, but you probably have a concussion. Wait until we get out of the smoke."

"I will bite your hand again if you don't put me down."

Nicholas sighed and placed her down. "Fine, but you have

236 | DAVID WEBB

to follow me closely. If you slow us down too much, or if it looks like you're going to drop, I will pick you up again. Deal?"

Aniya smirked. "Slow you down? I could outrun you if I wanted, and you know it." But she accepted his lead and followed him away from the wreckage.

They cleared the smoke, and Aniya paused briefly to look around. They were standing in a valley of dirt, heading toward a massive formation of rocks about a mile away. In the middle of the cliffside was a small hole near the bottom where the train tracks disappeared into the rock.

The landscape was so desolate that Aniya wondered if they were in a sector that was still under development, but as she turned around, she realized where she was.

Beyond the valley of dirt were hundreds of factories and smokestacks, laid out in a neat grid across most of the sector. But towering far above them all was a massive, silver tower that stretched seemingly all the way to the top of the sky ceiling. In fact, Aniya couldn't tell where the tip of the monument ended and the digital dome began.

It was the Citadel, home to the Chancellor and headquarters to the Lightbringers.

They were in the Hub.

She shuddered and turned toward Nicholas, who gestured with his head and continued walking toward the cliffs, which formed a bland, gray wall that stood around the entire perimeter of the Hub, shutting the sector away from the rest of the Web.

It was a far cry from the utopian paradise they had learned about in Assembly.

They climbed up into the cliffs, hugging the side of the rock wall and traversing over very thin walkways. Nicholas never let go of her hand, which grew increasingly uncomfortable. But he was right. The blow to her head had left her disoriented, a condition that proved dangerous as they got higher up in the cliffs. As angry as she was, she knew the stability provided by his hand was invaluable.

Finally, after several minutes, they rested on a large rock jutting out from the cliff.

Aniya took deep breaths of the air and noted that it still tasted like smoke. They were nowhere near the wreck now, but she deduced that it was a byproduct of the industrial grid across the valley. "Now that we're away from the train, what are you talking about? What contact?"

Nicholas shook his head. "I'm sorry, Aniya. I can't tell you that. What I can tell you is that you, me, William—we're all in danger. The Lightbringers are more dangerous than you or I thought."

"I don't know, I've seen enough that I believe it."

"Whatever you think, I promise you that it's worse. We need to get William and get out."

Aniya's heart raced. "Do you know where he is?"

"I have a general idea. Enough to get us started."

"Where would we even go? The Silvers are everywhere."

"According to my contact, as long as we can get to him, he'll take it from there."

"Do you trust this contact of yours?"

Nicholas shrugged. "I don't really have a choice. He says he wants to get rid of the Lightbringers."

"And you just believed him? The government specializes in manipulating people. What makes you think he isn't tricking you so you can bring me in?"

"He's the one who clued me in to the Operative's attack. I guess he was watching the security feed too. I doubt he would attack his own side like that to get me to bring you in when we were already on our way."

"Why can't you tell me who he is?"

"His orders. If you get caught, he doesn't want you giving him up to the Chancellor or his Adviser."

Aniya folded her arms. "I don't think we should be trusting anyone in this sector. Let's just go get William."

"I'm all for that. We just—" Nicholas's eyes narrowed, and he looked past Aniya, frowning.

Aniya turned around. In the distance, she spotted several small dots streaking across the sky in various directions. A few of them grew larger, heading toward the cliffs.

"Scanners!" Nicholas grabbed her hand again. "Get down!"

They dropped to the ground and crouched behind a boulder, shielding themselves from the flying machines.

Behind them, Aniya could hear an increasingly loud buzz, a mechanical hum that chilled her spine, but it also gave away the robots' positions quite obviously.

Her grip on Nicholas's hand grew tighter as the buzz grew louder. As he squeezed back, Aniya could feel her hand starting to get wet, and she couldn't tell if it was his sweat or her own.

"Do you have another one of those electric bombs?"

"I only had two, the one I used and the one you used. I do have this, though," he said as he readied his gun.

The buzz reached its loudest and then leveled off, maintaining a consistent hum that was nearly deafening. The noise moved around them, echoing against the cliff walls.

After another minute, the tension became too much for Aniya. She leaned forward to try to get a look, but Nicholas pulled her back as a large shadow fell over the rock in front of them.

Aniya landed on the ground with a thud, and she hissed in pain as her elbow made contact with rock.

In an instant, a large metal sphere shot into view, coming to rest directly in front of them.

Aniya held her breath. The machine wasn't facing them, but she wasn't taking any chances. Unfortunately, the noise of her fall had alerted the machine to their exact location, and it began to turn toward them, revealing a large red eye, pulsing with an angry glow. Aniya squeezed Nicholas's hand one last time.

Nicholas fired his gun, and the sphere emitted a loud whine as the bullet pierced its hull, sending the machine crashing to the ground. Its red eye blinked a few times, then went dark.

"We need to move. The other ones will have heard that." Nicholas stood up and searched the skies.

Aniya stood up with him and looked into the distance. Sure enough, several more scanners were headed their way.

"Let's go."

36

That night, in a hole in the cliffs, Nicholas sat on a large rock by a dying fire, munching on a chunk of mole jerky. Aniya had fallen asleep almost instantly, but Nicholas's sleep had been restless, plagued by regrets of the past and worries of the future.

Each time he closed his eyes to sleep, he saw Aniya holding her cheek in shock, staring at him with betrayal written on her face. So Nicholas chose to stay awake instead, hoping that watching Aniya's peaceful slumber would over-write the awful mental pictures that kept coming back.

To make matters worse, the quiet voice that had guided his every move was now gone. He was on his own now, blindly trying to finish his mission. But that wasn't the worst part. Nicholas had gotten used to the constant interruption coming from the radio in his helmet, and now that things were quiet again, there was nothing to distract him from the awkward-ness with Aniya.

She hadn't taken her eyes off him all day. In recent months, he would have done anything to get her to do that, but now she looked at him with a suspicious glare that he felt even when his back was turned.

Nicholas knew she had every right to not trust him after the way he had treated her. Even though she seemed to understand that he did what he had to, he couldn't shake the feeling that something between them had forever changed.

It had lifted his spirits to see her close her eyes, let her guard down, and temporarily forget about all the horrors behind her and the troubles ahead. As she slept, her face was washed clean of her anger and pain, and it was the same Aniya he had fallen in love with back in the Hole. Nicholas could only wish that it would be that way when she woke up.

He had seen her sleep several times. They had innocently spent the night together many times before. Sometimes, it was intentional. Aniya would often spend so much time talking with him that leaving his house was too dangerous, the consequences of getting caught while breaking curfew being too great to risk. Instead, she would sleep on Nicholas's cot while he arranged extra blankets to the side as a makeshift bed.

Other times, it was a happy accident, and they would fall asleep while watching the sky ceiling, its stars twinkling with an unnatural brilliance. The technology had fascinated him and was what originally inspired him to work in programming. It meant something else to Aniya, something almost mystical. Nicholas would often ignore the lights and simply watch her fall into a trance as she gazed at the twinkling lights above.

Even before all this started, those nights had long since come to an end. Aniya's parents didn't like that he was spending so much time training with Gareth and Roland, so they limited Nicholas's time with her as much as they could. She would still make an effort to sneak out to come see him, but it was never as frequent as it used to be.

Maybe it was for the best. In the last several months, he had wanted something different, something more. And it hurt to see her and know she didn't feel the same way.

She had once told him that it wasn't worth getting invested in each other when the Lightbringers would surely have someone else in mind. Whether or not this was her true reason, Nicholas was never sure, but she was right. Her candidates were never going to include him. They only knew each other because of her brother, and after studying the algorithms himself, he was dismayed to find that propinquity was a major factor in candidate selection. They may have spent a lot of time together, but as far as the Lightbringers were concerned, they were complete strangers. But even if the Lightbringers knew they were best friends, the daughter of Uprising instigators paired with someone in possession of advanced tech? It was never going to happen.

But now that they were no longer monitored by the Lightbringers, now that they had no way to enforce their stupid rules, maybe she would decide that things could be different.

They could turn around now. They could find a new sector, one in the far reaches of the Web where Lightbringer presence would be low. They could start a new life together and never look back.

It would be difficult to convince Aniya to leave her brother behind, but if he told her everything he knew, maybe she'd agree.

After all, he had enough doubts about his mission. Maybe, like Aniya suggested, his contact couldn't be trusted.

Get the girl and bring her to me.

The mission sounded identical to the Operative's, and Nicholas had nothing to go on but the word of a disillusioned idealist who claimed that he wanted to bring down the Lightbringers.

Aniya was right. Even as he had defended his contact to her earlier, Nicholas questioned how it was so easy to believe Kendall. But when the world is falling apart, you have to trust someone. This mysterious stranger seemed like the only option at the time, but now that Aniya was here . . .

It's not too late.

It wasn't.

He would never know.

He wouldn't.

Nicholas began to rise from the rock as he reached out toward Aniya. She was so close. Everything he ever wanted—

Aniya stirred, and Nicholas sat back down roughly and spun around on the rock.

He picked up the stick he had been using to stir the fire and began poking at the flames again. After the day they had, Nicholas couldn't imagine what Aniya's response would be if she woke up and found him watching her. After a moment, Nicholas started to turn around again but was stopped by Aniya's voice.

"Is it night yet?"

"Almost," Nicholas said.

Aniya joined Nicholas on the large rock, sitting next to him but keeping plenty of distance between them. "Couldn't sleep?"

"Got an hour or two, but no, not really."

"I guess we need to leave soon anyway."

"I guess." Nicholas poked the fire again.

They sat for several minutes.

Talking with her used to be the most natural thing in the world, but as hard as Nicholas tried to start a conversation now, he couldn't find the words to say.

Whether Aniya faced the same problem or she simply didn't want to talk to him, Nicholas didn't know, but she remained silent as well.

Finally, it was Aniya who broke the silence.

"I never thanked you."

"For what?" Nicholas spun on the rock and turned to face her, resisting the urge to laugh. "I helped them catch you, I hit you, and I shot you. What do you have to thank me for?"

"It's not like you chose to do any of that. They were watching you, right?"

Nicholas's face grew red. "I never apologized."

"I didn't ask for your apology." Her words came out harshly, and he saw the regret in her eyes as she looked away.

"It felt awful, every second of it. If I wasn't being watched, I never would have acted like that. I never would have— I never would have done those things." He winced as the image of her hurt face flashed in his mind again.

"I understand," Aniya whispered.

"No, you don't. Every second, I had to think and act like one of them, all while fighting the urge to turn on them. They killed that poor girl, and I had to stand there and watch, pretending not to care. They used me to get to you, and I let them. I could have refused."

Even now, I could refuse.

Aniya shook her head. "Then you would have died because of me. I don't want another person's blood on my hands."

"At least then I wouldn't have betrayed you. Maybe I could have found a way to escape earlier." Nicholas's voice grew low. "Maybe it wouldn't have been the worst thing for me to die."

"Don't say that, Nicholas. We're still alive," she said, placing a hand on his arm. "And the man who killed my parents is dead. We're alive and together, and I think we're in a better spot now than we would be if you were dead and never forced to be one of them."

He pulled away. "You really think it makes everything else okay?"

"I'm not saying that. I'm saying I understand. I'm saying I forgive you."

Nicholas shook his head. "I don't deserve that."

"It's not about what you deserve." Aniya touched him again, this time pulling on his arm, bringing him closer. She placed her other hand on his knee and gazed into his eyes as her voice began to shake. "Want to know a secret? I wish William had never escaped. I wish he had stayed in the Hub, forced to work for them for the rest of his life. You know why? Because then my parents would be alive. I wouldn't be running for my life all over the Web. They wouldn't have taken you. I keep telling myself that this isn't what I really want, but it is, Nicholas. I want more than anything to be back in the Hole, on your roof with you right now. Do you want to know what I deserve for wishing my brother was rotting in the hands of the Lightbringers? Because I don't. I'm forgiving you, Nicholas, even if you don't deserve it. And I hope that someone forgives me, too."

Nicholas sat, dumbfounded, staring at the rock they sat on, unable to look her in the eyes.

"You're all I have left, Nicholas." Her tears began to splash on the rock in front of him.

He could take her.

"My parents are dead."

They could run away together.

"William is probably being tortured."

She could finally be free to be with him.

"And I have no idea what happened to Roland."

He could at last have everything he ever wanted.

"Nicky, I don't know what I would do if I lost you too."

Nicholas finally looked up at Aniya. She was already looking in his eyes with an intensity that chilled him. Her eyes were wet, and her lips were trembling as he felt her hands slowly caress his own. Slowly, he brought his face toward her. Just as he closed his eyes, Aniya finally reacted, backing away with a gasp.

Nicholas froze. He opened his eyes again and stared into hers.

He had always been good at reading her, always able to tell what she was thinking. Even the first time he told her how he felt about her, he knew what she was going to say, her response written in her averted eyes.

But now, Nicholas was lost. He saw everything in her eyes,

from anger to sadness to shock to bitterness to something he
had never seen before.

Does she know?

As Nicholas studied her eyes, he realized that despite her
claims, she would never truly forgive him.

Nor should she.

Dejected, Nicholas backed away. As awful as he felt, he
knew he didn't deserve anything from her. He had made his
choice.

But as he relaxed and leaned back, Aniya leaned forward.
Gone was the confusion in her eyes, and she leaned toward
him intently, her eyes fixed on his lips.

The one kiss they shared years ago in the darkness of a
Black Day had been enough to permanently seal that passion
in his heart, and ever since that day, he had dreamed of
kissing her again. But out of the thousands of times he had
played the scene out in his head, it never went like this.

This time, with a sigh of passion, he took her chin and
pulled her closer, meeting her lips in a long-awaited embrace,
letting a small moan of contentment out as he locked lips with
her in passion.

His head spun as sparks danced across his closed eyelids.
His moist hands stroked her hair and rested on her warm neck
as he held on for dear life.

Chills raced over his body, and his skin tingled in pleasure
and excitement as his heart raced within, pounding so hard
that he could feel his heartbeat in his fingertips.

And as he opened his eyes and watched her kiss him back,
he saw his love reflected on her face, and he let himself melt in
her arms.

But as Nicholas snapped out of his imagination and
leaned forward to make this fantasy a reality, the orders he was
given came back to him as guilt crashed over him in waves.

Get the girl and bring her to me.

Nicholas knew it could never happen now, not with the

gut-wrenching condemnation that ravaged his heart. No matter how much he wanted to express his love for her, even now that she presented herself to him, finally ready and willing to give him what he had always wanted, he couldn't bring himself to do it.

I've made my choice. Now I have to live with it.

Nicholas shook away the imagined kiss and backed away from Aniya's advance. It looked so good in his head. Even now, he could feel her lips, remnants of the fantasy he had enjoyed for a split second. If he thought hard enough, he swore he could taste her lips, and he wished more than anything for it to be real.

But he couldn't. He could never.

Nicholas stood up and turned, leaving Aniya behind, her lips unkissed.

"We need to get going. It's dark enough now, and we need all the time we can get."

He kicked dirt over the fire, extinguishing the glowing embers. He heard Aniya get up behind him, but he refused to turn around and let her see his eyes beginning to water.

"I'll pack our bags." Her voice came from behind. She walked past Nicholas and picked up the leftover jerky, and in the torchlight, he saw her cheeks glistening with tears.

I hope you know what you're doing, Kendall.

37

R oland held on to Tamisra's waist for dear life.

Every movement of the mole beneath his body threatened to throw him off and send him crashing into the dirt and rock wall on either side. He found himself realizing that instead of practicing various forms of combat with Tamisra, he should have spent the last two weeks learning to ride the moles. His lack of experience meant that he had to double up with Tamisra, and the lack of control made the ride nauseating.

"You okay back there?"

In response, Roland pulled her closer and let out an "uh-huh" that came out in a much higher pitch than he would have liked.

Tamisra only laughed.

They had been riding nearly non-stop for the last eleven hours, resting only for the benefit of the mole. As it turned out, their mole had the kind of endurance Roland had hoped for, an endurance he wouldn't mind having himself. The two times they rested, he had collapsed in exhaustion until Tamisra woke him.

"We're almost there," she shouted back at him above the thundering footsteps. "Just a bit longer."

Roland moaned and watched the cave walls as they raced by. It wasn't much better than watching the ground below, but at least glowworms populated the walls, softly illuminating the tunnel in a twinkling green glow where the torchlight was scarce.

Despite Tamisra's reassurance, it was another hour before they slowed down. Meanwhile, Roland had resumed his normal position of laying his head on Tamisra's back, his eyes closed tight.

"Do you see this?"

Roland looked up again as the mole slowed to a brisk walking pace. The walls of the cave were no longer illuminated by the glowworms or the occasional torch. As they continued further into the darkness, the light behind them fading, Tamisra lit a torch and held it as they lumbered on.

"Aren't these tunnels supposed to be lit?" Roland examined the dark walls closely. A few torches hung from the walls, but none of them were lit.

"They are. The Lightbringers must have disabled them when they collapsed the tunnel exit. Guess they scared away the glowworms at the same time."

They finally reached the end of the path and stopped in front of a large rockslide that reached all the way to the cave ceiling five feet above their heads, blocking off the rest of the tunnel.

Tamisra dismounted and approached the blockage, leaving Roland still on the mole. "This is going to be fun to get through."

"Still think the mole will be able to get through in time?"

"Curry," she said, correcting him. "And it's not a matter of whether Curry will be able to get through in time, but whether he can get through without killing all three of us."

Roland dismounted. "I thought you said the moles would be able to dig straight through."

"Technically, yes, but I was hoping the tunnel exit would be dug by a smaller one. This is one of the larger tunnels I've seen." She shuddered. "I'd hate to meet the mole that dug this out. Curry's only a pup. If he digs through debris that's only a couple weeks old, it might just collapse on him. Might even trigger another cave-in that will fall on us."

"So we came all this way for nothing?" Roland threw his hands in the air and walked away from Tamisra and Curry.

"No, we can still try. We'd have to be a safe distance away, and we run the risk of losing our only means of transportation, but we can try. We can help him to the top of the rock slide and let him try to dig his way out near the top. It would definitely lessen the chance of death for all of us."

Roland heard Tamisra approach from behind and felt her hands on his shoulders, massaging them gently.

"We could even go back and take another side tunnel. There's plenty of those. I don't know if you saw, but we passed one not too far after the tunnel went dark. There's a chance that one of those leads to the Hub. And if all else fails, we can go back and take the train tunnel into the Hub."

He laughed dryly. "Take the most dangerous route, the one that's sure to get us caught and killed? Stop it, that sounds almost too fun. Besides, it would be way too late by that point."

"We have to do something, Roland."

After a long pause, he turned around again. "I know. Tell you what. We're all tired, even that beast of a mole."

"Curry."

"Right, Curry." He continued, "We made good time, but I don't think there's any way we've beat the train to the Hub. Let's rest tonight, and tomorrow we'll figure out our next step. We're getting into the Hub one way or another."

Tamisra nodded.

"Deal."

It didn't take long for them to fall asleep. Though they had done practically nothing, the constant vibration from the lumbering mole had worn them out and left them exhausted. Even Curry was asleep within minutes, but not before Tamisra fed him a special treat of glowworms for his hard work.

They slept soundly enough, almost straight through a troubling sound five hours later.

Roland sat up slowly and rubbed his eyes. He looked around, gathering his surroundings. Whatever had made the noise that woke him up was not obvious. Roland only saw Curry in the light of glowworms from a glass container on the ground. Tamisra had placed them out after feeding a few of them to Curry, and they now softly illuminated the immediate area of the tunnel. As Roland became more alert, the thought of the noise all but disappeared.

By his side, Tamisra was still asleep. The mole, however, was wide awake, and it stared into the green light blankly.

Roland grabbed the glowworms and approached the mole, waving the light in front of Curry's snout.

"You like that? Enough to let me ride you?"

However, the mole was shaken from its stupor suddenly. Its snout bunched up as a low growl emitted from its throat.

"Hey, relax. You like Tami, so you're going to have to get used to me."

The mole continued to growl as Roland backed away. The farther he moved, the more he realized that Curry's growl was not the only sound disturbing the silence.

The sound of footsteps.

Roland's eyes flew open, and the last of his grogginess faded instantly. He shook Tamisra roughly, hissing in her ear, "Get up!"

Tamisra shot up, grabbing for the gun at her side. She looked up at Roland. "What is it?"

"Listen," he said.

Tamisra froze, cocking her head to the side.

Nothing.

She shrugged. "What are you talking about?"

Roland didn't answer.

The sound had vanished. Even Curry's growl had quieted to a soft rumble.

Finally, he sighed. "Nothing. I guess I was still a little tired."

Tamisra punched his shoulder in a not-so-playful fashion. "That's for waking me up." She punched his other shoulder. "And that's for scaring me."

She sat up and reached for her sack nearby. "Now that I'm up, we might as well get ready for . . . whatever we're going to do."

But Roland was still looking down the tunnel toward where he had last heard the sound, and he staggered backward as he was blinded by a bright, white light.

The canister of glowworms fell from his hands to the cave floor, smashing open and freeing the already-dead worms inside.

Another light flashed on.

Then another.

And another.

Then, they began shooting.

38

Aniya had nearly expected the Hub to be constantly lit in a state of everlasting day, but as she stepped out of the cave and into the darkness of the Hub, her breath was taken away by the beauty of the dark capital sector.

The cliffs in which Aniya and Nicholas had found shelter were shrouded in darkness, thanks to the starless sky ceiling above. A shadow hung low over the dirt valley before them, stretching on and seeming to disappear into nothingness in the dead of night.

The only source of light in the Hub was the Citadel, the towering building that loomed before them in the very center of the Hub, its tip vanishing into the dark ceiling above. It shone like a beacon in the distance, its white light so bright that it cast a visible halo around the massive obelisk.

A large grid of industrial buildings completely surrounded the Citadel. Smokestacks stood tall, scattered throughout the grid, but even the tallest one was dwarfed by the massive tower. The grid was silent and unmoving, production seeming to have halted during the night hours. But they were not without purpose on this night in particular. Tonight, they would serve as cover for Aniya and Nicholas as they approached the Citadel.

But first, they would have to make it past the valley, a vast stretch of dirt where there would be nowhere to hide from the scanners.

Aniya could see them in the distance, their positions given away by several red dots that slowly hovered back and forth. The scanners were still out there. Now that the light of the sky ceiling was gone, Aniya could see glowing red spots on the ground of the Hub, each of them below a brighter red light in the sky, indicating the drones' gazes.

At least they would know if they were about to be caught and killed.

After waiting for a patrolling scanner to turn and head toward the center of the Hub, they climbed down the cliffside without a word.

Nicholas still hadn't spoken since they had almost kissed back in the cave. Aniya still didn't understand why he hadn't kissed her, and the more she thought about it, the more frustrated she grew. She knew he had always liked her, even when she made it clear years ago that he was simply a friend. Of course, she hadn't done much to discourage him. He had been her first kiss, after all, an innocent brush of the lips when the power was out one day. After that, his feelings were no secret. So why had he changed his mind now after pining for her for so many years?

She mentally kicked herself. He had hit her, shot her, almost got her killed, and here she was, all torn up that he wouldn't kiss her? What made things worse was she couldn't figure out why she cared so much.

Maybe it was her fault. Aniya had spent the last several years going out of her way to make sure he knew that he was no more than a friend. And now that she had thrown herself at him, he had refused. In hindsight, maybe she brought it on herself.

As she almost tripped over a rock hidden in the shadows, she forced herself to focus on the path ahead. Nicholas would always be there tomorrow.

They eventually reached the ground below and began to make their way across the valley of dirt.

"We need to move quickly here." Nicholas finally spoke, keeping his voice low. "If the scanners get too close, there's nowhere to hide, and I only have a few bullets left."

Aniya increased her speed until she heard Nicholas begin to struggle. Regardless of her frustration toward him, she knew he needed his strength, so she slowed down just enough until they were both running at a comfortable pace.

They made it halfway across the valley when Aniya heard Nicholas whisper something to her. But the wind rushing by her ears obscured his words, and she couldn't quite make them out. She turned to ask, but he was no longer by her side. What she did see, however, was a large red glow lighting up the dirt several hundred feet away from her.

She dropped to the ground and lay as flat as possible. Turning her head, she saw Nicholas assuming the same position not too far behind her. She looked back and watched the scanner slowly move across the valley, its gaze darting back and forth. At its pace, the machine would spot them in a matter of seconds.

For a moment, Aniya questioned Nicholas's choice to hide rather than run, but as it grew closer, she realized that the scanner was moving much faster than she thought. Maybe even faster than she could run at top speed. As it bore down on them, Aniya's hopes fell. It was headed straight for them. Maybe they were already spotted, and it was too late to do anything.

Maybe not.

She grabbed her rucksack slowly, pulling it off her shoulder. There wasn't much left inside except for a few pieces of jerky and the radio.

The movement made enough noise that the scanner now began to move directly toward them, its gaze now fixed in one direction.

"What are you doing?" Nicholas hissed.

She ignored him and reached to open the pack to get the radio. They would need it if they had any hope of surviving in the Hub. But the scanner was moving too quickly, and there was no time.

Aniya jerked her arm to the side and threw the rucksack as hard as she could.

It soared through the air. With the radio inside, her only defense against the watchful eye of the Lightbringers, the pack disappeared into the dark.

Just as the red glow was about to land on her, the rucksack fell several yards away with a thud, and the robot turned and darted off toward the noise.

Aniya's hand was suddenly grabbed and pulled, and she turned to follow Nicholas toward the center of the Hub, hoping that the distraction would keep the scanner occupied long enough for them to reach shelter.

"Don't look back," Nicholas said between heavy breaths, obviously pushing himself harder than before.

Aniya looked over her shoulder and was blinded by a bright red light.

The scanner had been distracted for mere seconds, and it was bearing down on them again, its red gaze now washing over their bodies.

Looking past the scanner, Aniya spotted several more red lights fall in line behind the lead machine. They all knew where she was now. She turned and willed herself to run faster, pushing away the thought of what would happen to her when they finally caught up.

Aniya and Nicholas neared the edge of the factories, which Aniya thought would provide enough hiding places to lose the machines, but she quickly began to lose hope as they drew closer to the buildings. The industrial grid was spaced out more than she had guessed, leaving way too many wide open spaces that were lit up sufficiently thanks to the light of the Citadel. Anywhere they would run, the scanners would have plenty of room to follow.

She looked beyond the buildings, and her spirits fell further as she saw several more scanners headed toward them from the opposite direction, metal arms now protruding from their spherical bodies. It seemed there was nowhere left to go.

They finally cleared the valley and broke through the edge of the buildings, running past smokestacks and warehouses by the droves. Aniya felt herself pulled left and right in seemingly random directions. She realized that it was intentional, that Nicholas was trying to evade the logical machines with unpredictable movement.

It was working, but not as much as she hoped. The machines were not getting any closer, but they weren't getting any farther away either.

Finally, Aniya spotted something out of the corner of her eye in the opposite direction. She pulled against Nicholas, trying to take the lead. "Follow me!"

However, Nicholas had chosen that exact moment to pull her behind another smokestack. Their fingers slipped from the stress, and they stumbled apart, momentum carrying them yards away from each other.

Aniya stopped briefly and turned, looking for Nicholas. She spotted him trying to make his way over to her, but a large, red glow appeared on the ground between them, and he skidded to a halt.

Over the whir of the machines, she heard him yell, "Split up!" Then, he turned and disappeared into another collection of smokestacks.

Aniya had no time to argue or think. Half the scanners followed Nicholas while the rest of them turned to chase her. She turned and ran, following her original plan.

Free from Nicholas's hand, she ran faster now, but she knew she could never match the speed of the flying robots.

One of the machines suddenly appeared as if from nowhere, descending directly in front of her and again blinding her with red light.

Aniya did not stop. Instead, she let her feet fall out from underneath her, dipping down to the ground in a graceful dive. She slid directly underneath the scanner and smoothly transitioned to an upright position again. She took off running again, but not before a metal arm shot out at her, lunging toward her head.

Sharp metal dug into Aniya's cheek, and blood poured down her throat and over her chest as she staggered for a moment, her vision blackening briefly as her head spun.

But the whir of machinery shook her from her disorientation.

It was right behind her.

Ignoring the blood that freely flowed from her face, Aniya spun on her feet and took off to her right, hoping to create a small amount of distance between herself and the machines, just enough for the final stretch.

Pumping her legs with all that she had left, she made a beeline for a large building ahead of her. If she had had any breath to spare, she would have sighed in relief. The door was indeed open.

Not caring what was on the other side of the door, she ran into the building and pushed the large steel door closed behind her.

Dozens of crashes came from the other side of the door, the clang of metal on metal. Thankfully, the scanners seem to have been constructed with speed in mind and not force, and they barely budged the door as Aniya pressed her body up against it from the other side.

The crashes stopped, and Aniya carefully cracked the door open just enough to look outside.

Hunks of metal lay just outside the door. The scanners were now in pieces, some melting in flame.

She closed the door again and let herself slide to the floor, catching her breath. As she recovered, she looked around and realized why the door was open.

Several wires hung from the ceiling in front of massive metal frames, meant to hold some sort of large, round object. These structures lined the walls of the hangar-like building, going down as far as Aniya could see in the glow of dim electronic screens. This must have been where the scanners were stored, waiting for activation.

She smirked at the irony and stood up, now breathing normally again.

Nicholas was still out there somewhere, probably still being chased by the scanners. Aniya knew the odds were slim that he had been able to escape like she had. If she went after him, she'd probably wind up in the same situation all over again. If she left and tried to find her brother, she would have to do it alone.

Aniya turned around and faced the door, already knowing her decision. She had come with Nicholas, and she wasn't leaving without him.

She opened the door wide, and standing among the remains of the scanners was a man dressed in black. Large red scars marred his face, making his smile even more disturbing.

The Operative pointed his gun at her. "Hello again, Ms. Lyons."

39

Aniya hung from the ceiling, suspended by chains wrapped around her wrists.

Her cell was pitch black, leaving Aniya to her imagination. Try as she might to focus on the problem at hand, all she could see in the black were faces, the faces of the people she'd failed.

Roland, who had warned her of the Silvers and helped her in the caves. She had left him in the tunnels, bleeding out from two gunshots, his fate unknown.

Nicholas, who had held back the Silver Guard just long enough for her to escape Holendast. She had left him to be captured and forced to work for them against his will, putting his life at risk.

Kira, the girl who had sheltered her and befriended her. Aniya had watched as she was executed in front of her grieving father.

Her parents, loving and loyal until the last possible second. They had given their lives to protect their children, who wound up in the hands of the Lightbringers anyway.

It was all for nothing.

All the hurt, all the pain she had carried from Holendast to the Hub now seemed meaningless.

Desperately trying to escape the Lightbringers, she had inadvertently left a trail of death and destruction across the Web. But all she had done was just delay the inevitable. It was all over now, and all Aniya could do was bitterly wish that she had given herself up back in Holendast.

The Operative was right. Had Aniya known that she was always going to end up here, at the mercy of the Light- bringers, she probably never would have run to begin with. She may have been imprisoned for the rest of her life, tortured, killed—but at least Roland and Nicholas would be safe. At least Kira would be alive.

The crystal around her neck had gone unnoticed by the Operative this time. The Silvers had shown up and taken custody of her before he could search her.

Aniya still had the gem, all that remained of Kira, but the beautiful rock was now coated in her blood and hung heavy, dragging her head down to match her defeated spirit. She had done everything she could to save herself, her family, Kira . . . but it seemed like all she accomplished was ensuring their deaths at the risk of staying alive for just a few more days.

Now, all she could do was let herself hang limply, her hands numb and her wrists bleeding. All she could do was wait.

The worst part of it was that Aniya didn't know what she was waiting for. Her natural assumption was death, but if they wanted her dead, they surely would have killed her by now.

Relocative servitude?

Well, now that I'm in the Hub, I guess it would just be servitude.

Or maybe this was her fate, to hang in a windowless cell for the rest of her life, however long that may be.

If that's the case, just kill me now.

Her only hope was Nicholas, still out there somewhere.

Maybe he found some way to evade the scanners. Maybe he found his mysterious contact and was working to save her. Maybe there was still a chance.

Aniya's imagination halted as the door to the room opened and the lights flashed on. She winced at the harsh florescent light and blinked rapidly.

She could hear more chains rattle, accompanied by a grunt of exertion.

By the time her eyes adjusted to the light, the door closed, and the room was dark again.

But not before she saw Nicholas hanging next to her, his clothes soaked in blood.

"Nicholas?"

She heard a pained grunt.

"What happened to you?"

"Well, they got me, Aniya." Nicholas's breath was ragged. "What did you think happened?"

"I mean, why are you covered in blood?"

She heard a moan.

"Their operative wanted his own revenge before turning me in. I guess I messed his face up pretty bad when I wrecked the train." He started to laugh but ended up coughing.

Aniya heard liquid spatter on the ground as he coughed. "How bad is it?"

"It's not as bad as it looks. Or sounds, I guess."

"I thought you said he was dead."

"Well, he wasn't breathing. I guess I shouldn't have assumed. Anyway, I'm glad all he did was beat me to a pulp. I bet he would have loved to kill me, but I'm pretty sure the Lightbringers want to save me for servitude. Both of us, probably."

"Wonderful," Aniya said. She tugged on her chains again. "I don't suppose they'd be up for just killing us?"

"Come on, it can't be that bad. All the rumors we've heard are nothing but that—rumors."

"Yes, but we've only heard rumors because no one has ever come back to tell us what actually goes on here." She looked at Nicholas. "You mean they never told you what relocative servitude actually means?"

Nicholas shook his head. "I didn't ask about it much because I was being constantly watched. For all I know, the Silvers don't even know. I'm not sure the Operative even knows. If he does, I doubt he cares."

"If you don't have any insight, I think I have reason enough to be afraid of it. You saw William. It looked like he aged forty years. Whatever they're doing to their recruits, it's not healthy. Gareth said the Lightbringers are probably working them to death."

"We might be able to escape."

"Would you really want to? Look what happened when William escaped. My parents were killed, we're being hunted, and an innocent girl died. If that's what happens every time a recruit escapes, the Web would be better off if we stay where we are."

Nicholas swung his leg toward her shin weakly. "After all this, you're just giving up? You just want to suck it up and die? If we're forced into servitude, you'll roll over and take it just like that? Doesn't sound like the Aniya I know."

"I'm not the Aniya you knew, Nicholas. That girl died when her parents did. I don't know what I am anymore. Maybe it would have been better if I had died with the rest of my family."

"Please," Nicholas said, the exasperation in his voice clear. "There's no point in feeling sorry for yourself. You were meant for great things. I always knew it. You were never happy where you were, always looking for something more. There's still a chance for that. We were close to getting that something more back during the war, and I believe that we can still accomplish it."

"What do you mean? Who is we?"

Nicholas took a deep breath. "You know how I feel about the Lightbringers. I haven't exactly kept it a secret. To you, at least. If they knew how I talked about them, they would have taken me years ago. Luckily, other people found out how I felt a few years ago and taught me various things that could help me. That could help us."

"What people? You're not making this any clearer."

"People like your parents, Aniya. If you don't already know, they were very active in the Uprising."

Aniya looked down. "Funny how everyone knows more about my parents than I do. Even Salvador, who hadn't seen them in years."

"He would know them best. They started the Uprising and turned it over to him."

"If my parents were so important, why didn't they just lead it?"

Nicholas grunted in pain. "They had just started a family, so they weren't willing to jeopardize their only child by becoming the public faces of the rebellion. That's where Salvador came in. Ironically enough, that's why your parents think the rebellion failed. The people followed a madman out for blood, but what they really needed was a stable leadership, one built on the ideals they were fighting for.

"In any case, we lost. Your parents were lucky enough to be spared, along with a few others, but for the most part, the movement was eliminated or trapped in the caves in the middle of the Web. When I got older and wanted to learn more about the Uprising, Gareth was the first one to reach out to me, and he taught me and Roland the ins and outs of the Web, along with all he knew about the Lightbringers. I would also meet with your parents occasionally, but they didn't like me very much."

Aniya scoffed. "What are you talking about? They loved you."

"They did until they found out that Gareth had basically

indoctrinated me. I had already made up my mind, and they understood that, but they dreaded the thought of me influencing you into repeating their mistakes. They also asked Roland to stay away from you. If they had known you spent several of your nights at the bar, they probably would have had a talk with Gareth."

"Influence me? I'd like to think I'm a free-thinking individual, thank you very much."

"That's exactly why they were so concerned. The Web's free-thinking people don't make it very far along in life. They liked me less when they found out how I felt about you."

Aniya fell silent.

"They didn't want you marrying into another rebellion that would end with one or both of us dead."

Before she could speak, Nicholas continued, "And the more I think about it, the more I agree with them. It's not safe for us to be involved like that. I was foolish to think it could ever work. If another uprising begins, especially if I have any kind of leadership role, it's unlikely I would make it out alive."

"We can take care of ourselves, Nicholas. It doesn't have to be like that."

"In any case, everything kind of hinges on my friend now. I've gone as far as I can, and so have you."

"Nicholas, who is this friend you keep talking about?"

"I told you, I can't tell you. If they find out who it is before it's time, it poses a serious threat."

Aniya groaned in frustration. "You keep saying that, but you're telling me everything else, things you never bothered to tell me before. And now that none of it matters, you'll spill your guts? Except, of course, for the identity of your friend. God forbid that you—"

"I'm telling you all this because you need to hear it. You're no good to yourself or anyone else if you're willing to give up and accept servitude or death. I'm telling you because there's still a chance. There's something greater out there that you can be a part of. I hate that your parents are gone now, but what they represented isn't dead yet. We have a chance to give new life to the Web."

"I don't care, Nicholas. I don't care about your something greater. I just want my brother back. What part of that is unclear to you? I don't want to be part of your rebellion, and if that's all you're living for, then I don't want you either. I just want my family back. That's it. That's all I—" Aniya broke down. Everything came crashing down as she finally gave in. Tears flowed freely as if she had no audience, and she let herself hang from her chains like a rag doll, letting her tears splash in the pooled blood on the floor.

After a moment of nothing but Aniya's sobs, Nicholas spoke again.

"I know, Aniya. I want him back too."

She continued to cry, not expecting or necessarily wanting any more words from Nicholas.

Hours dragged on.

At her side, Nicholas seemed to be sleeping. Either that or passed out from the pain. Aniya simply hung limply, phasing in and out of consciousness but too uncomfortable to fully fall asleep.

Finally, the door opened again, light spilling in from the hallway and blinding her again.

Two men stepped inside and unlocked their chains.

Nicholas, awake now, was the first to break the silence. "Well, it looks like we won't have to wonder about our fate for much longer. Just know that whatever happens, Aniya, I'll stay by you no matter what."

She felt a hand slip inside hers, and she didn't pull away.

"Let's go face it together, then."

40

Aniya and Nicholas were led through the white halls of the Citadel, guided by men in silver armor.

Their silver-armored escort surrounded them, but they didn't bother to lay a hand on their captives. They, like Aniya, must have known that there was truly no escape.

They even walked at a slower pace to accommodate Nicholas, who limped down the halls. Aniya fidgeted and wished they would hurry it along anyway. The longer their walk, the longer she had to imagine the horrible fate the Lightbringers had in store for them.

She had long since reasoned that whatever "servitude" was, it was the means by which the government produced its electricity. Maybe it was a new energy source from the mines, and they needed people to gather and process it. In the past, Aniya would occasionally decide that if it meant the entire Web would be supplied with free light, heat, and power, then maybe it was for the best. But seeing her brother at death's door had banished any benefit of the doubt she had ever given the Lightbringers.

Finally, they reached the end of the hallway, and the Silvers opened two huge doors in front of them.

Aniya and Nicholas stepped inside, and the doors closed behind them.

They stood in a massive room, at least thirty feet tall. It was not as wide, but it was still an impressive sight. The room was white, floor to ceiling, and on one side of the room was a full-length window that spanned from one end of the room to the other, overlooking the Hub.

A man in a gray cloak stood in front of the window, his back to them.

"Welcome."

Aniya turned her head to the left and saw another man in a white suit sitting at a long table. He was smiling at them widely, his teeth flashing a color almost as white as his clothing.

"I wish I could say that I'm sorry for the circumstances which brought you here, but for the first time in years, they were entirely out of my control. You forced my hand at every turn." He waved his hand, his smile remaining unnaturally still. "No matter. You're here now, and that's all that matters."

The man stood up and walked over to them. He took Aniya's hand and gave it one firm, simple shake. Shivers ran down her spine as the man's tongue darted across his lips.

He then took Nicholas's hand, his smile growing a fraction wider when Nicholas winced in pain as they shook.

"I am the Chancellor, as you may have guessed. This man is my trusted Adviser."

Aniya and Nicholas made no effort to introduce themselves, and neither did the Adviser, whose back remained toward them.

"My, what an unlively bunch you are this morning. I myself had a wondrous breakfast and am in the best of moods." His smile inched back down slightly. "Lucky for you, I must say."

The Chancellor walked back to his table and sat down, gesturing to two chairs across from him. "Please, sit."

Aniya, despite her distrust, gave in to her exhaustion and sat down, Nicholas close behind.

"Annelise Lyons—"

"It's Aniya," she spat.

"Aniya, then. I must say, in another life, I would have loved to have worked with you. Not since the ill-advised Uprising have I seen such . . . spunk." He laughed. "You would have made for a good Adviser. Lord knows mine lacks your personality."

Aniya glanced toward the man by the window. He remained motionless.

"I'm sure you'll be happy to know that we don't plan on killing you. If our Operative had his way, you would be dead by now, but we've found that he's a little too trigger-happy sometimes. To his merit, however, his instincts are good. If I had listened to my intuition, your parents would have died along with the rest of the rebels years ago. Maybe I was right after all." The Chancellor shot an annoyed glance at his Adviser. "But perhaps things worked out for the best. As I understand it, certain individuals were growing restless with the current state of affairs." At this, he stared directly at Nicholas. "Their removal serves as a reminder of what happens when you take advantage of the good graces of the Glorious Bringers of Light. Not that I intend to have you killed. Like I said, I'm in a good mood. You will both be allowed to live and serve the Web for the remainder of your lives."

The Adviser spoke for the first time. "I'm not so sure that's wise, your Excellency. I think the boy should die."

At this, Nicholas, who had been hunched over in his chair in pain, looked up, eyes wide open.

The Chancellor narrowed his eyes and licked his lips. "If I remember correctly, you were the one who insisted on his survival in the first place. He helped us find the girl, didn't he? And whatever happened to laying off the killing in times like these?"

"We were kind enough to let him live once, even offering full benefit among our ranks," the Adviser said. "He repaid our kindness by turning on us and damaging government property. It will be several weeks before the train is running again. I think he has served his purpose, and I believe a swift punishment is appropriate for a traitor of his stature."

The Chancellor frowned. "Perhaps you're right."

"No!" Aniya shouted, slamming her fist down on the table. "He may have tried to help me, but only because he cares about me. If you're going to punish him, then punish me too."

The Adviser shook his head before the Chancellor could respond. "There's no need for that. His death will serve as an effective demonstration of power and authority. Your time in servitude will benefit the Web and help you understand the futility of rebellion."

"It's decided, then." The Chancellor's smile was gone, his expression now somber. "Nicholas, you will be executed immediately. Aniya, you will serve the remainder of your life dedicated to the Glorious Bringers of Light and your fellow citizens. You should be honored. As we have been gracious to only accept males into our . . . rigorous program, you will be the first female in hundreds of years, a landmark occasion if I do say so myself."

Without hesitation, he pressed a button on his desk, and the large doors opened on the opposite end of the room. Four Silvers entered the room, two of them grabbing Aniya, who protested vehemently, and the other two grabbing Nicholas, who remained silent.

As the officers dragged them away from the table and out of the room, the Chancellor nodded toward Aniya.

"The Web thanks you for your service."

The doors closed with a resounding slam.

41

Nicholas let the Silvers drag him down the hallway, the heels of his shoes scraping across the floor.

"I'm sorry, Aniya."

Aniya looked up at him, but he stared dejectedly at the floor, his spirit crushed. There was no way out anymore.

"I should have just helped you escape. They would have remotely terminated me, but at least we wouldn't be stuck here now."

Aniya grimaced. "Hey, at least we made it to the Hub."

"A fat load of good that did us." Nicholas looked down and shook his head. "I'm sorry about your brother, Aniya."

Aniya gave a small smile. "At least this way I'll see him again. We'll be serving together until we die, so there's that."

One of the officers smirked. "Is that what you think? You're in for quite the surprise."

"What exactly will I be doing?"

The other officer tightened his grip on Aniya's left arm. "You'll be fulfilling your role in society, supplying free energy to the entire Web. Now shut up."

Suddenly, the two Silvers holding Nicholas changed direction and headed down another long hallway, while the officers with Aniya turned in the opposite direction.

"Aniya!" Nicholas began kicking helplessly, pulling at his captors.

"Nicky . . ." Aniya began to cry again.

"Tell William I'm sorry. I'm sorry for bringing you here. I'm sorry for your parents. I'm sorry for everything." His voice began to fade as he began to disappear into the long white hall.

Aniya nodded as she was dragged away.

The officers carrying Nicholas opened a door and pulled him inside the room, and Aniya disappeared from view.

"Aniya, I love you! I'm sorry for not telling you before now, but I love you!"

"Nicholas, I—"

The door slammed.

Nicholas's heart sank as he was dragged to his fate.

42

An intense sensation of vertigo raced through Aniya's body as the elevator zipped down at breakneck speed. If it weren't for the officers standing calmly on either side, she would have been convinced that this was how she would die, in a fiery crash at the bottom of an elevator shaft.

Finally, the descent slowed, and the elevator came to a smooth stop with a beep. Almost as if on cue, she vomited on the white floor.

The Silvers ignored this as three sets of six-inch doors opened, and they pulled Aniya out of the elevator, dragging her through her own bile.

Aniya looked around and found herself in a dark tunnel, lit only by small fluorescent lights mounted in the rock walls.

Rather than letting the officers drag her, she walked on her own, finding it painful to let her shins skid across the rock walkway.

The officers guided her to a metal sphere at the end of the path, and one of them opened what looked like a door and pushed her inside.

Aniya tumbled into the sphere and looked around. It reminded her of the train car she had shared with the Operative. There were two large cushions across from each other, and a few buttons were laid out on the opposite wall.

The Silvers climbed inside, shut the door, and pushed one of the buttons.

Aniya lurched as the sphere took off, whizzing down the tunnel almost as fast as the elevator had gone. She held her head between her knees as the vertigo only got worse.

Finally, the sphere stopped, and the Silvers helped her back out into an identical, dark tunnel. From further down the tunnel came a dim green glow, not unlike the light of the glowworms.

They continued away from the sphere and through the tunnel until they passed into a massive, glowing cavern, stretching deeper and farther than Aniya could see.

Dozens of pillars ran up and down the depth of the cavern, descending into darkness, but glowing with an eerie shimmer and bathing the rock walls in a bright green wash.

The sight was hauntingly beautiful.

Aniya looked around and noted that the wall of the cavern behind them was pure black and did not seem affected by the green light, but instead loomed blankly over the entrance she had just walked through.

The officers pushed her forward, interrupting her stare. She reluctantly continued, stepping onto a narrow walkway that protruded from the cavern wall and extended as far as she could see. She looked down at the infinite depth and felt her head rush with dizziness. Her stomach churned, and she wobbled slightly.

Behind her, one of the officers chuckled. "Thinking about taking a shortcut? We could meet you down there if you'd like."

Aniya shuddered and stepped back to the middle of the pathway but felt herself career forward again as a boot viciously met the base of her spine. Helpless, she stumbled forward, teetered on the edge for what seemed like an eternity, then lost her balance entirely and fell off the edge.

She closed her eyes tight, feeling a mixture of dread and relief. Falling to her death was almost certainly preferable to whatever torture awaited her.

However, she did not feel air rush by her like she expected. Instead, she heard the officers laugh behind her as if she hadn't moved an inch. She opened her eyes to find out that this was indeed the case.

Aniya was suspended in mid-air, floating just to the side of the walkway. After a moment, an invisible force pushed her roughly, and she landed back on the walkway, the rock floor scraping her face as she rolled.

The officers picked her back up and continued forward, still chuckling.

One of them said, "We installed that a long time ago. Many people decided they would prefer death over servitude." He stopped laughing. "I can't say I blame them."

They continued down the long pathway, heading directly for the largest of the glowing pillars. As they neared, Aniya got a better look at the source of the green light.

Rather than a seamless wash of light, each of the pillars hosted thousands of individual lights, clumped together tightly and covering the surface in a conglomerate of green light.

Each light came from an outward-facing tank, each tank housing a luminous green liquid and a dark form floating inside.

Aniya gasped.

Naked men floated in the tanks, wires protruding from various points on their bodies and long tubes attached to their mouths.

She stared in horror as the bodies in the tanks took one synchronized breath of air from the tubes. The green color of the liquid grew richer, and the wires from their bodies pulsed red.

The pillar grew brighter and then dimmed rapidly, and a pulse of green energy descended from the top of the cavern, shooting down into infinity. A few seconds later, she saw a bright yellow light respond from the depths, flashing once and then vanishing. A vibration shook the chamber, and then everything went still.

"Welcome, Aniya."

Aniya turned around and saw the black wall of the cavern come alive, revealing a massive screen.

The Chancellor looked back at her, grinning broadly.

"By now, you must have surmised the true nature of your servitude."

Aniya remained silent, her shock rendering her speechless. As the Chancellor continued, the officers led her down another pathway to the left, toward another, smaller pillar.

"Centuries ago, we found a way to harness the strongest and most pure form of energy: the *Homo sapiens*. Humans, we found, were the ultimate solution to the energy problem, one person offering more energy in a minute than our most valuable resource in its natural lifetime. As it turns out, you, our beloved citizens, are the true Lightbringers. Of course, it takes a toll on the body, as you may have seen from your brother, but we are now able to keep a host alive much longer than it could by itself. You'll outlive everyone you've ever known, so you might say we're doing you a favor."

"Gee, thanks," Aniya said, finally able to form words again.

They reached the next pillar, and the officers guided her halfway around, stopping at an empty tank.

"You will be reunited with your brother, in a way. This was his pod, and it will now be yours. It normally takes our engineers weeks to calibrate a pod to a specific individual, but since you and . . . what was his name again?"

"William!" she shouted.

"Ah yes, William. You share much of the same DNA, so

you should be a compatible host without much consequence. Or at least we hope."

Already dreading the answer, she asked, "Where is he?"

"I honestly don't know, and I truly don't care. Last I heard, we gave him to our Operative for questioning. He could still be alive, but I'm sure you've noticed that our Operative is not the most merciful individual."

Aniya's head dropped.

One of the officers accessed a computer terminal by the pod and pulled out a keyboard.

"Name?"

Aniya glared at the man.

"Annelise Lyons," the Chancellor said from the screen. As Aniya looked up at the wall, he smirked. "Forgive me. Aniya Lyons. The least we can do for the poor girl is call her by her preferred name."

The officer pecked at the keyboard and placed it back under the computer as the tank in front of her came to life. The glass barrier descended and disappeared into the floor as machinery behind the tank buzzed and lit up with green lights.

"Place her inside."

The second officer stripped her naked, taking the crystal and pocketing it after a quick examination. He then escorted Aniya onto the platform as a long tube dropped down from above. The officer placed the end of the tube over her mouth, fastening it with a strap behind her head.

"Enjoy your bath," he said, stepping off the platform.

The other officer pressed a button near the terminal, and the computer receded into the wall as the glass wall began to rise again.

Holes appeared at the bottom of the tank, and liquid gushed upward, submerging her body slowly.

The Chancellor spoke one last time. "Good night, my dear." Then the screen went dark again.

Aniya felt the warm liquid race up her body. In seconds, her body was completely engulfed in the thick, green solution.

A sharp sensation shot through her arm, and she looked down to see a red wire now embedded in her right wrist.

She looked around to see dozens of wires appear around her, each one lunging toward her body and sticking themselves into her skin.

As each wire pricked her, the pain was soon replaced with a numbing sensation as her body began to fall asleep slowly, one body part at a time.

The wires reached her head and began to jab at her. Her ear, her chin, her cheek . . .

Aniya's eyes fluttered closed, and she succumbed to the black.

PART IV

LIGHTBRINGER

43

It had been a week since Salvador's daughter had disappeared with Roland.

When he had learned of their departure the next day, Salvador of course sent a team of scouts to retrieve them. If Roland was determined to seal his fate at the hands of the Lightbringers, that was his prerogative. But Tamisra belonged in Refuge.

The scouts had come back after two days, reporting that the tunnels were empty. The blockage at the end of the tunnel hadn't even been disturbed.

Either they found another way through or they were taken long before they reached the Hub.

Whatever happened, all Salvador could do was wait. He wasn't about to send his men into the most dangerous sector in the Web on the chance that something went wrong. He had to keep telling himself that he made the right choice, that to do so would be sending innocent men to their death with no promise of Tamisra's return.

Though the guilt of potentially losing his daughter to the Lightbringers crushed him, Salvador knew he wasn't the one to blame. He cursed Roland for getting his daughter involved in a fight he had sworn off decades ago. He cursed himself for not doing enough to stop the madness in the first place when William had first come stumbling into the tunnels.

And then there was Kendall.

Kendall and his "plan."

Forget where he came from. Sure, they had resources, not to mention all the time in the world. But the plan was absurd, not to mention impossible.

Salvador wanted nothing to do with it. Not anymore. A long time ago, he had seen an opportunity to rid the Web of the Lightbringers, and so he agreed to become their symbol, the Scourge. But anything beyond that was something he had never been fully comfortable with. Even if it did work, he could never condone it.

And yet, he had sent a child to die.

Maybe this was his karmic punishment.

Blood for blood.

Whatever the cost, Salvador would have been happy to pay it years ago when he had no family, when Refuge lay in disarray. Now, for the first time since the executions, he truly regretted everything.

The knock on his door went unheard as he buried his face in his hands.

"Sir?"

Salvador looked up, not bothering to speak. Corrin stood in his doorway, holding a metal device in his hand.

"We captured one of them."

He stood up, blood flowing to his fists.

"We caught a Silver."

Barely containing the rage that consumed the guilt inside, burning it to a crisp, Salvador uttered one word. "Where?"

"The Hub tunnel, sir. He's down in the war room now, blindfolded, gagged, in a sack, the whole deal."

Salvador stepped toward the door, but Corrin didn't move out of his way. Instead, he held out the device.

"He was carrying this."

It was a tablet, a mobile video player. Not found with your typical Silver supplies.

Salvador took the tablet and pressed the play button.

"Would you like some privacy, sir?"

Salvador didn't respond. Instead, he staggered backward and let himself fall to his bed.

On the tablet, he saw his daughter hanging upside down by her toes in a dark room.

A flash of light.

His daughter screamed in pain as her body convulsed and her hair shot outward.

The room went dark again.

"No."

Another flash.

Another scream.

Salvador watched it three more times, knowing that the video was only a few seconds long and would continue to replay itself, but he was unable to look away.

Finally, he threw the tablet against the wall and screamed in rage.

"Sir?"

Corrin still stood in the doorway.

His scream had died out into a whimper, and Salvador, defeated, looked up again.

"Are we going to go get her?"

For the first time in decades, the Scourge had nothing to say. In the war, it was his job to speak for the resistance. He would inspire the rebels with rousing speeches, publish anti-Lightbringer propaganda, even hijack the sky ceiling and make Web-wide announcements to rally thousands to his side.

But now, his enemy owned him, and he truly had no words.

"We're ready, sir. We can fight if you give the command." Corrin stepped inside slowly. "We love your daughter and will

die if it means bringing her back. And Aniya . . . you know
I would do anything."

Salvador shook his head. "You would die for the chance to
save them? Because that is what you can expect. You will all of
you die. This is an obvious trap, one they would not lay for me
if they were not ready." With considerable effort, he held back
a tear. "Tamisra is surely dead already. They do not need her
anymore, now that they have attempted to use her as bait.
And Aniya? They have taken her for a much darker purpose.
That is all we are to them, you see? Tools waiting to be used.
Led to the slaughterhouse so they will have meat. Hung on
strings for their entertainment. Plugged into the wall so we
can be their light. *Que será, será.*"

He rocked back and forth. The device was dark, lying
shattered on the floor, but he could still see his daughter's
body, hear her screams.

"They don't know how strong we are," Corrin said finally.
"There will be a price, but we will gladly pay it. We knew
what we were signing up for when we started this all those
years ago. Those younger have agreed to the same risks
because they believe in what you once believed in. A world
without the puppet masters."

Salvador looked up. "You would not be so ready if you
knew the true cost."

"It doesn't matter. If we have a chance to be free, then we
will pay that cost. And if your daughter is truly dead, then
don't let it be in vain. She believed in you. It's time you believe
in yourself again." Corrin motioned to the window. "There
are people out there that need you back. Not only in Refuge,
but a whole world."

"I do not remember casting that tablet aside," Salvador
said, pointing at the destroyed device. "I know only the feeling
of coming to as my screams died. That was the remnant of
the Scourge, not the man who sits before you now.
The Scourge is dead."

"That guy was a jerk anyway," Corrin said, grinning. "The Scourge was vicious, insane, a necessary evil. What we need now is a leader to make sense of the battle before us and tell us that we can win, even if we can't. We need a father who is willing to move mountains, fight impossible odds, even give his own life to save his daughter. We need Salvador."

After a long pause, Salvador nodded. "I think I can do that."

With those words, his exhausted limbs began to stir, his fingers twitching. He got up, opened his dresser, and pulled out a massive golden sword. He could barely hold the weapon up, but the strain it put on his arms felt good.

"I think I can do that," he said again, turning the blade over and examining the steel.

He turned around.

"I think," he said, a spark in his eyes, "it is time for war."

44

Aniya's eyes flew open as a surge of energy jolted her from head to toe. She grabbed at her throat as air was forced through the tube strapped to her head, cramming her lungs with oxygen. She squirmed as the wires in her body roughly pulled themselves out of her skin, tugging at her naked body in dozens of places.

Then, the green liquid drained from the tank with a loud hiss. As Aniya's feet touched the ground, and she stood on her own, she had to grip the sides of the tank to keep her balance.

After a moment, the glass barrier sank into the floor.

Aniya removed the tube from her head and carefully stepped outside on unsteady feet as her head spun.

The cavern was empty, save for the tens of thousands of men imprisoned in similar pods.

She looked down and noticed a neatly folded robe on the ground, with a piece of paper resting on top. After looking around again to make sure she was alone, she ignored the robe and picked up the paper.

"Take the elevator back up. Fourth room on the right."

Aniya studied the handwriting. It didn't look familiar, crushing her hopes that Nicholas had found a way to escape

292 | DAVID WEBB

death. She turned the paper over, but dropped it when she heard footsteps echoing across the cavern.

Grabbing the robe, she quickly dressed and stepped into the space between two neighboring tanks, wincing as her stiff muscles complained.

"Thank you for your patience," she heard a man say, echoing along the rock walls. "I know you've been curious as to what kind of work you'd be doing, but we had to wait until your blood sample was processed by our scientists."

"Please, I just want to go home." Another male voice piped up, this one much younger.

"Sorry, kid." Another man spoke up. "You drew the short straw, so you get to serve the Web from the Hub."

The footsteps grew louder, as did the boy's protests.

Aniya grew nervous. Thanks to the cavern walls reverberating all sound, she realized there was no way to determine the newcomers' position. She stuck her head out from between the pods slowly but saw nothing.

"Are those . . . people?" The boy's voice turned to panic.

No one responded, and Aniya could hear the boy begin to cry.

"Told you."

Motion appeared out of the corner of her eye, and she pushed herself farther back into the pillar, her ragged breath racing.

"Don't worry, kid. It'll be over soon. It's just like sleeping, I'm told. A long nap. Just one you don't wake up from."

The voices were close.

Two men and a boy walked by the pod she had just left, passing directly in front of her. They didn't seem to care that the pod was empty, nor did they notice the piece of paper on the ground beside them.

"Step inside, please."

Aniya frowned in confusion. She hadn't seen any other empty pods nearby.

A latch and a quiet hissing sound emanated from Aniya's right, then a loud, rapid whoosh that quickly diminished.

Then nothing.

Aniya carefully stepped out from between the pods and nearly collapsed. The adrenaline that kept her moving was beginning to wear off, giving way to exhaustion. After taking a moment, she looked around but didn't see any sign of the group. She backtracked around the pillar to the walkway, walking as quickly as her shaking legs would allow.

She almost got back to the mouth of the cavern when she stopped in horror, realizing that the paper that had been left for her was still sitting on the ground where she dropped it.

The officers must have been distracted by their captive, but when they returned alone, they would surely see the paper next to her empty pod. Worse still, the instructions on the paper may have seemed vague to her, but they might not be as indecipherable to the officers.

Aniya spun around and ran back to her pillar, pushing the limits of her exhausted body. Her vision began to grow cloudy, and she shook her head, fighting just to stay awake.

She reached her pillar and froze.

The whooshing sound resonated throughout the cavern again, and she identified its source: on the side of the pillar was an elevator that allowed access to the seemingly infinite number of pods.

And the elevator had nearly finished its ascent.

Aniya ducked back between two different pods, still on the opposite side of the pillar from her own pod. She held her breath as she hoped the officers would come back around the circular pillar the other way, inadvertently avoiding the paper on the ground.

She heard the elevator open on the other side of the pillar, then footsteps beginning again. Of course, thanks to the echoes of the chamber, they could have been walking either way.

"You owe me dinner tonight. Told you that kid was a crier."

"Can't believe I let you sucker me into that. Like he was going to fight back. Whatever. He only—"

The footsteps abruptly halted, as did Aniya's heart.

"Did you see this?"

Aniya closed her eyes and cursed her luck.

"Do you know if this pod is down for maintenance?"

"I don't know, but this note means that something is up. We need to let the boss know immediately."

"You do it. I don't feel like winding up in one of those green baths myself."

"Seriously? You're afraid of the suits? You're lucky that kid wasn't a fighter because he probably would have taken you out."

"Come on, man. There's a difference between fighting a kid and having to tell the Operative that one of the donors got out."

"The Operative? You really think he'd get involved?"

"Oh yeah. After what happened with the girl, you can bet he'd want to know about this."

"I guess all the more reason to tell them now instead of waiting to do it in person."

"Fine, I'll radio up."

This was her only chance. Aniya darted out from between the pods and raced around the pillar, nearly falling off the edge in dizziness. She yanked at the string at her side and pulled her robe off in one motion.

Rounding the corner, she saw the officers, one of them with a radio and the note in his hands.

The two men looked up and froze in shock and confusion at the naked girl running toward them.

"What the—"

Aniya rushed the officer with the radio and wrapped her robe at his head, blinding him and choking him at the same time. Turning to the other man, who was drawing his weapon, she kicked as hard as she could, pushing the officer off the edge of the walkway and into dead space, where he hovered helplessly, his weapon drifting away from him.

The man under Aniya's robe clutched at her hands weakly as he gasped for air.

Aniya held on tight, forcing the man to his knees, then letting him fall to the stone floor, unconscious. She grabbed his weapon and turned to face the officer who had been floating in the air, just now being launched back onto the walkway.

The man landed, and as his weapon flew back toward him, he grabbed it out of the air and pointed it at Aniya.

Without checking to see if the weapon was set to tranquilizing pellets or live ammunition, she fired at the man, who froze, then dropped to the ground.

Tossing the gun aside, Aniya grabbed her robe and clothed herself again, took the note and radio from the unconscious officer, and ran back to the entrance. She looked up, half expecting the screen to come alive, but the ceiling remained dark.

Aniya ran up to the main walkway, then to the mouth of the cavern, gaining strength as adrenaline again coursed through her veins. As her vision cleared, she ran harder, dashing through the cave and to the sphere that would lead to the Citadel's elevators.

She didn't remember the journey through the sphere, and the next thing she knew she was standing in the open elevator, facing the wall.

The doors closed behind her, and she turned to see a massive display of buttons on the wall. There were hundreds, maybe thousands of small buttons, laid out neatly in rows of twenty and spanning almost from floor to ceiling. Confused, she froze.

What now?

Before she could make any choice, the elevator began

moving, taking off at an impressive rate, knocking her to the floor.

A minute later, the elevator finally stopped, and the doors opened smoothly and silently.

Aniya looked into a bright, empty hallway, completely identical to the rest of the building that she had seen so far.

How do people get around in this place?

She glanced at the note again to make sure she wouldn't wind up in the wrong place. And in the Citadel, the wrong place would probably be a very undesirable location.

Fourth room on the right.

One, two, three . . .

Aniya reached for the handle but froze. Whoever left her the note also woke her up. She was completely helpless, and someone chose to bring her back. Whoever it was wanted to help her, right?

Nicholas said he had a friend inside, but he wound up dead anyway. If his friend couldn't—or wouldn't—stop the Adviser from killing him, would he really have her best interests in mind?

A noise behind her made her jump, but a quick look around revealed nothing. It was enough to force her into action, however.

Aniya took a deep breath and opened the door.

A man in a gray cloak stood inside, facing a large control panel and studying the digital display with a hand to his chin. At the sound of the door opening, he turned and faced her.

The Adviser to the Chancellor of the Web, the one who had sentenced Nicholas to death, stepped away from the screen and toward her, a smile on his face. "Good morning, Aniya. I hope your rest was pleasant."

45

A niya found herself unable to move. Half of her wanted to turn around and run while the other half wanted to punch this man as hard as she could. One thing was certain. She wished she hadn't left the gun back in the chamber.

The Adviser bowed his head slightly. "My name is Kendall, and I'm glad to finally speak to you away from the facade of the Adviser."

Kendall. Where had she heard that name before? She racked her brain, but it was still addled from her time in the tank.

He stepped away from the control panel and toward her, and Aniya instinctively stepped backward.

"I'm sure you have many questions. We don't have a lot of time, but I'll answer as many of them as I can."

Finally, it clicked. *Trust no one but Kendall,* Roland's last words to her. *Is this Nicholas's friend? How could he sentence him to death just like that? Or did he?*

Slowly, Aniya asked, "Where is Nicholas?"

"He's safe. He's in position, waiting on my signal."

Aniya's heart soared, and she took a deep breath.

"To do what?"

"Free your brother."

Aniya's eyes widened. "William's still alive too?"

He nodded.

"Can I see him?"

"That depends on how quickly we execute our plan." Kendall gestured toward a chair. "Please, sit. You've been in the pod for a week. Your body needs to rest."

"A week?" Aniya sat in the chair, and sure enough, her head felt like it was floating as she let herself relax. "What plan?"

Kendall walked back over to the control panel. "Everything has to happen at once. One of the reasons we failed when it was just me and your brother was that I was working under pressure, and we were interrupted. But now that so many pieces are in play, with plenty of disasters to distract the Silvers, we have a much better chance of succeeding."

"You helped him escape?"

"Twice, actually. I woke him up and sent him to be with Salvador, whom you know. The idea was to reconfigure his pod and set up a chain reaction that would use William to disable the reactor. That part worked. I did some calculations, and by the time William returned, we were able to partially execute the plan."

"Salvador said he didn't know who William's partner was."

Kendall shrugged. "I don't know why he would keep that from you."

"So he knew you were trying to stop the Lightbringers? Aren't you the closest person to the Chancellor?"

"Making me perfect for the job. Unfortunately, it wasn't enough, and we only succeeded in shutting down the reactor temporarily. Due to his weakened state, he wasn't capable of pushing enough energy in the final phases of our plan to shut it down permanently. I was able to get your brother out of here alive, barely, and I put him on a train to Holendast, but

I couldn't escort him any further. I needed to stay here and redo the calculations. Admittedly, I was taking a risk, since the power was out and the train had to run on diesel, making for a much slower journey."

"You put him on one of your own trains? He could have been seen!"

"I marked the cargo as sensitive and forbid passenger admittance. He went to Holendast alone. In hindsight, I should have sent an armed guard with him. My only thought at the time was to get him as far away from the Hub as possible."

"What now? Are you going to try again?"

"Yes."

"You said that everything has to happen at once. What did you mean by that?"

He paused. "Your brother and Nicholas are going to break out of the Hub. That's the first piece that will raise the alarm as well as secure their safety. The second is an explosion on the border of the Hub and the subsequent attack. That will further confuse the Silvers and draw them far away from the reactor."

"Attack?"

"The third is you, the most crucial step. This is where it gets complicated. We need you to take your brother's place in the pods. You may have noticed that once a host is placed in a pod, it becomes part of a hive mind, a collective body of energy. We need a conscious person inside the loop to break the cycle and start a chain reaction that will, in a sense, change the instructions that each host unconsciously follows. Their new directive will be to then pump three bursts of energy into the reactor. The first one is normal and expected. The second will be too much for the reactor to handle so soon after the last one, and it will trip a failsafe and send it into reserve. The third will disable the reactor."

"Permanently?"

"That will require one final step. Let's see if we even get that far, and then we can finish the job."

Aniya paused. "So, your plan was to bring me here the whole time?"

Kendall nodded again. "We can't use your brother again. His body is spent from years in the pod, and he doesn't have the physical endurance to complete the process. He barely made it the first time. As soon as I knew you were on the run, the plan was hatched. I requested Nicholas be used to bring you in because that's the only way I could ensure your survival. Of course, derailing the train was not part of the plan. That was a dangerous move we had to make before the Operative could harm you or Nicholas."

"Why did he come after us? Couldn't you tell him to bring us in alive?"

"I did. But the Operative was growing increasingly suspicious of my motives. He was never comfortable with my order to use Nicholas against you, and he got dangerously close to figuring out my secret. I didn't have a choice. I told Nicholas to bring down the train to give you both a chance to escape. In the end, everyone ended up where they were supposed to be. We're on track, so long as things go according to plan from here on out. But first, you should take a moment and rest. Waking up from that state is quite disorienting, and you need all the strength you can get."

"I'm not sure we have as much time as you think."

Kendall frowned. "Why not?"

Aniya pulled the radio from the pocket of her robe. "I ran into trouble on my way up here."

"What happened to them?" Kendall grabbed the radio, his peaceful demeanor disappearing.

"I knocked one of them unconscious and shot the other one."

"Dead?"

Aniya shrugged.

"Where was this?"

"Right next to where I woke up."

Kendall spun around and started tapping away at the control panel. Seconds later, camera footage of the chamber appeared.

Aniya squinted and saw the two officers, one of them floating in mid-air and the other lying still on the ground next to her empty pod. The first officer suddenly flew back onto the ground, but he just rolled back off into the dead space after a few seconds, floating once again.

He appeared to be unconscious, stuck in some kind of loop.

"My apologies. I should have been, but I wasn't watching when you woke up. I was preoccupied. But at least we can get rid of one of them." Kendall grimaced and pressed a button.

On the screen, the floating officer suddenly dropped, vanishing into the dark.

"Did you just kill him?"

"We can't take any chances. Timing is everything, and we need to make sure we get it right this time." Kendall pressed the button again, then relaxed and turned toward Aniya. "Unfortunately, while I can turn the gravity shafts on and off, I can't push the other officer into the pit from here. We'll have to move sooner than I planned."

Aniya didn't respond. Instead, she stared over Kendall's shoulder. She could have sworn she saw something move.

"You need to get back down to the chamber. Once you're inside the pod, I'll send the signal to Nicholas and order the attack. That should give us enough time to execute our plan."

"What attack are you talking about?"

Kendall smiled. "I'll show you."

But no sooner did he say that than Aniya's radio crackled to life in Kendall's hand.

"We've got a problem down here with the—"

Kendall's hands flew across the keys under the control

302 | DAVID WEBB

panel, and the radio went silent. He and Aniya looked up at the screen to see the second officer, now awake, speaking into his own radio.

"Did you turn off his radio from here?"

Kendall shook his head and turned to her with a grim look. "I can't do that. I had to shut down all radio channels. Unfortunately, they've already heard part of the message, and they'll get the channels back up and running shortly. We need to move now." He pressed a button on the control panel, and the screen changed again to show a white hallway that bobbed up and down with the camera's movement. "Are you in position?"

"Almost there." Nicholas's voice came over the screen, and Aniya's heart leapt. "Did you hear the radio transmission just now?"

"Sadly, yes. Our schedule just got a little tighter. Go get William."

"What if he doesn't go with it?"

"Just get him out of here. Aniya's already agreed to it anyway."

"To how much of it?"

"Get William and get out." Kendall pressed the same button, and the screen disappeared.

Suddenly, the white room turned to red as a loud alarm sounded. Kendall typed at the panel again, and the screen showed the reactor chamber, now flooded with dozens of officers.

"Great. Change of plans." He pulled a gun from his holster and shot Aniya in the chest.

46

A drenaline coursed through Aniya's body, and she opened her eyes to find herself back in the pod, suspended naked in the green liquid. She floated gently, the tube strapped to her head and supplying her with a steady flow of oxygen.

"Aniya, can you hear me? I can't see you from up here, but nod if you can hear me."

Kendall's muffled voice barely penetrated the tank, but she nodded.

"Good. I'm picking up movement in your pod. Sorry for shooting you, even if it was just a tranquilizer. I had to make it look like I found you wandering the halls and caught you. You're now alone in the chamber because the entire Hub is now looking for your brother and Nicholas."

Aniya peered through the murky green liquid, up at the cavern wall, and saw Kendall's face stretched across the giant screen.

"As soon as I start this process, it won't take long for the Hub to be put on full alert, so it's time to distract them. I thought you might want to see this."

Kendall's face disappeared, and the screen showed a wide

view of the cliffside of the Hub. The image seemed static, but after a few seconds, a large explosion shook the earth, rock flying away from the cliffs, followed by a steady, large stream of smoke. From the smoke appeared dozens of moles with riders, followed by hundreds of running men and women with guns and spears.

One of the riders looked directly at the screen, and Aniya's heart soared as she recognized Salvador. She saw him launch a spear toward the camera source, and then the screen went dark.

"That should keep the Silvers busy enough. In the meantime, let's get started."

An incredible heat surged through Aniya's body, and she cried out into the tube in pain.

"I imagine that hurt a little. That was the link being broken between you and the other pods. Your body was mostly awake, but still working in tandem with the rest of them. I had to shock it, if you will, to finish waking it up and break the chain. Now I have to change your pod's programming, which will then re-sync you and update every single other pod. To do this to each pod at the same time would be impossible."

Aniya simply floated in the liquid while Kendall typed away. Her mind was beginning to wake up again, and she could hear the individual keys over the screen.

"You'll now feel three ebbing and flowing waves of energy. I have to warn you that this is not going to be pleasant."

Without giving her time to think, every part of her body suddenly went cold as the wires protruding from her skin glowed red. Then, just as quickly, her body heated up immensely. Her mind and body disoriented, she vomited into the tube what little food was in her stomach. Instead of letting her breathe it back in, however, the tube sucked up the vomit and the air in her lungs. The bile disappeared, and she hyperventilated as new oxygen came back down the tube.

"That was the first wave. You and your brother are the only ones who have been conscious during one of those. I don't envy you. Get ready for the second one."

Aniya groaned as her mind spun.

The cold feeling returned, this one seeming to last longer. Aniya curled up her fists and tensed her body, feeling energy suck out of every pore. Then the heat came, and her gut wrenched. She didn't vomit, but only because there was nothing left to spit up. The tube did not seem to sense that, however, and it sucked away the air from her lungs.

"Very good. Just one more."

Aniya's vision began to go dark again.

She tried to speak but only had strength to think. *Wait. Please, just wait a second.*

There was no delay, however, and all energy that Aniya had managed to muster back up vanished once again. She screamed into the tube in agony as her body trembled. Within this wave, however, there were several mini-pulses that sucked her dry over and over and over, keeping her in a perpetual state of cold and pain for several seconds.

Finally, the heat came again, and Aniya went limp. Her vision was now completely black. Her extremities, though warm again, were numb.

"Aniya, can you hear me?"

Kendall's voice came to her as nothing more than a whisper.

She heard, she understood, but she could not muster the strength to even nod.

"Aniya?"

She had nothing. She couldn't even feel the liquid receding around her, her body collapsing to the ground, or the taste of fresh air as the tank door descended into the floor. Now that she wasn't submerged, she could hear a bit better, though.

"Aniya, I can't hit you with any more adrenaline. Your body wouldn't be able to handle it. You need to wake up."

She slowly opened her eyes. *Aren't we done? Can't you just leave me here?*

"Take a moment if you need to, but don't wait too long. We're running out of time. The reactor is temporarily disabled, but after the last incident, they routed the reactor to backup generators so it wouldn't take as long to get started again. Besides, the Citadel is now under full alert. They'll all know by now that the reactor is down, so even with the battle outside, it's only a matter of time before reinforcements show up. So please, Aniya. Wake up."

With all her strength, Aniya slowly pulled the tube off her head, letting herself breathe natural air again. That helped greatly, and her vision began to clear.

"That's it. You're getting there. We could have proceeded with the next step, but you'll need your strength for that one. Besides, I can't bring myself to do it without asking you first."

Aniya finally spoke, but in a raspy voice barely above a whisper. "What more could you possibly do to me?"

Silence.

"Aniya, you have to die."

47

"Well, at least it can't get any worse than this," Roland groaned as he hung from his feet.

Tamisra laughed, blood pouring from her open wounds. "You're right. I think we've hit an all-time low."

Shaking his own blood from his head as it trickled down his suspended body, Roland grinned. The details of Tamisra's face were beginning to get a bit fuzzy, probably a side effect of the massive blood loss, but she looked just as beautiful, even upside down and blood-soaked. Knowing the pain he felt paled in comparison to hers, he kept trying to distract her.

"You know, if I look at you at just the right angle, you kind of look like Curry. Just as fierce, loyal, and don't get me started on your nose."

"Are you calling me a mole?" Tamisra laughed again.

"If it looks like a mole, talks like a mole . . ." He trailed off, giving into laughter himself.

The room echoed their forced mirth. When the laughter subsided, complete silence fell on the room again.

"Do you think Aniya ever escaped?" Tamisra finally spoke.

"I don't doubt that she can, but since we're still hanging here, I'd say she hasn't gotten around to it yet."

"That's if she even finds us. I can't hear anything out there. I wonder if we're even in the Hub. If we are, it'd be nice of her to hurry up."

At least they weren't dangling from the ceiling with cords around their toes anymore. That had been incredibly painful. But hanging by their feet wasn't much better.

Tamisra piped up again. "Can't you die if you hang like this for too long?"

Roland sighed. "Probably. But I'm really trying not to think about it."

"Sorry."

Trying unsuccessfully. Every breath was a battle thanks to the increased weight on his lungs. Every gasp for air just made Roland more and more sure that if they stayed hanging like this for another few short hours, they would indeed die.

"Are you hungry?"

Roland groaned. As much as he cared for her, Tamisra hadn't stopped talking for more than a minute since their captors last left them. He was grateful for the company, but it was trying his patience after the three hours they had been alone.

"What I wouldn't give for some mole right now," she said, audibly licking her lips.

He smirked, trying to at least enjoy the talk. "Yeah, some Curry sounds real good right now . . . or maybe some Brisket!"

"Stop it!" She shrieked and laughed at the same time. "That's insensitive."

"It's not my fault that you give them names like Curry and Brisket."

Tamisra smiled. "It's a habit we got into. For the longest time, we captured them and kept them for food, but our parents knew we would get attached to them. So instead of letting us name them, they would give them names of food so it wouldn't hurt so much when they would eventually be slaughtered and eaten. I don't know why they thought that would work, but they did it anyway. We didn't figure out how to ride them until a few years ago, but I guess the habit had already stuck."

It went silent again.

Seconds later, he heard Tamisra sigh in frustration.

"I almost forgot about the whole torture thing for a second there."

Roland smiled. "Thinking about food?"

"Yeah . . ."

The door opened, and light flooded inside, along with the sound of a blaring alarm. When the door closed again, the light and sound vanished.

Roland blinked away the spots of light furiously as Tamisra began to scream.

"Let me go!" Her shrieks echoed throughout the room. "I'm going to get down from here, and I'm going to rip you limb from limb!"

Roland began to thrash, letting his body swing violently from the rope as he fought to get free.

Tamisra's voice moved across the room as she continued to protest.

"Where are you taking her?" Roland turned to follow the noise, but still couldn't make out any details.

The door opened again, and he closed his eyes tight.

A man spoke. "Get her out of here safely. Take her to the cliffs."

Then silence.

Roland opened his eyes again and looked around. "Hello?"

A few seconds later, a voice spoke next to his ear.

"Hello, Roland."

He turned his face toward the voice, making out faint details of a face in the darkness.

"I need your help."

Roland gritted his teeth as he recognized the voice from the sky ceiling transmissions they occasionally received in Holendast. "Our glorious Chancellor. What makes you think I would help you?"

"Because I just let your girlfriend go. This entire building is about to be bathed in radiation, and she will be safe on the edge of the Hub. You have my word."

"Why should I believe you?"

The Chancellor's voice turned sickeningly sweet. "Because now I'm offering you a chance to save another girl you care for."

"Aniya."

"She stands to destroy everything we've worked for. This entire sector, maybe more. Even I can't guess the full ramifications of her actions. But they will be catastrophic."

"You're asking me to help you win?"

The Chancellor laughed. "There are no winners here, Roland. Damage has been done. Irreversible damage. But it's not too late. We can still salvage the Web. We can still have peace."

Roland shook his head. "Forget it. Peace through slavery isn't much of a peace."

"I don't believe you understand. She's not posing any risk to me, or even the Lightbringers. Rather, she threatens our very way of life. Admittedly, it's not ideal for everyone, but it's worked for centuries. She also threatens the safety of everyone in the Hub, including herself. She plans to take her own life in order to bring about the destruction of thousands more, all for the perceived safety of the Web, which would be forever without power, a governing body. The world will be plunged into darkness, both literally and figuratively."

Roland shrugged, ignoring the amusing mental image of an upside-down shrug.

"I'll forgive you for your short-sightedness. I know you,

Salvador, and your merry band of misfits are bent on revolution, but I don't think you've bothered to consider the consequences." The voice moved away, and Roland realized that the man was pacing. "I blame myself, really. I saw the signs. Despite the efforts of certain conspirators, I knew what was going on. I've had a good idea of their plans for the better part of twenty years. Thankfully, I have prepared, more than they can imagine. I will humbly say that it took me longer than it should have to realize that my trusted Adviser was at the root of it all. That discovery was only today, far too late. But let me assure you, Roland, that whatever happens here today, I will live. However, the Web will never be the same again. So, trust me when I say that I need your help not to save me, but to save this world."

Roland spat. "You're wasting your breath. If it means our death to bring about the end of your tyranny, so be it."

The Chancellor laughed again. "You really don't get it. The people who sent me, who sent Kendall—they don't change. It's the same wheel, only a different spoke. The Web will be just like you left it, only without power. Worst case scenario, this colony will be destroyed, and they will move on to the next." He leaned in close again. "If nothing else, dear boy, don't do it for me. Don't do it for this world, this Web that you claim to love so much. Do it for Aniya. Even if everything else I said is a lie, Aniya is below the Citadel right now, about to give her life away for nothing. If you don't believe anything else I said, believe that. She will die for no reason, and you can stop it."

"That's just the problem. I have no reason to believe you."

"And I have no reason to lie to you. If you get down there and are unsatisfied with the information I've given you, feel free to come back up and kill me yourself. But you're wasting time. For your sake, mine, and everyone's in the entire Web, it is of the utmost importance that she lives."

Roland glared at the Chancellor, his grim face barely visible in the shadows.

"Cut me down."

48

Aniya couldn't decide if she was shocked or hearing what she knew all along. All the secrets, all the half-truths she had been told, everything added up to this. She had to die.

Kendall continued after a moment.

"Your brother and I failed the first time because I was not aware of the reactor's final failsafe. You see, when the reactor receives too much power, it defaults to a restricted reserve as a way of further limiting any incoming power. I knew this. What I didn't know was that if the reactor somehow manages to overload, like it just did, it shuts itself down completely and redirects all power back to its source to avoid overloading the core and destroying the entire reactor. I discovered this final failsafe with your brother, but by the time I realized, he was too weak for a fourth blast, and the Silvers had already interrupted us."

Regretting the words the instant she said them, she cleared her throat and spoke a little louder. "But if we wait a little bit, you can just use me for a fourth blast, right? The last three were awful, but I don't think another would kill me."

"I'm afraid not. Like I said, the reactor has shut itself down and is prepared to reverse any incoming power. Any energy we fire at the reactor would just be redirected right back to you and do nothing but hurt you. A lot. The only solution is to jumpstart the reactor. This will stop the energy redirection because it needs to accept reserve power to start back up. It won't even have time to activate the failsafe that shut down the reactor to begin with. We are then free to bombard the core. The only way to do so is by diverting all power into a single source and then blasting the core all at once. It will also confuse the reactor because it expects a small amount of power from thousands of different pods and won't expect so much from one source."

"And I'm that one source?"

"That's right. Unfortunately, even though I've prepared your body for this while you were in the tank for a week, containing the combined energy of several thousand hosts all at the same time for even just a second will kill you. It might make you stronger for a few seconds, but your body simply can't handle it, let alone your mind."

Aniya shook her head. "I don't know if I can do that."

"I understand. It's a lot to ask. We can try it with any of the other pods, but it requires a conscious host. We would have to wake them up and ask them to sacrifice their life instead. Besides, it has a very low chance of success that way. Your body has been conditioned to temporarily handle that much energy due to changes I made to your pod before you were first placed inside, and again by keeping you awake during the surges just now."

"There has to be another way."

"I'm afraid not, Aniya. If there were anything else we could do, I'd be open to suggestions, but we're running out of time."

Her body wasn't even strong enough to cry. "I just wanted my brother back. That's all I wanted."

"I know, Aniya." Kendall's voice grew quiet. "And you can still have him back. I'm not going to make you do it. I can't force you to do something like this. If nothing else, we've temporarily disabled their reactor again, and by the looks of the battle in the city outside, we've struck a huge blow to the Lightbringers. They won't forget this, and we might be able to come back and finish what we started with someone else. But maybe not. The Operative is catching on to my game, especially after the incident on the train, so it's only a matter of time before I'm discovered. This is the single best time we have to end the Lightbringers for good. Their entire authority is based on the fact that they can provide free power. Once that's gone, once we blow their precious Hub to pieces, they'll have nothing. I know you only came here to get your brother back, but he is committed to finishing the work your parents started years ago. He can't do that, but you can. Right here and right now."

Aniya turned her head to face the empty pod. Going back inside . . . the thought filled her with dread. Even if the pain would eventually stop and release her to death, the thought of going through the torturous process again horrified her.

But this was the only way to truly save her brother. If the Lightbringers remained in power, they would hunt her, Nicholas, William, and Roland for the rest of their lives.

This way, she might not ever see them again, but they would at least be alive.

Even if she chose to run and save her own life, what kind of life would it be, knowing her friends and remaining family would never live in peace again? Knowing that she could have done something to put a stop to it?

It was the only option.

"I'll do it." Even as she said the words, a peace flooded Aniya's mind. She came here to save her brother, and she would finally succeed.

"Are you sure?"

"Yes. I've been fighting to stay alive this entire time, and I guess it's worked. But only because other people get hurt, even die because of me. The only way to keep them safe now is to die for them."

"Very well. The Web will be eternally thankful for what you're about to do, Aniya. I'll make sure they all know of your sacrifice."

"Just make sure Nicholas and my brother get out before the Hub is destroyed."

Kendall nodded. "You have my word. Just one moment." With that, he disappeared from the screen on the ceiling.

Aniya took a deep breath and pulled herself to her feet carefully, gripping the computer monitor attached to her pod with shaking white knuckles.

The monitor still bore two words: "Aniya Lyons."

She had chosen the name years ago, giving up the name Annelise for a moniker that seemed more suitable to her personality. Annelise sounded like a girl who would always be wearing a dress, refusing to go outside in the artificial rain for fear of getting her feet muddy.

It had crushed her father. He loved the name Annelise. He said it was a special name for a special girl, the light of his life. Aniya, on the other hand, always preferred the dark and was frequently chastised for extinguishing the candles in the house during Black Days.

But Aniya was the girl who brought nothing but trouble. She asked for it, always breaking curfew, skipping classes. And now, she was the girl who got people killed.

No more.

With some effort, she carefully pecked on the keyboard with one finger, finally changing the display to read "Annelise Lyons."

She released the monitor slowly and let her legs bear her full weight. Her knees knocked together, and she fell back toward the ground.

But she didn't hit the rock below. Instead, a set of arms caught her and lowered her gently to the ground.

Aniya opened her eyes again and saw a fuzzy Roland kneeling above her, taking off his cloak and covering her naked body. He had snuck up on her, an easy task in her disoriented state.

"Gotta say, Aniya," he said, a mischievous grin on his face. "You're not looking too great."

Aniya laughed, but it came out as a long wheeze.

"Don't hurt yourself." Roland's grin disappeared as he looked around. "What's going on?" He looked around at the columns of green light. "What is this place?"

Rather than answering his question, Aniya clutched his hand weakly. "How did you find me?" She traced the dried blood on his face with her other hand. "And what happened to you?"

Roland ignored both questions. "What happened to me? Aniya, what happened to you?"

Before she could answer, Kendall reappeared on the screen.

"All right. William and Nich—" He froze. "What are you doing here?"

Roland narrowed his eyes in suspicion, but he said carefully, "Kendall?"

"I assume Salvador told you about me?"

Roland nodded. "What's wrong with Aniya? She looks like a ghost. And what is this place?"

"You're not too far off. The cavern you're sitting in, put simply, is a giant machine the Lightbringers constructed to extract natural energy from humans to power the worlds we live in. Aniya has agreed to sabotage the machine, but the process requires her body to be used as a catalyst to overload the reactor. Unfortunately, while it will permanently disable the machine and destroy a large part of the Hub, it will also kill her."

"What?" Roland glared at Kendall, then looked down at Aniya in disbelief. "You agreed to this?"

Aniya nodded.

The silence that followed stretched on as Roland seemed to process this information, and time slowed to an exaggerated crawl due to Aniya's half-conscious state.

"No."

Roland shook his head repeatedly, either in denial or disbelief. Aniya couldn't tell.

"There's no way I'm letting you do this. We didn't come all this way for you to die in a hole."

Aniya quietly laughed again. "We've lived our entire lives in a hole, Roland. It was bound to happen sooner or later."

"She's already agreed," Kendall said. "This noble act of sacrifice will end the tyranny of the Lightbringers for good and ensure the safety of you, her brother, Nicholas . . . the entire Web."

Roland looked back down. "Nicholas? You found him?"

"Don't let your feelings for her stop her from finishing the work her parents started."

"My parents would never have wanted this for Aniya." Roland gently laid Aniya's head on the ground and stood up, clenching his fists. "They would have fought tooth and nail to keep her away from this place and away from you."

"Roland—"

"I'll do it. I'll take her place. Get Aniya out, get William out, get everyone out. If my death means the end of the Lightbringers, I'm okay with that."

Aniya reached up and grabbed his arm. "No, you can't. It has to be me."

"That's ridiculous." Roland brushed her hand away.

"No, she's right," Kendall said. "The pod is genetically programmed, assigned to William's DNA and recalibrated slightly to allow his sister's. If you stepped in there, it wouldn't do anything but kill you."

"No, it'll work." Roland gave a sad smile. "She's my sister."

Aniya gaped and spoke in unison with Kendall. "What?"

Roland looked down at her and nodded. "We were born as twins, and rather than let the Lightbringers take one of us away from your parents and William because of the two-child limit, our parents gave me to Gareth, whose family was killed after the war. They didn't tell you or William for my safety. Gareth didn't even tell me. Salvador told me and warned me not to tell you, but of course I would have if we didn't get separated."

Roland looked up to face Kendall again. "So, I'll work just as well as Aniya. Just make sure she gets out of here."

"But you won't. Not only did I have to recalibrate the machine and customize William's old pod to match her DNA as close as I could, but her body has been given a week to acclimate to the machine and the energy transfer process. You haven't been prepared and therefore wouldn't survive nearly as long as she would. And if the host dies or even falls unconscious before the process is complete, it won't work, and we'll be back where we started."

Roland gestured toward Aniya's shivering body. "Look at her. She's close enough to death as it is. Do you really think she'll survive long enough to finish it?"

Kendall began to speak again, but Roland cut him off.

"Forget it, Kendall. She won't be dying today. I'm taking her place, and that's final. If you have a problem with it, come down here to push her inside yourself, but we'll be long gone." Roland looked down at Aniya. "Besides, I don't have anyone left. You have William and Nicholas, even this Kendall guy who apparently doesn't care if you make it or not."

Aniya shook her head. "William's your brother too."

"Not really. I didn't know until just recently. I don't think William even knows. I don't have anyone."

Tears finally began to surface as Aniya found energy to cry, and she touched his face. "You have me."

Roland smiled again but clutched her hand firmly. "Not if

you give yourself up now. One of us is going to die today, and I'm not going to let it be you."

They gazed at each other for a long moment before Kendall finally spoke again.

"Fine. Get in the machine. Aniya, you'll have a few minutes while the machine cold starts and the process begins, but if you're still here in ten minutes, I can't promise your survival."

"What about you?"

Kendall shrugged. "I'll try to make it out, but I have to stay until the process is finished. After that, between the battle outside, the radiation that will be seeping up from underground, and the Operative looking for a traitor, I'm not sure I'm getting out of the Citadel. Besides, when the reactor blows, there's no telling what it will do to the Hub. Things are already falling apart up here thanks to the work we've done so far. In all likelihood, this is it for me."

Aniya looked at Roland again. "I'm not in any condition to run, Roland. If you do this, we'll probably both die. Let me do it, please."

Roland clutched her hand. "You'll make it, Aniya. I have no doubt in my mind. But you'd better leave now."

After another pause, Aniya nodded. She kissed his cheek gently. "Thank you."

With one last smile, Roland stood up and took a deep breath.

Then, a blast echoed against the rock walls, and Roland fell over on top of her, blood flowing from a hole in his back.

49

S alvador opened the large door and peered inside. Seeing the man standing on the other end of the room, Salvador closed the door behind him and approached the large window overlooking the trembling Hub, joining the man standing alone.

It was a strange sight. One man was in an elegant, white suit. The other one was fully covered in ornate, golden armor.

Neither man spoke, instead watching the ground crumble as sinkholes formed and fault lines opened. The destruction of the Hub was imminent. It was now only a matter of time.

Pieces of the sky ceiling fell thousands of feet down onto the dirt valley, the buildings, the streets. The falling sky burst as it hit the ground, sending sparks flying. Even in collapse, the artificial sky provided some form of light.

Men fought on the ground below, ignoring the debris falling around them. Muzzle flashes reflected off silver armor. Fire illuminated the piles of dead bodies—Salvador's men, the Silver Guard, and mole alike.

Corrin had been right. The cost was great, but victory would come at last. They might all of them die, but they would take their oppressors with them. The Uprising would finally come to a bloody, well-deserved end.

The man in the white suit spoke.

"I was wondering how long it would take you to make your way to me."

"Is that why you are still here, Noah?"

"I knew you couldn't resist one last visit to gloat." The Chancellor walked back to his desk and sat down. "So, what do you have to say? 'I told you so?' No need for that."

Salvador remained by the window. "That implies that you already knew how your road would end. I see hundreds of bodies out there that prove otherwise."

"A waste, I agree. But by the time I realized the inevitability of it all, I also knew that it was too late to try to stop it. *Que será, será*, Aram. Your favorite words." The Chancellor drank from a glass, then licked his lips. "Sorry. Salvador." He laughed.

Salvador shrugged. "I did not give myself that name. Call me what you wish."

"You taught me a valuable lesson, I'll give you that. But I was prepared for this, and it is not the end for me or those who still believe in what I've created. A setback. A change of scenery. Nothing more."

"The Director may have a thing or two to say about that, Noah."

The Chancellor waved his hand. "The Director does not care for the politics of the Underworld. He only cares that we provide for him what we promised him. And given that these tragic times are a direct result of his involvement, he apparently doesn't even care about that as much as I thought."

"You know how it works," Salvador said. "This had to play out naturally. Any involvement would destroy the illusion that he has worked hard to protect. I sincerely doubt that this was his plan."

"I wouldn't be so sure. How long ago was it that he asked you to spy on me?"

Salvador paused.

"Yes, I know he came to you first. It was all a little too convenient. Your departure, Kendall's arrival, the Uprising. And don't pretend there was anything natural about this. I know you've been in contact with Kendall. You sent the girl here to finish her brother's job, didn't you? There's no way you would have done so unless my oh-so-loyal Adviser told you that it would work. The Director's hand has been at work the entire time. Do you really think that any of this is a surprise to him?"

"If you remain so sure of the Director's sovereign hand, what makes you think that he will allow you to live?"

The Chancellor licked his lips again. "Kendall could have killed me at any time. But in the end, no one in the sectors cares about the Hub or who governs the Web. As long as they have their power, they're happy. Even if it means that a few of their children must leave to serve their leaders, they understand in the end. No, I doubt very much that the Director cares whether I live or die. I think he assumes that even if I live, I will have lost all influence in this world. I believe, in this regard, that the Director is wrong."

"For someone who respects his power so much, you place a terrible amount of trust in your own will. Even if you do live, if you prove that you still have power in this world, he will ensure that you do not survive."

"So be it. I've enjoyed the position I've been given for a long time. If it's really my time to go, then I wish the best of luck to Kendall. But I do not intend to go quietly."

"As you wish," Salvador said. With that, he drew his massive sword from the sheath on his back and made a broad swipe toward the Chancellor, slicing his chest and sending him rolling off his chair and onto the floor.

Salvador approached the supine man calmly.

324 | DAVID WEBB

The Chancellor lay on the floor, writhing in pain as he bled out. But despite the wound, his words were calm. "And here I thought you came for an amicable conversation."

"You lost that right when you took my daughter, Noah."

The Chancellor laughed, coughing up blood. "Your daughter is of no concern to me. Why do you think I let her go?"

"I know how this works. She outlived her usefulness. I am truly surprised you did not kill her. When she showed up in the hands of your men out there, I knew you realized you were beaten. You hoped I would take her and leave, did you not?" Salvador stepped on the Chancellor's chest, pressing his heel down on the blood-soaked tear in the dictator's suit.

"Whether you leave or not is of no consequence to me. The survival of you and your daughter has no bearing on my plans."

"Says the man under my boot." He pressed harder. "You took her and lured me here. Why? You had to have known that my family has grown in the last two decades. Even if we lose today, it would be devastating to you. Why pick a fight you might not win? Why now?"

The Chancellor gave a pained smile. "Why indeed? There's a question you're not asking, Aram."

"What are you talking about?"

"You keep asking why. That implies that I took your daughter to begin with."

Salvador's eyes narrowed. "Did you take my daughter?"

The Chancellor laughed again. "I think you know the answer. I think you knew before you stepped into this room. I remember who you were, and I remember what you turned into. I would not be alive if you truly believed that I took your daughter."

"But you freed her. You could not have done that if you did not know if she was here."

"Little happens in the Web that escapes my attention.

I was notified that your daughter and her boyfriend had been captured." He stuck out his lips slightly and clucked his tongue. "And my heart went out to your poor daughter, which is why I set her free."

Salvador shook his head. "You are but a snake. Your precious Hub is crumbling around you because you were deemed unfit for your position. To trust you is foolish."

"Then don't trust me." The Chancellor shrugged. "It doesn't matter. But now I have a question for you. Why didn't you tell anyone our secret? You could have turned the entire Web against me long ago."

"Panic is a powerful thing. Look out your window again. Your men are scattered. They realized their defeat, and now they are in disarray. If I had told the Web how you harvest electricity, what you do to their children, they would be angry, yes. But they would be scared."

"Liar."

Salvador glared into the Chancellor's eyes but said nothing.

"You can lie to your flock all you want, shepherd, but you cannot lie to me. They still believe that it was the Light-bringers who cut off your finger, don't they? That we tortured you? It's a shame the smartest of them can't tell the difference between an injury and a birth defect."

Salvador remained silent.

"I see through you, Aram. If you had won eighteen years ago, I can tell you what would be three miles underneath us right now. I know how you would sustain power." The Chancellor reached up and grabbed Salvador's legs, blood splashing over the Scourge's golden armor. "I can tell you what would have changed. Nothing. Because you know that while our system is cruel, it works. It keeps the world alive. If the Light-bringers go, the rest of the world goes with us. No, you would have carried the secret to your grave. You would have been a wiser ruler, a kinder one, but you would have maintained our one true purpose. You knew it when you were my Adviser, and you know it now. It's so much bigger than this Web. It's so much bigger than me, and certainly so much bigger than you."

Salvador's heart sank as the Chancellor's words echoed in his ears. He held a hand to his eyes and shook his head. Then blood flowed from his shoulder as a bullet made its way through the cracks in his armor and ripped through his body. He staggered backward and fell to the ground, grabbing his shoulder in pain.

Behind him, a second bullet fired. Glass shattered.

Salvador turned in time to see the Chancellor stagger his way toward the open window. He had a white backpack on now.

"So long, Aram, Salvador, whatever you choose to call yourself. I hope to see you again, no matter what the world is tomorrow." With that, the Chancellor stepped through the open window and fell.

Salvador scrambled toward the window, trying to ignore the pain. He watched as the Chancellor fell, opening a parachute halfway down and gliding slowly toward the trembling ground below.

"A parachute?" He rolled his eyes. "He really was prepared."

Salvador turned and let himself sprawl out on the floor as he bled, looking up at the white ceiling.

He had spent so much of his adult life despising the man he knew as the Chancellor. He was famous for his hatred of the dictator, and he had built a platform on the promise that he would kill the man and change the Web for good.

But was Noah right? If the Uprising had been successful, would anything be different?

He couldn't say for sure. The thought terrified him as he realized that there was more truth to the Chancellor's words than he cared to admit.

And if Noah was right, then Salvador was an even bigger fraud than he thought. He had promised to free the Web, but if he had succeeded, just how free would they really be?

Even his name was a lie. Theodore had thought it was appropriate for the savior of the Web, but what kind of savior would willingly imprison and torture his followers?

The one thing he knew was that he wasn't Salvador anymore. He wasn't even Aram. Both names had lost their meaning.

Salvador was a fighter, a symbol for freedom, a lie.

Aram was a trusted Adviser, a dutiful employee, a lie.

Somewhere in the middle was a loyal friend, a father to many, a leader . . . a lie.

As it turned out, Salvador never had the chance to prove the Chancellor right. He had not betrayed the Web, but he also had done nothing to fix it. He had only made it worse. Even now that he had learned from his mistakes, now that he had helped Kendall end the lie for good, would the world be any better?

And at what cost? The Web would forever change, finally free of the Chancellor, but only because he sent an innocent girl to her death.

And now that he had committed his unforgivable crime, the Web no longer needed Salvador, and he no longer wanted the Web.

With a grunt of pain, Salvador stood up and began walking, letting blood drip to the ground as he staggered forward.

His one regret was Tamisra. Salvador didn't know which he regretted more, the fact that she was born into an awful world he had helped ruin, or the fact that she would now have to live without a father.

She deserved better.

Roland would make a fine companion, assuming his survival.

If nothing else, he trusted Corrin to take over in his stead and be a good leader for Refuge, a good father to Tamisra.

It was only fair, after all.

He smiled as blood poured from his shoulder.

It was better that he leave this place and live on in the Web as no more than a memory, a tribute to a war that would finally be over. He would never have to face the consequences of betraying a world he had promised to save. He would never have to explain his willingness to send a child to her death.

There was no place for Salvador in a Web without war. His purpose had been fulfilled, he had made up for his sins, and his time had come to move on.

Yes, it was a fitting end to the life he had lived, and the Scourge welcomed it with open arms.

Salvador stepped forward and descended into darkness as he left the Web once and for all.

50

Aniya lay on her back, looking up and watching the stars. These were her favorite moments, resting on the roof of her shack and watching the skydome above slowly turn, revealing a dazzling display of stars. It was a sight so intricately designed that it was easy to forget that the Glorious Bringers of Light, who took time to place each star in an aesthetically pleasing manner, were also responsible for so much pain in her life.

The only thing that made these getaways any better was when Aniya would stay out late enough to break curfew and watch the stars with Nicholas by her side. It was a pastime that had begun innocently enough years ago, when their hands would meet and embrace with no thought beyond mutual comfort.

In recent years, even as Aniya rejected Nicholas at every turn, she would still hold his hand in the dead of night, entranced by the stars, artificial though they were. The beautiful sight always put her at peace. Nicholas would often fall asleep, but Aniya could not bring herself to close her eyes, insisting to watch every second.

But these stars were different. They moved and pulsed brightly, obscuring her vision.

"Nicholas?" Aniya tried to speak but quickly realized that she had no breath. She tried again, but air refused to come.

Concern turned to panic, and she gasped, reaching for air with her lungs and for Nicholas with her hands.

Nicholas.

Suddenly, a weight was lifted off her body, one she never realized was a burden. As her chest was relieved, she inhaled deeply, managing to draw in air with a heavy wheeze.

Fluid glided over her neck, tickling her, and Aniya glanced down to see that although a cloak was wrapped around her body, her chest grew wet and warm as liquid seeped through the cloak and dripped onto her bare skin.

"Aniya, are you okay?"

William's face came into focus.

"Hey, you." She smiled, the gravity of the situation somehow a distant memory.

Her hand became warm, and she realized that another hand rested in hers, stroking her thumb slowly.

"Are you okay?" The words came again, but this time from Nicholas.

"Just peachy."

"Hello there, Ms. Lyons. I thought you had left us."

Another voice ignited the four corners of Aniya's mind.

The pain returned, and her consciousness came crashing back down into her body.

The stars disappeared, and Aniya's vision cleared to reveal the dark chamber that she had accepted as her tomb. Kendall had vanished, leaving only a dark screen that loomed blankly on the wall before her.

She turned to see the Operative standing nearby, his gun emitting a small wisp of smoke that drifted away carelessly.

Aniya screamed in horror as her eyes fell to Roland's limp body at the Operative's feet.

When her scream died away, the Operative simply laughed. "I was afraid you left us for a moment there, girl. It would have made the next few minutes quite boring, honestly."

"Just put me back, okay?" Aniya held up her hands, her strength returning rapidly now. "I'll go back in my pod, and you can keep me here. Just let them go."

The Operative smirked. "Oh, I'll put you back. You and your brother both. I don't have any need for this one, though." He raised his gun and pointed it at Nicholas's head.

"No!" Aniya shouted, the full force of her voice returning. "Take him to the Adviser. You can't just kill him."

"I don't trust the Adviser. Besides, what he doesn't know won't hurt him. It would defeat the purpose anyway. I brought him down here just so you could watch him die."

Nicholas held up his hands and stepped toward Aniya. "Just give me a moment. There's something I need to tell her."

"Sorry, you've run out of time." The Operative grabbed Nicholas's shoulder and dragged him away from Aniya, readying his gun again.

Nicholas looked at Aniya, his eyes moist. "I'm sorry."

But before anyone could move, the screen on the cavern wall came to life again.

"A moment, please."

The Operative glanced behind him. "What do you want?"

Kendall raised an eyebrow, seeming almost bored. "You so rudely interrupted us. We have work to finish. I'm afraid I must ask you to leave."

The Operative laughed again. "I don't report to you anymore."

"So be it."

William kicked the Operative's hand, and the gun flew away as Nicholas spun around and jumped on his attacker.

"Aniya, run!"

The order came from Nicholas. Or maybe William.

It didn't matter. She didn't plan on following it.

Aniya turned.

The empty pod loomed before her, seeming bigger than before.

A gunshot sounded.

"Go!"

She dropped Roland's cloak to the ground, pressed the button on the outside, and stepped bare inside the tank as the glass barrier began to rise.

"What are you doing?"

Aniya turned around to see William banging on the glass. He pressed the button repeatedly, but the water was already beginning to seep in from the floor, and the barrier refused to go back down.

Aniya placed a hand on the glass. "I'm sorry."

Another gunshot.

A bullet bounced off the tank, just over William's left hand.

As William stepped away from the glass, Aniya saw Nicholas sprawled on the ground, alive but wounded.

The water reached her knees, and Aniya took a deep breath, resolute but terrified as she prepared for her imminent death.

Beyond the glass, William charged at the Operative, knocking him to the ground.

The liquid reached her chest, and Aniya attached the hanging tube to her mouth.

William shoved the Operative off the rock floor, letting him drift away in dead space.

Her head was completely submerged.

William shouted, "Kendall, shut off the anti-gravity shafts!"

The wires began to prick Aniya, sending tiny jolts of electricity racing through her body.

Time stood still as the Operative remained suspended, reaching for the gun that floated nearby, just beyond his fingertips.

Her extremities went numb again as the wires quickly covered her body.

"Hurry!" William's voice took on a panicked tone.

Her vision began to go dark.

The Operative finally grabbed his gun, and almost instantly, his body was propelled forward by an invisible force, right before Kendall shouted from the screen, "Done!"

Aniya's vision cleared one more time just in time to see William jump away from the pillar, meeting the Operative in mid-air and stopping his momentum. She watched in horror as the two men collided and fell as one into the depths of the cavern.

She screamed into the tube, the numbing sensation giving way to pain as her anguish cleared the brain fog. Her rage and grief flowed out in one guttural cry before finally going quiet.

As her voice died, she felt her body go limp, the last of her energy spent on her grief.

Her vision completely blackened, and she gave herself up.

Aniya drifted, miles away from the horrific cavern beneath the Citadel. She was back home, in the arms of her father, who stroked her hair and whispered, "Welcome home, Annelise. The light of my life."

She gave herself over and collapsed in his loving embrace. It was over. It was finally over.

No more running, no more fear. Safe in her father's arms once more, never to leave again.

Her home around her faded away, leaving only Aniya and her father.

Then, with one last kiss on her forehead, her father slowly disappeared.

There was only black.

Aniya gave one last breath.

. . .

S *plash.*
        Aniya pushed against an unseen force, trying to see the source of the noise. She realized that her eyes were closed, and she opened them with significant effort.

She was back in the Hub, in the pod, but now there was someone else in the tank with her, gazing at her and caressing her cheeks.

Nicholas.

Everything became clear once again, and her body woke in alarm as she thrashed her legs in the thick liquid.

What are you doing here? Get out!

Aniya would have given anything to speak, but she could only push Nicholas away in desperation, shaking her head.

The tank's liquid took on a red tint as blood flowed from Nicholas's shoulder.

Get out, you fool. Get out.

Dry heaving into the tube, she shook Nicholas as hard as she could.

Nicholas didn't fight back, his only response a sad smile. Slowly, he reached behind his neck and pulled a necklace from his shirt. The clear crystal, washed free of blood, looked like an emerald as it floated in the green liquid.

He tied the necklace around Aniya's neck, letting it drape over her bosom.

As Aniya began to lose energy again, he wrapped his arms around her, leaned close, and spoke through the thick liquid.

"I love you."

Aniya was almost grateful for the tube secured to her mouth because the emotions she felt for Nicholas were too many to express in whatever time they had left.

Friendship, frustration, tenderness, anger, gratefulness, rage . . . and, yes. Love.

She felt his arms go limp around her, and she pulled back to see Nicholas's eyes looking back at her, empty. Void.

With no energy left to cry or scream, all she could do was stare at his lifeless body drift away slowly.

Then, lack of energy was no longer an issue.

Heat flooded through Aniya's body, a furious energy filling her from head to toe. Every atom of her body swelled and burned as the wires emerging from her skin pulsed an angry red, making the crystal on Aniya's chest sparkle with crimson highlights.

Nicholas's face grew bright, and Aniya grew hopeful, but she quickly realized that the light was coming from her own body. She looked down and saw that her entire body was glowing with white light.

Looking back up, Aniya watched as Nicholas's skin grew more and more pale. She noticed that many of the wires that had attached themselves to her had detached and were now embedded in his skin, and they pulsed angrily, sucking beams of red light from his body. With each throb of red that left his body, Aniya felt herself grow stronger and stronger. But as energy coursed through her veins, she watched, horrified, as Nicholas's hair and skin turned a ghostly white.

Aniya looked back at her body as it grew brighter, the luminosity rapidly growing until she could no longer make out the details of her hands.

Suddenly, beams of light burst forth from her feet, shooting straight into the floor. Tendrils shot from her hands, piercing the glass and the surrounding machinery. Her eyes grew incredibly hot, and her vision went white. A sensation of fullness built up inside her, stretching her insides, her guts, her lungs.

Aniya opened her mouth, and a massive beam of light spilled out, narrowly missing Nicholas's face and bursting the glass wall of the tank into thousands of pieces.

Her vision cleared just in time to see Nicholas's body spill out of the tank and onto the ground in front of her, but her own body remained suspended, supported by absolutely nothing.

Aniya gasped as one final surge raced through her body. She no longer could tell the difference between her own body and the light that consumed her.

As the light shot forth from her skin, it pierced the crystal around her neck and split into infinite colors, bathing the cavern in a beautiful rainbow.

Then, in one instant, everything went black.

And then she fell.

51

Roland lay in a pool of blood and green liquid, his breath ragged.

Meltdown imminent. Evacuate immediately.

Robotic voices echoed throughout the cavern, urging him to leave.

But Roland wasn't going anywhere. Even if he wasn't bleeding out, miles beneath the Hub, where was there to go? His friend's pale body lay before him, dead. His brother was at the bottom of one of the anti-gravity shafts, dead. His sister lay crumpled up in a ball on the floor of her broken tank . . . dead.

He cursed Nicholas under his breath. It should have been Roland to step into the tank in a final effort to keep Aniya awake. He was as good as dead anyway.

"I owe it to her," Nicholas had said as he climbed into the tank to be with Aniya.

What does that even mean, anyway?

It would have been just as easy for Nicholas to boost Roland up and help him in through the open top of the tank. No need to waste a life when people are dying left and right.

Even Kendall was gone. The tangible, deadly beams of

light that came blasting from Aniya's tank had not only destroyed her glass prison but also the screen on the cavern wall.

With considerable effort, Roland climbed to his hands and knees, ignoring the glass shards that bit into his hands. Nicholas lay a few feet away, but the journey may as well have been a mile.

Wincing in pain, Roland pulled himself toward his friend. Nicholas was completely white. Not pale—white. His skin, his lips, his hair, all stark white. In contrast, his eyes were a pure and empty black.

Roland dragged himself past Nicholas and closer to his sister, who lay sprawled out in the open tank.

Aniya's body was white as well, but not quite in the same way. The unearthly color came from a vibrant white-green glow that covered her body, gently pulsing. A crystal lay around her neck and over her chest, pulsing green in time with the light.

Roland reached for his cloak, which was soaked in blood and green liquid. He placed it on Aniya's naked body, almost taking it off again when it sizzled loudly. But the hissing eventually stopped, and he sat back and stared at his sister's face. Slowly, he touched her bare cheek and shuddered as his hair stood on end.

Aniya's skin was cold, but the light surrounding her body was quite warm. Her icy skin was not completely devoid of life, however. As his skin made contact, Roland felt tiny jolts of electricity racing up his arm, causing his heart to beat just a bit faster and his vision to clear slightly.

Probably residual energy left behind by the machine.

Roland pulled Aniya out of the tank and toward Nicholas, doing his best to keep her body away from the scattered shards of glass. Though it took all the strength he had left to pull her, the contact with her skin continually sent shocks through his body and gave him tiny bursts of energy. He laid her body next to Nicholas and jumped back as Nicholas's hand grazed Aniya's arm, sending sparks flying.

Meltdown imminent. Evacuate immediately.

He shook himself out of his stupor and focused again on Aniya. After years of learning from Gareth, he had a good grasp on many medical techniques, but if Gareth had ever brought someone back from the dead, Roland was not around to see it. Severely injured, yes. But dead?

Roland pinched Aniya's nose and pressed his lips against hers, breathing firmly into her lungs, then again. He pressed down on her chest once, twice, thirty times.

Nothing.

He breathed into her mouth twice again, then compressed her chest several more times.

Still nothing.

Roland repeated this, ignoring the rocks falling around them as the cavern began to shake.

After several cycles of this, Roland began beating on her chest, crying.

"Come on, Aniya. Wake up. Wake up!"

Suddenly, Aniya's eyelids flickered open, blinding Roland as bright light shot forth from her eyes.

Roland stumbled backward, shielding his eyes and blinking furiously. "Aniya?"

She didn't respond.

Slowly, Roland lowered his hand and looked at his sister as the light receded back into her eyes.

The girl sat up and stared back at him, unmoving and silent.

"Aniya?" he said again, this time with caution. Whether it was the way it stared at him, eerily still, or the fact that its eyes glowed and danced, embers crackling from within—whatever was looking back at him did not seem like the girl he had come to know.

"Roland," the ethereal being said, matter-of-factly. As it

spoke, light freely flowed from its mouth and spilled on the rock below, which quivered at the resonating power of the being's voice. It was masculine now, with hints of Aniya's feminine voice seeping through. Her speech carried a childlike tone, but the timbre of her voice seemed ancient. It was like nothing Roland had ever heard before.

Above, more rocks began to fall. Whether it was due to the overloaded reactor or the being's powerful voice, Roland couldn't tell.

"You're hurt," it said plainly.

He laughed, wincing as the blood flow increased. "Just a nick somewhere in my spinal column. No big deal, right?"

The being did not react to this, but instead cocked its head and stared.

In an instant, the light vanished, and it was just Aniya.

His sister turned to him and gasped as her eyes moistened. She opened her mouth to speak.

Then, just as quickly, the light returned, changed now from a brilliant white-green to a deep, rich, sickly green.

The being uttered a shriek that violently shook the pillar they sat on. Roland slapped his hands over his ears as the screech nearly deafened him, sending shivers down his spine.

Debris now fell like rain around them. Roland looked up in fear, but saw that as rocks fell directly toward them, they disintegrated upon entering the glow emanating from the being.

The pillar, however, seemed to be dangerously close to breaking apart, and Roland could feel himself beginning to sway.

He gripped the being's shoulders and shook them, ignoring the searing pain from the wound in his back.

"Aniya! Aniya, you've got to stop!"

The light diminished again, reduced to a faint glow around Aniya's skin.

"Roland."

Her eyes opened, and Roland recognized his sister once again.

He smiled.

"You're back."

Aniya smiled but then shuddered as tears began to fall. "They're so loud. Make it stop, Roland. Please make it stop." She covered her head and rocked back and forth.

Roland gently wrapped his arms around his sister and let himself rock with her, now comforted by the warm spark coming from her body.

Meltdown imminent. Evacuate immediately.

"You need to get out of here, Aniya."

Aniya pulled herself away from him. "What do you mean? You're coming too."

"I don't think I'm going anywhere," he said, smiling weakly and turning to show Aniya the hole in his back.

She examined his body. "You're hurt," she said again as if just now noticing his injuries, this time her voice laced with genuine concern. Her gaze traveled to Nicholas. "Oh," she gasped, a fresh round of tears streaming down her face. She raced to his side, seemingly unaffected by the torture her body had endured just minutes earlier.

"Nicky, please wake up." She spoke shakily through her tears, which fell on his body and sizzled, wisps of steam rising from his skin.

"Aniya," Roland said again. "You have to leave."

She ignored him and stroked Nicholas's hair, kissing his forehead gently.

Roland crawled over and sat by Aniya's side as he placed his hand on hers. "Please, Aniya. I can't watch you die again."

In response, Aniya squeezed his hand tightly but refused to move.

"No."

That voice. Terror gripped Roland's heart as the pained, angry voice shook his very soul.

"No."

It came again, rumbling the ground beneath him. Her voice morphed, taking on a depth and gravitas that was hauntingly unnatural. It wasn't human. But it wasn't inhuman. It was somehow . . . more than human.

Meltdown imminent. Evacuate—

"No!" The voice burst forth, and the shout rattled the cavern again. The pillar Roland sat on finally shook free from the ceiling, and it slowly tilted toward the wall.

Roland grabbed the being's face with his other hand, forcing it to look at him. "Aniya, come back! You have to stop!"

But it wasn't listening to him any longer.

The pillar continued to tilt slowly, then careened toward the wall, tilting the ground in the wrong direction as Roland felt his body start to fall off the edge.

"Aniya!"

The being made no move to save him, and his body dropped off the side. Roland closed his eyes in preparation for the fall.

But it never came.

He opened his eyes and watched the pillar crash into the wall. Thousands of pods shattered as unconscious men were freed from their prisons, helplessly falling to their deaths in a morbid freedom after a lifetime of slavery.

The pillar rocked back and forth for a moment, then crumbled under its own weight and fell into the depths below.

The entire pillar had missed him somehow, but what was more remarkable was the fact that Roland remained suspended in the air. His hand was still holding on to the glowing phantom, which sat on thin air as well, still holding Nicholas.

Did Kendall turn back on the anti-gravity shafts?

But instead of vaulting to safety, propelled by an unseen force, they instead rose slowly to the main walkway. The surrounding light gradually grew, now a sphere that encompassed them.

They came to rest on the main walkway, and Roland yelped, startled by an intense heat racing up his right arm. He turned to see the being, now glowing a shimmering gold, one hand on Nicholas's chest and the other clutching Roland's right hand.

Tiny veins of yellow light danced across the being's body, from its heart, down its arm, into Roland's hand, and disappearing around his side.

Suddenly, his back grew hot, and the pain coming from the bullet hole was replaced by a warm feeling that calmed his spirit and slowed his heart.

Roland felt the bullet still embedded in his back slowly drill itself backward, passing bone and muscle that stitched itself up behind the foreign object. Within seconds, the bullet dropped to the rock behind him with a *clink*.

Then the heat was gone as the being released his hand.

Roland opened his eyes after the initial shock wore off. The light was now focused in a different direction, now channeling itself from Aniya into Nicholas. The yellow tendrils were brighter now, and the light seemed more intense, racing faster and spreading over Nicholas's entire body.

The being shuddered as the light took on a reddish hue. It mumbled, almost whimpering. For several minutes, crimson light coursed over Nicholas's body, its intensity growing with every second. Soon, the light was so bright that Roland could no longer see him.

Roland covered his ears again as the noise emanating from the being escalated into a deafening, howling wail. Terrible pain throbbed in his ears, and warm, thick liquid bathed his palms as he moaned in pain.

The light reached its peak, and almost instantly, it began to diminish rapidly, dwindling back to its source as the being's cry turned to a whine.

He could now see Aniya's face once again. His heart broke as her face strained in agony. For a moment, it seemed like she was about to give up. The light had almost completely left Aniya, and Nicholas reappeared as the light bathing his body vanished as well.

Aniya looked up at Roland as tears streamed down her face.

"I can't."

She looked down at Nicholas.

"I'm sorry."

As Aniya's eyes grew dark again, she leaned over and kissed Nicholas.

The light returned instantly, bursting into a white blaze and lighting up every nook and cranny of the cavern. Roland felt his eyes grow hot, and smoke rose in his vision as he realized that his eyes were quite literally burning. But there was no pain, and he could not bring himself to look away from the incredible sight.

Then his eardrums burst as a colossal explosion shook the cavern once again. Fire rose from the depths below, shooting upward in a pillar of flame and surrounding the trio as they sat on the walkway, which remained unnaturally still despite the powerful quakes.

And just like that, it was over.

The fire vanished, the roaring boom ceased, and the white light vanished. Roland's eyes were normal, and his ears were restored. In fact, as Roland ran his hands over his body, he felt perfectly fine.

Aniya sat before him, faint streams of light coursing over her body. The crystal around her neck glowed green, pulsing in time with her breath. Several streaks of white highlighted her black hair, and her eyes held a sharp green sparkle that took Roland's breath away.

Nicholas's body, now flush with color, was shaking in her

lap. After a moment, he opened his eyes and gasped loudly. His eyes darted between Aniya and Roland.

"What happened?"

Aniya looked back at him and smiled.

Then, her eyes went dark again, and her crystal drained of color, turning black. All that was left was a tiny, dim speck of green light, barely visible in the dark gem.

Aniya toppled over and fell to the ground.

52

The next day, Aniya finally opened her eyes again, groaning at the pain coursing through her body. She was in a small room, lit by a candle that flickered just out of sight.

"Good morning." A voice came from her side.

Aniya tried to turn to the source of the voice but found that it was simply too painful to move.

Roland's smiling face came into view as he leaned over her. "How are you feeling?"

"Like death," Aniya muttered, wincing as her words revealed a sharp headache.

"Yeah, Kendall said that might happen. You're fine. A picture of perfect health, apparently. You're just feeling the effects of the electrotherapy they used to bring you back after we lost you the second time."

"Electro—" Aniya searched her mind, but her memories were scattered and blurry. "Where are we?"

"Back in Refuge. Xander and Malcolm found us in the Citadel and brought us out."

"What happened?"

Roland took a deep breath. "A lot. What do you remember?"

Aniya closed her eyes and tried to push the pain out of her mind. "I remember you getting shot. I remember stepping into the tank. I remember the pain. I remember Nicholas . . . I remember Nicholas dying." Suddenly, the darkness provided by her closed eyes turned from comforting to crushing, and she opened her eyes again as tears spilled out.

"That's the last thing you remember?"

Aniya nodded.

"Nicholas is alive."

Aniya choked on her tears as a cry of joy escaped her lips. "But I watched him die."

"I know. I watched *you* die too."

"I died?"

"Or at least I thought you died. I pulled you from the tank and revived you. You woke up, and then you . . ." Roland looked down.

"I healed you."

Images came flooding back, exacerbating Aniya's headache as she relived the trauma in the Hub.

"I healed you, and then I healed Nicholas. But it wasn't me," Aniya said. "I didn't do any of it."

"That wasn't you? But I saw—"

"I know what you saw," Aniya said. "I saw it too, but I don't think I was in control. It felt like I was outside of my own body, watching myself do things without any say in the matter. It scared me, not knowing what my body was going to do next."

"So if it wasn't you, what was it?"

"I don't know. Maybe it was me. Maybe I just don't remember. I do remember being surrounded by light, almost like it trapped me and made me watch. And then there were the voices."

"Voices?"

Aniya closed her eyes again, remembering the hair-raising feeling of a thousand voices pervading her mind. "I don't know what they were saying, but there were so many of them." She opened her eyes. "If you're alive, and if Nicholas is alive, is William—"

Roland looked away and bit his lip.

Aniya's throat closed as the tears started to come again.

"He died to save you, Aniya."

"You don't get it," she said, spitting out her words as her chest heaved with the sobs. "I was supposed to die to save him, and I failed."

"No, Aniya. I'm alive because of you. You went to the Hub to save your brother. You didn't fail. You saved me. I just wasn't the brother you set out to save." Roland smiled. "Nicholas is alive. The man who killed our parents is dead. Their awful machine is destroyed. The Hub is in ruins. The Lightbringers are scattered. We won, Aniya. We won."

As Aniya's tears subsided, she felt a hand in hers, and she looked down to see Roland's hand gently caressing hers, a green glow faintly shimmering as their joined hands exchanged warmth. She looked up again before Roland could notice her stare.

"What now?"

"Now, we finish the job," Roland said. "No one's seen the Chancellor since the battle in the Hub. He could be anywhere, so Kendall is organizing a full-scale attack on the remaining Silvers spread out among the sectors in hopes that we find the Chancellor. We lost Salvador in the Hub, so Corrin has taken command of his army. Combined with a few hundred Silvers loyal to Kendall, we'll have an army that will quickly take care of the remaining Lightbringers. Hopefully, we can restore the Web to normal in a few weeks at the most."

"Normal? What normal do you think could possibly be waiting for us? The power is out now for good now."

Roland shrugged. "I think Salvador put it pretty nicely. We

got along without the Lightbringers for centuries. We can do it again. The rest of it should fall into place. Of course, Kendall plans to hold special elections for a new chancellor as soon as the war is over . . ." Roland trailed off and looked away.

"But?"

Roland looked back at her and frowned. "I'm not sure about Kendall."

"What do you mean?"

"We don't know anything about him. He was the Chancellor's right-hand man for almost twenty years, but beyond that, we know nothing. For all we know, Kendall just wanted to pick a fight with the Chancellor so he could take his place."

Aniya shook her head. "That doesn't make any sense. He helped us blow up the reactor that powered the entire Web. The Lightbringers were only in control because they knew how to provide power. Without that, they have nothing."

"Yeah, but people need leadership. Now that they've gotten used to having a leader, they won't know how to live without one. And the one who got rid of the dictator that everyone hated would seem like a pretty good fit."

"You said there would be a special election."

Roland scoffed. "An election with only one candidate is pretty special, don't you think? I just don't trust him."

"The last thing you told me before we got separated was to trust no one but Kendall. What changed?"

"I said Kendall because Salvador told me about him. He said Kendall was the one Nicholas was working with on the inside. But if Salvador knew Kendall, that must mean that he had some idea of what Kendall was up to. And since Kendall's plan was to use William to end the Lightbringers, Salvador had to have known that he would try again, maybe with you."

"That sounds pretty circumstantial."

"That's the whole point. Nothing about this adds up. And since the story we know doesn't make sense, we can't know for sure who to trust. Salvador either lied to us or didn't tell us the whole story. He even told me not to say anything about being related to you. Why hide that from you? It just doesn't sit right with me. And if we can't trust Salvador, we can't trust Kendall."

"You're not making sense, Roland."

Roland threw his arms in the air. "Nothing about this makes sense, which is why we can't trust anyone until we learn more."

After a long pause, Aniya said, "Nicholas trusts him."

"Yeah, I know that Nicholas will follow him to his death, but I'm not quite there yet. I'm just saying that we should be careful with him."

"What do you want me to do?" Aniya rolled her eyes. "It's not like I can refuse to go along with his plans. My part is done. He doesn't need me anymore."

"For starters, maybe we shouldn't tell him about everything that happened under the Citadel," Roland said slowly. "After all, we're not sure what happened ourselves."

"Why would it make a difference if Kendall knows?"

Roland paused. "I know you don't have a clear picture of what happened down there, but I saw it all. The light that came out of you didn't just heal me and Nicholas. It shattered glass. It blasted a hole clear through the wall of the cavern. I don't know if whatever that was is still in you, but it was terrifying. And it was dangerous. I'm afraid Kendall will see it that same way and want to use you as a living weapon."

"You really think he'd do that?"

"I'm not sure. That's what I'm saying. There's no telling what he'd do to fulfill his agenda, and we don't even know for sure what that agenda is."

Aniya nodded slowly. "Maybe you're right. So we don't tell Kendall about what happened in the cavern. We should tell Nicholas before he says something."

"I already talked to him. He agreed, but probably only

because he wouldn't be able to explain it even if he wanted to. I was intentionally vague when I told him what happened anyway."

"We can trust Nicholas," Aniya said, narrowing her eyes.

"Can we?" Roland asked quietly. "In any case, he knows enough that I made him promise not to say anything to Kendall until I talked to you. Now that you agree, I'll let him know that we're all on the same page."

Aniya glared at him. "And I'll tell him myself what happened. You may not trust him, but I do."

"I didn't say I don't trust him. I'm just . . ."

"Not sure," Aniya finished, sighing and leaning back on her cot. "Do you trust anyone, Roland?"

Roland took her hand again. "I trust you."

She looked at her brother. "Then trust Nicholas."

After a moment, Roland nodded.

"Where is he?"

"He was watching over you earlier, but Kendall insisted that he report for a full medical evaluation. I'll send him up to see you as soon as I can, but I think they're running tests on him for the rest of the day. Kendall may not know much of what happened, but he knows enough to realize that none of us should still be alive." Roland stood and started walking toward the door. "As for me, I'm going to go check on Tamisra. She's still recovering from a nasty bit of torture."

"Are you going to tell her anything?"

Roland turned around and gave a sad smile. "No. I love her, but like I said, I don't know who to trust anymore."

He turned again and left.

Half-truths, lies, conspiracies—Aniya felt it would have been so much easier if she had just stayed dead. She wouldn't have to look over her shoulder, wondering who she could trust.

She tried to sleep several times over the next several hours, but the pain in her body would always keep her from finally drifting off.

Finally, hours later, the pain began to dissipate, only to be replaced by a new feeling that spread throughout her body. Restless life buzzed inside her, tingling every inch of her skin as her insides felt like a balloon beginning to expand.

She looked back down at her hand. Sure enough, the green glow was still there. It was almost imperceptible, but in the dimly lit room, it was just bright enough that she could see the emerald tint that covered her body.

The more the pain vanished, the stronger this strange vibration grew. The more she felt as if something inside was beginning to grow.

Aniya touched her thigh, and her skin seemed to respond with a tiny spark of green and a quick buzz that drowned out the immediate tingle.

She traced the feeling from her waist to her stomach to her chest—but she paused as a hard object halted her examination. She reached underneath her shirt and pulled out the crystal, still draped around her neck where Nicholas had placed it.

The crystal was no longer clear as she remembered it, but it was now green, the same emerald hue that covered her body. As she turned the crystal over in her hand, the light shifted, glinting in unusual ways as it caught the candlelight. But even as she held the crystal still in her hand, the light still seemed to move slowly.

The beauty of the gem held Aniya's rapt attention, and she suddenly realized that she had been holding her breath. Aniya let her breath go, and the crystal gave off a shimmering light, its color growing much richer, a bold green that flickered with her ragged breath.

A whisper startled Aniya, and she gasped, dropping the crystal. It was caught by the necklace and hung from her neck, draped off to the side. The whisper came again, and it was joined now by many more voices.

They were back.

The voices grew louder, plaguing every corner of Aniya's mind. She reached her hands to her head and clutched her temple, wishing away the intruders.

Go away, go away.

The voices were now almost shouting, and one of the voices grew louder still, rising above the rest but still unintelligible.

As the collective voice became deafening, the solitary voice strained even harder, fighting for attention.

Aniya's ears rang with a screech that rattled her bones and sent daggers of pain through the nerves in her teeth. Tears running down her cheeks, she let out a scream of pain, a cry she just barely heard above the din that raged inside her mind.

She ran out of breath and fell backward in her cot. As she gasped for air, she realized that her mind was quiet once again. The conglomerate of voices was silenced.

But as she sighed in relief, a single feminine voice whispered one final time, its speech now clear.

"Aniya."

EPILOGUE

"**R**eport."

Kendall glanced back down the tunnel behind him. Aside from the obvious, they were alone. But it wouldn't be long until someone realized the jammer had been disabled. He had to hurry.

He cleared his throat and spoke into the earpiece. "Mission was a success, sir."

"Good." A smooth, pleased voice crackled in Kendall's ear. "And the girl's status?"

"You were right. They found her almost dead in the reactor chamber, but we were able to resuscitate her using electrotherapy, just like you said."

"Well done." His voice was smooth and low. "And the rest of the main players?"

"They made it out as well. Except for William, that is. You were right. They survived. But how could you have known all this?"

"You should know by now not to waste your breath with that question. In any case, what matters now is what happens next."

"Understood."

The man's voice lost its cheeriness. "What became of the Chancellor?"

"He's gone. Escaped in the middle of it all. No one knows where he is because all surveillance is down. I saw just enough to know he's still alive."

"You must waste no time finding him. When you hunt down the rest of the Silvers still loyal to the Chancellor, I want him dead."

"Understood."

His voice was soft again. "Run full medical diagnostics on the girl and report back as soon as you find something."

"Already ordered them, sir."

"Very good."

Kendall shifted his balance uneasily. "But, sir . . . Nicholas was inside the tank with her."

The man's voice took on a new tone, one that Kendall had never heard from him. "And he's still alive?"

"Yes, sir."

"Interesting. Where is he now?"

"All three of them are with me in the caves," Kendall said. "You were wise to send someone back into the Citadel to check the remains of the reactor or we never would have found them. I should have never questioned your judgment."

"Indeed. And you've ordered diagnostics for Nicholas as well?"

"Yes, sir."

The voice crooned. "Good. Did you see what happened in the cavern?"

"Nothing past the main explosion."

It went silent for a moment.

"Keep a close eye on them."

Kendall nodded. "Yes, sir."

"I'm sending another operative to you."

"I was hoping we would not have to resort to using one of them."

"In an ideal world, we wouldn't, but you know I cannot afford to rely simply on hope."

"Understood, sir. Aren't you concerned about the children's survival?"

A chuckle came across the line. "I am concerned with everything that happens in the Underworld. That's my job. How I react to things, however, is what determines my effectiveness. I choose reason, logic—not panic."

"Yes, sir. Anything else?"

The mirth in the man's voice vanished. "When the girl recovers, bring her to me."

"Sir?"

"Is that a problem?"

"No, sir. Sorry. What of the asset?"

A long pause. "Keep him close. If you see any change in his condition, send him to me immediately. Make sure he stays alive for now."

"Yes, sir."

K endall took off his earpiece and looked up at the asset. "What did he say?" The asset spoke slowly, almost cautiously.

"Keep an eye on Aniya," Kendall said. "And report to me instantly with any new developments."

"Yes, sir."

The asset turned to leave.

"One more thing."

Kendall leaned forward in his chair.

"Emotion is a dangerous thing. You must not let your feelings for her get in the way of what we've worked so hard to accomplish."

"That won't be a problem, sir."

"Good." Kendall sat on the floor of the small cavern and stared into the fire. "You did well. I know it must have been hard for you, leading her to a death you knew was certain. You have proved your loyalty as a valuable asset, and it seems that fate has rewarded you with her miraculous survival. But don't be tempted. If a time comes when you must choose between Aniya and this new world, I have to trust you to make the right choice."

The asset said nothing.

"Can I do that, Nicholas? Can I trust you?"

After a long moment, Nicholas nodded. "I live to serve the Glorious Bringers of Light."

TO BE CONTINUED...

THANK YOU

Thank you for reading my debut novel, *The Light Thief.*

As you may have noticed, the story isn't over. Aniya will return in *The Phoenix Mandate* (March 2020). Would you like to be the first to know when it drops? How about a free book? Do you want to read about William's adventures, his escape from the Hub and heroic attempt to destroy the reactor?

Go to jdavidwebb.com/free-book and sign up for the mailing list to be notified of all new releases and special offers, and you'll get a **FREE** copy of *The Saboteur*, a book that expands the *Light Thief* universe. I would like nothing more than the opportunity to get to know you!

I promise not to fill your inbox with spam or share your contact information with anyone, ever.

P.S. *The Saboteur* is a prequel to *The Light Thief*, but it contains spoilers for the main story. So if you managed to get to this page without reading the 300-some pages before it, first of all, what are you doing? Go back to page 1, or whatever page you were on before. Secondly, don't read *The Saboteur* unless you want to be spoiled!

Enjoy this book?
You can make a big difference.

If you enjoyed *The Light Thief*, the single most helpful thing you can do is leave me a review on Amazon. To explain how grateful I would be for this would take another hundred pages.

Suffice it to say that I can't afford to take out an ad in some big-name newspaper. You probably haven't seen a billboard with my face on it. If you've met me, you're probably grateful for that.

But while big publishing companies are buying out digital signs on Times Square and forcing raunchy books in your face every time you leave the comfort of Gmail, there is something much more powerful that money can't buy. Reviews.

Honest reviews of my books help bring them to the attention of other readers.

So, if you wouldn't mind, take about 30 seconds to leave a dazzling review encouraging others to check out this book! How? Just go to your Amazon order history and click "Write a product review."

Thank you,

David Webb

THE PHOENIX MANDATE

Get it now!

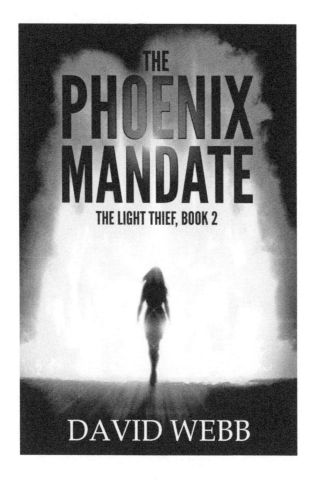

Made in the USA
Middletown, DE
02 December 2024

65957634R00223